SURVIVORS OF THE DEAD:

FROM THE ASHES

TONY BAKER

***

Edited by Monique Happy Editorial Services
http://www.moniquehappy.com

***

CONTENTS

ACKNOWLEDGMENTS

I began my writing journey in September of 2012 after harboring that desire for years. Although I have faced some interesting hurdles, and many learning curves, I would not change one single thing that I have been privileged to experience. Meeting incredible people, both fans of the genre as well as other amazing authors, are just two of the highlights of this adventure so far. I have so many people to thank for their unwavering support throughout this adventure.

First to my family: nephews, Eric and Jimi, sister, Tommi, and brother-in-law, Jeff. You are the center of my universe and without your support over the past year I am not certain I could have made it. I love you all more than I could ever put into words.

To the incomparable Monique Happy Lewis. Not only is Monique one of the best industry editors, I am proud to call her my friend. A simple 'thank you' will never be enough to express the deep appreciation and gratitude I have for her taking on my work.

To Wanda and her granddaughter Nevaeh. Not only did they grant permission for me to create characters based on them, they are steadfast supports and true friends.

To David P. Forsyth for granting permission to include a few minor references from his *Sovereign Spirit Saga*. Although Mr. Forsyth had no direct participation in writing *Survivors of the Dead: From the Ashes*, nor is my book a spinoff of his series, it was a pleasure to add a sequence directly from the second book of that series, **Flotilla of the Dead*, along with a few of the events found in the SSS and one character. In addition, I am pleased readers will find an excerpt I wrote pertaining to Angel Island for the third book of the SSS, *Deluge of the Dead*, which was used with my permission. I also wrote, with Mr. Forysth's approval, a sequence between one of my characters and his toward the end of my book.

Finally, and just as importantly, once again to all of the wonderful people I have met and who have supported and shared this writing journey with me. This includes many authors and readers of the genre. You all initially accepted me with little more than a book cover and a Facebook page, as I talked about a concept while writing this book, but you stood with me along every step of this adventure. To list each of your names would take pages. You know who you are, so please also know that each of you have my most sincere heartfelt gratitude, appreciation and admiration.

"From the ashes a fire shall be woken,
a light from the shadows shall spring.
Renewed shall be blade that was broken,
the crownless again shall be king."

— J.R.R. Tolkien

1

Harold Lancaster woke to screaming and that incessant moaning again from the street outside his bedroom window in the San Francisco apartment building he managed. Or, more specifically, had managed. He was not certain what rule of law applied in a zombie apocalypse, but it was still his building for now, and he wasn't allowing an apocalypse to change that just yet. After all, he had been forced to kill several of the residents in the first few days of the madness, even wittily concluding that little endeavor might have given him some form of property ownership. "Yep, I'm taking adverse possession of the building," he'd thought at the time.

Harry had been in the bathroom getting ready to shower on the morning the madness began, that date being set to memory quite clearly: April 1st. As he finished using the toilet, he heard an obvious squabble erupt in the unit above his. That was unusual, as the upstairs tenants were a very nice young couple that both travelled extensively in their professions. Harry had rarely heard them in the past, which raised an immediate red flag. There was yelling and thumping; it sounded like items were being thrown on the floor. Then came a heavy thud, like a body falling, and a long, drawn-out scream that raised goose bumps on Harry's body.

Rushing out of the bathroom, he pulled on a pair of jeans, a sweatshirt, and his slip-on shoes. Without thinking, he also grabbed the Glock handgun that he kept in a nightstand by the bed. Harry had never felt the need to arm himself in the building before, but something made him pick up the weapon this time. Tucking the gun in the rear of the jean's waistband, grimacing slightly at its coldness against the bare skin at the small of his back, he pulled the sweatshirt down over it and rushed out of his apartment door into the hallway. His plan was to proceed down the hall and take the stairs located just before the lobby up one flight to the second floor. From there he could quickly reach the couple's unit. Harry almost immediately forgot that plan after only taking a few steps outside of his apartment.

The first thing that hit Harry was an odor so rancid it nearly brought tears to his eyes and actually caused him to gag. It was as if rotten meat had been left in the sun for days while sitting in raw sewage. Breathing through his mouth, he walked toward the lobby area and the stairway. As he got closer, he began to hear what could only be described as a wet, ripping sound, and a low moaning that was coming from the lobby, just out of his line of sight. Curiosity getting the better of him, Harry continued on past the stairway.

As Harry walked around the corner and into the lobby, the scene that met him was like something out of a nightmare; it shook him to the very core. He had been witness to some gruesome things in his career as a cop, but what he now observed was incomprehensible. Lying next to the mailboxes was a body so mangled that the person was unrecognizable, although the brown tattered shirt and pants probably meant it was a UPS driver that had been making an early morning delivery. The face had been completely torn away, and the only discernible feature was a bloody, whitish skull with a few tatters of flesh, muscle, and hair remaining.

The upper portion of the body had not fared much better. What little of the brown shirt remained had been shredded, exposing the abdominal area which had been eviscerated, its contents spilling out and across the floor. Hunched over the corpse, next to several packages lying in a spreading pool of blood, were two elderly women he immediately recognized as Katy and Edna, tenants of the building.

Harry said, "What the fuck?" which garnered the immediate attention of Edna. Katy ignored him, continuing to rip bloody strips of flesh from the body with gnarled, claw-like hands and then stuffing the grotesque tidbits she had liberated into her mouth. Bile quickly rose in Harry's throat but he did not have time to actually vomit because Edna, who had been sharing this ghoulish meal, began to struggle to her feet, staring right at him.

Edna was a long-term tenant in her late 70's, robust for her age although hard of hearing and nearly blind. She was the epitome of that 'nasty old lady' everyone has met at one point in their lives, with never a pleasant word and always complaining about something. She was renowned for her loud, screeching 'fingernails on a chalk board' voice, and would corner any unsuspecting person with venomous avowals as to the current state of the nation or her categorical disapproval of San Francisco politics. It was the long-held conclusion by most of the building tenants that she should be avoided at all costs.

Tenants with the misfortune of running into Edna while trying use the elevator could always look forward to another of her pleasantries. In that loud, screeching voice, much like a herd of cats in heat, she would shriek, "Hold the elevator! Hold the elevator! I've gotta get my mail!" Edna had the ability to make strong men cringe, women weep, and small children run screaming in horror.

Harry immediately saw that Edna was definitely the worse for wear as she struggled to regain her feet, all the while emitting a low, menacing moan. The tattered housecoat she wore, which had been her ever-present trademark fashion statement, was hanging open, exposing torn flesh and a missing breast. The remaining one sagged almost to her stomach, which, in and of itself, was enough to give Harry nightmares for weeks. Her hair was disheveled, with clumps missing, and both bruised arms bore what appeared to be numerous and severe bite wounds. What chilled Harry the most were her bloodshot eyes and a foamy reddish-white substance which dripped very slowly from her slightly opened mouth.

Once on her feet, she raised bloody, arthritic hands, resembling the same claw-like appendages as her cohort Katy, and moved toward Harry with purpose in an impossibly fast manner for someone of her age and current physical condition. As she quickly closed the short distance between them, years of training took over and Harry delivered a front leg kick that sent her crashing back into Katy and the corpse. Katy, whose physical condition rivaled that of Edna's, now turned her full attention also on Harry. To his horror, both of these monstrosities began to struggle to their feet, and he knew their intentions were not to discuss a plumbing issue or why the elevator was not working.

With more adrenaline flooding his system than he had experienced in years, he screamed at them, "What the fuck is the matter with you!" Harry then withdrew the .45 caliber Glock, quickly pulling the slide back to chamber a round, and shouted "STAY DOWN! For the love of God, stay the fuck down!" He took several steps backward, bringing up the Glock and depressing the first trigger safety, took a standard firing stance, and lined the sights up on the first target.

His words only seemed to agitate them more as they continued to stand, slipping a few times in the pool of blood that now covered a large portion of the lobby floor. Once again his reflexes and training took over, as he realized this was a failure-to-stop scenario and deadly force was required.

That thought passed through his mind within seconds as he rapidly fired the Glock four times in succession, delivering two of the heavy rounds center mass first into Edna and then Katy. Harry wondered how he was going to explain shooting two old ladies in the lobby of an apartment building. *This will look good on KRON News tonight*, he thought.

Over the years Harry had heard the various forms of public condemnation that were usually generated from police-involved shootings that resulted in a death. "They should have just shot him in the leg," and even once during a very emotional witness deposition, someone had said, "The cops could've just shot the gun out of his hand!" Police officers are trained, and have drilled into their very souls, that the use of deadly force is an absolute last resort. But unfortunately there are situations in which a cop has no alternative.

Police officers do not start their shift with the wanton desire to take another human life, even those of the worst of violent criminals. But if innocent people are in a life-threatening situation—if indeed the officer is in fear for his own life—a cop is trained to shoot. They shoot to permanently eliminate the mortal danger that required that decision in the first place. Hollywood theatrics of shooting a person to wound them or shooting a weapon out of someone's hand are simply not realistic in the adrenaline-filled moments leading up to the use of deadly force.

In the 1980's when Harry first began his law enforcement career, there was not the concern over terrorist activity that had grown over the years since, nor were there as many heavier caliber assault-type weapons in the hands of those seeking to conduct nefarious activity. But the use of deadly force was very much a part of the instruction and training recruits had to master.

The Mozambique Drill, also known as the failure to stop drill, or just failure drill, is a close-quarter shooting technique in which the shooter fires twice into the center mass of a target, momentarily assesses the results of the hits, then immediately follows up with a carefully aimed shot to the head of the target. The third shot is aimed to destroy the brain or brain stem, killing the target and preventing the target from retaliating.

This technique was first developed in the mid-1960's during the Mozambican War of Independence by Mike Rousseau, who had been a mercenary hired to fight in that war. At some point Rousseau had found himself engaged in a fire fight, armed only with a Browning single-shot bolt-action rifle and a pistol; as he rounded the corner of a building, he came face-to-face with an enemy combatant armed with an AK-47.

Rousseau had been too close to the target at that point to use his rifle, so he quickly drew his pistol and fired two rounds into the enemy's chest. Unfortunately, the soldier not only stayed on his feet but also managed to hang onto his rifle. Rousseau realized he was in serious trouble as he quickly assessed that the first two shots had been ineffective, and decided to deliver a third shot to the man's head, killing him instantly and removing Rousseau from mortal danger.

Over the years this technique was perfected and became part of military forces training, and in the late '70s was incorporated into law enforcement. With the advent of body armor becoming readily available to the general public, along with the higher accessibility of assault weapons and the ever-growing terrorist threat, this technique has become vital training for police officers. In the new zombie-permeated world this technique would prove how vitally important, and effective, it truly was—many times over.

Harry had not delivered the fatal kill shot to the little old ladies. Two to the chest should have snuffed out any chance at life for those two. *Yeah, this is definitely going to look just great on the news tonight*, he thought as he closed his eyes momentarily to clear his thoughts. However, it seemed as if all the rules had been tossed as he opened his eyes to see that both Katy and Edna were struggling to stand again, with wounds that would have instantly killed a normal human being!

2

Harry had not changed his stance since the first four rounds had been fired; his training and experience took over once again as he fired two more rounds into Edna and Katy, this time obliterating each of their heads in turn. Both bodies crumpled to the floor and lay motionless.

Thinking the worse, and in a moment of near panic, he aimed the Glock at the corpse that had been Katy and Edna's breakfast and put a round into its head. "Probably better safe than sorry," Harry said with an almost maniacal giggle. He then dropped to his knees, having been given a momentary reprieve from the waking nightmare he was in, and emptied the contents of his stomach.

He wasn't sure how long he had been kneeling, but the dry heaves finally subsided enough for him to get slowly to his feet. Staring at the carnage in front of him, Harry knew he had to get back to his apartment and report this mess. What he couldn't shake was the tremendous pounding and ringing in his ears from the six shots he had fired in the small lobby area. That was until he realized that some of the ringing was coming from the building fire alarm, which had extremely loud bells. *Must have set off the system with the rounds*, Harry thought, referring to the shots he had fired and the resulting cordite lingering in the air.

He walked over to the fire panel, needing to step over one of the headless bodies to do so, and silenced the alarm. That helped the ringing in his ears a bit, but the pounding persisted. Turning back toward his apartment, he walked the short distance in a complete fog. All he could think of was getting to the phone he had left on his desk and calling 911. As he passed one of the other apartment doors in the hallway, he abruptly realized that the pounding sound he thought had been in his ears was actually originating from that door. As his head cleared a bit more, and he was better able to focus, he realized with rising alarm that the pounding sounds were also coming from several other doors. What caused his blood to run cold was the underlying sound of moaning that also emanated behind those doors.

"What the hell is going on?" Harry said, rushing into the already open door to his apartment, slamming it shut and throwing the two deadbolts into place. "I've got to get some help here." With shaking hands, he picked up his cell phone from the small table in the foyer and dialed 911. It rang at least a dozen times before the number finally connected and a recorded message began: "*All circuits are busy now. Please hang up and try your call again later.*" Frowning, Harry hit the 'end' button, then 'redial'. As the phone began ringing again, Harry started pacing. "Come on, come on ...." After ringing once more at least a dozen times, it finally connected and he heard the same recorded message.

Harry hung up and immediately opened the directory on the phone. He located Central Station, deciding to call the report in directly, and pressed the speed dial number he had assigned to the station. Once again he started to pace as the line began to ring. He happened by the coffee table where a universal remote control lay, and absently picked it up and turned on the television. Harry normally started his day by watching the morning news on KRON, Channel 4, but as he stared at what was on the 52" LED flat screen TV, it looked as if the location being televised was somewhere in the Middle East. It did not register just yet that what he saw was actually taking place, live, on Market Street in the middle of downtown San Francisco.

"Central, O'Leary," a voice on the other end of the line finally answered after ringing more times than Harry could remember.

"Bob?" Harry responded to Robert O'Leary, a desk sergeant he had known for years. Continuing before O'Leary could reply, he said, "Bob, it's Lancaster. I've had trouble in my building. Jesus, I had to shoot two of my tenants!"

"Listen Harry, there has been a department-wide call-in for every officer and reserve as of 0745 hours this morning. I tried calling you but only got your voice mail," Bob replied. "There's some serious shit going down and it's going down all over the City. People are going crazy and attacking anything that moves. We've even had to lock down the station. Nobody knows what the hell is going on, but you listen really carefully. DO NOT come in! It's too dangerous and we're losing our people left and right. Make sure your place is buttoned up tight and don't let anyone in under any circumstances. If you see anyone acting even remotely odd, and believe me you'll know what that means when you see it, do not hesitate! Take them out immediately! Do you copy me?"

The events of the morning thus far with what he'd had to do in the lobby, and now hearing what O'Leary had just said, nearly pushed Harry over the brink! "What do you mean, shit's going down all over the City?" Harry demanded. "I just had to blow away two old ladies in my lobby that were gnawing on a fucking UPS guy! Now you're telling me if anybody acts odd I should take them out? What the fuck, Bob!"

With an exasperated tone, Bob immediately said, "Turn on the TV, Harry, see for yourself." Harry started to respond, but only got a couple of words out, before O'Leary interrupted him. "Listen Harry, I gotta go. You button up tight and you stay put until we can regroup and get the City back in control. We've got SWAT backed up with calls and every car is in a different location all over the City. There's nothing you can do right now, so you wait for further instructions." With that, O'Leary hung up. Harry could only look at the cell phone in his hand in complete astonishment.

Staring intently at the television that was directly in front of him, he turned up the volume and started to surf the channels in total disbelief. What he saw was total anarchy.

There were indeed scenes of mass rioting not only in San Francisco but also apparently all over the country, according to the national news networks. He settled on network news channel when he ran across them in some sort of heated debate over what was happening.

3

Harry watched the new for the better part of two hours, alternatively switching between that and the local channels. They all told the same story: something about a worldwide bioterrorist attack that had affected a large portion of the population. Those infected seemed to then attack and either kill or infect others. It didn't make any sense to Harry, and obviously it didn't make much sense to the talking heads reporting the information. As is normal in an emergency involving unknowns, everyone had an opinion on the cause. Shouting matches erupted on some networks between so-called respected experts generating conflicting reports, which seemed to only create more confusion. But the televised images themselves spoke volumes, overshadowing anything the experts or the studio anchors were relaying. Harry finally muted the television to allow what he had seen and heard to be absorbed a bit, and to gather his jumbled thoughts. That was also when the unrelenting pounding that seemed to resound throughout the building came crashing back into focus. He had only one thought: "What is this, fuckin' Cujo meets Dawn of the Dead?" Walking over to the closed, heavy curtains in his bedroom and pulling back a small section, Harry peered out onto a scene of horror much like what he had been watching on TV.

After viewing the craziness unfold on the street below his window for several minutes, Harry finally stepped back from the window with sudden determination. "Okay, so first things first; I need to check on the rest of the building." Although he knew what he was assuredly going to find, he prepared himself as best he could. Walking over to a dresser, he opened the uppermost drawers, revealing several boxes of

.45 caliber ammunition and four empty magazines. Pulling these items out of the drawer, he carefully lined them up in front of him on top of the dresser.

Opening the boxes of ammunition, and then picking up the first empty magazine, he started to thumb in rounds. When he finished loading the four mags, he reached to the back of his jeans and pulled the Glock out from where it had been sitting in the small of his back since he had replaced it after the lobby incident. Dropping the mag from the weapon, he reloaded the rounds he had fired. Harry suddenly realized he had not noticed the slight discomfort caused by the large weapon pressing into his skin until that moment. He also realized that the minor discomfort must have subconsciously kept him a bit more grounded in the otherwise surreal last couple of hours of hell in which he had found himself. "No time to sit in the corner babbling incoherently about the possibility of large slobbering dogs or zombies roaming the streets of San Francisco," Harry said absently, slipping the freshly reloaded mag back into the grip of the Glock, then pulling back the slide to chamber a round. "Work to do right now."

Harry retrieved the master key that would unlock any apartment in the building from the hook he kept by the door, and ventured out. The first door he approached was only about ten feet from his, but he could hear the pounding and that moaning almost as soon as he entered the hallway. Walking up to the door and using the tenant's name he called through it, "Jean, its Harry, the manager, are you okay?"

The only response was a more insistent pounding.

"Jean, step back away from the door so I can open it. I want to help you."

Furious pounding was the only response to Harry's pleas.

Inserting the master key with his left hand, tightly holding the Glock with his right, he quickly assessed what he was actually going to do. He was afraid that as soon as he unlocked the door, the tenant would surely come out and set upon him.

"Jean, please step back from the door so I can help you," Harry once again pleaded as he turned the key in the lock, standing just to the left of the door in a standard police door knock position. He clearly heard the key turn the deadbolt with a distinctive click; the pounding continued, with an increase in the moaning, but nothing else happened.

Not understanding why the tenant had not rushed out of the door, Harry grasped the doorknob, still standing to the left side of the entry, and slowly turned it. The pounding became more frantic, if that was possible, which only increased Harry's anxiety. He pushed the in-swinging door open just a fraction, maybe two or three inches, and was instantly met with the tenant, or whoever was on the other side, slamming their body into it and causing it to slam shut. Harry nearly pissed himself but quickly recovered. With a slightly trembling hand, he once again grasped and turned the knob, going through the same procedure as before, and again the door was slammed shut with the heavy thud of a body impacting it from the inside.

"God damn it! I'm trying to help you!" Harry shouted in frustration. No intelligent response was given in return from the tenant other than the constant pounding and moaning which was beginning to really grate on his nerves. Staring at the door for several moments, Harry finally said, "Fuck it," turned the knob once again, and shouldered the door with everything he had. The door flew open, knocking the tenant to the floor some feet back.

Harry was able to see clearly that this was, in fact, the tenant of the apartment. Jean was a young woman in her mid to late 20's, athletic and in very good shape – a stark contrast to Edna and Katy – although it was quite evident that she had the same reddish eyes and what appeared to be a pinkish white froth around her lips.

Jean quickly regained her feet, nearly jumping up as she rushed Harry, who had already had the Glock aimed in her general direction after he forced the door open. Without hesitation he fired twice into Jean, who was literally thrown back across the room from the impact of the rounds. Although Harry's experience in the lobby earlier that morning should have prepared him for what happened next, he watched in absolute horror as Jean got up. It was much slower this time, but she still got to her feet, staring at Harry all the while, and started at him again! All Harry could think as he fired a final round into her head was, "Oh my God, oh my God, oh my God."

After obliterating Jean's head from her body, he took several deep breaths, glancing at the carnage briefly. Turning, he walked back into the hall, leaving the door ajar slightly behind him. He leaned back against the doorframe and wiped his forehead with the back of his right hand, which held the gun, to remove the nervous sweat that had quickly developed. This time he did not get sick. "Okay, let's review here, Harry ole boy," he said in a weary tone. "You've now killed three people and mutilated the corpse of a UPS guy by blowing its head off. What have we learned from this so far?"

What began to finally sink in given the lack of response from Katy, Edna, and now Jean – regardless of how much he had resisted the thought – was that these 'people' were obviously so out of their minds that they didn't understand what was going on. Or he was truly facing something from the depths of hell as he had seen on TV a short time ago. "It looks like these things may not be smart enough to open a door." That was in line with what he had learned watching the news broadcasts. They had said these things, these zombies, were mindless creatures, reverting back to very primitive instincts. Harry took a few more deep breaths and allowed the years of training to take over. Moving with determination, he approached each door where he heard pounding along with the now all-too-familiar moaning; he identified himself and offered to help, unlocked the door and forcefully shouldering it open; and immediately shot whatever he found on the other side. With practiced ease he finally began to administer just headshots, as he understood this was truly the only way to kill them.

This went on for what seemed hours: Going methodically through the building, door-to-door, opening each where the pounding emanated and putting down whatever was behind it. Searching the apartment for any additional nasty surprises, then leaving the door ajar slightly so he would know which units he had cleared. Harry went from apartment to apartment until finally the building was quiet, other than the hammering of his heart and the slight ringing in his ears from the rounds he had fired. Out of forty-six units, twenty-eight had been occupied by tenant/zombies, and two of the units had belonged to Edna and Katy. He'd thought the rest were empty of any form of life, or 'unlife', but as he reached the door of the very last apartment on the sixth floor he could hear muffled voices. Knocking loudly twice, he excitedly said, "It's Harry, Harry Lancaster! Open the door!"

After a few moments the door to Apartment 67 opened and the very frightened tenant peered out, the security chain on the door still attached.

"Harry, what, what's happening?" The young woman asked in her usual whiny voice. "I've been calling you for hours! Why haven't you answered the phone? You need to do something!"

Harry looked at her in amazement. She'd always been a pain in the ass. Mom and dad paid all her bills, and she was nothing more than a spoiled brat. She was always complaining about something.

"Are you serious? Things have been a bit hectic around here lately if you haven't noticed!" Harry said while attempting to keep his building anger in check. What he wanted to do was pull her through that eight-inch gap and slap her.

"Well, you need to do something! The electricity has gone out and nobody is answering at PG&E," Miss Brat said, large tears rolling down her face. "I tried calling my mom but she isn't picking up."

Harry wanted to tell her that mommy was probably dead. Either that or running around infecting others. But he didn't have the opportunity.

"Who is that?" said a familiar male voice that Harry unfortunately recognized all too well. Miss Brat's boyfriend; a short, balding man in his early thirties, with oily hair and the onset of a gut. Harry was convinced, after dealing with him on several occasions, that he lived off the support of people like Miss Brat. Harry didn't understand what women could possibly see in this guy. Then again, he couldn't really understand what men saw in women like Miss Brat. The old saying *'there is someone for everyone'* surely applied in this couple's case. This guy never held a job long, always whining about something, and was a general pain-in-the-ass on many levels. Harry had taken to referring to him as Mr. PITA.

Harry watched the door to the apartment close and heard the chain being removed. When the door opened again, sure enough he was greeted by Mr. PITA.

"Look," he began, "we have been trying to call you for hours! We don't have electricity, the phone went out a little while ago, and can you please do something about that smell!"

Mr. PITA had begun his rant before taking in Harry's general condition. Not to mention the handgun that he held. Like a light bulb being switched on, Mr. PITA did a quick head-to-toe inspection of Harry and paled quickly.

"Umm, yeah, why do you have a gun, Mr. Lancaster?"

"Listen slick, if you aren't up on current events here, the world is in a shitload of trouble right now!" Harry said with obvious sarcasm. "I don't give a damn about your electricity or anything else involving you two right now! If you value your lives, you will close and lock that door, stay quiet, and wait for me to finish securing this building! Lock your door and do not open it for any reason until I let you know it's okay to come out! Do you understand that or do I need to draw you a fucking picture with bright colors to maintain your attention?"

Mr. PITA slammed the door in Harry's face. Harry heard the deadbolt being thrown and the chain put back into place. He waited a few moments but there was only dead silence from the other side of the door.

"Hmm, maybe I won't have to break out the crayons after all," Harry said to himself as he turned and headed toward the stairs leading to the roof – the last area of the building he needed to secure.

Thankfully, Harry did not discover any further surprises in the open common areas of the building. He had no idea how Edna or Katy had gotten out of their apartments, but he had found both of their doors locked. He decided that whatever was affecting people, causing them to turn into these monsters, probably had not turned the old ladies until they had made it to the lobby. He began to wonder just how long it did take that change to occur. The network news information didn't really discuss that much. Regardless, and to his immense relief, at least he knew his building was now free of those things.

As he was descending the last set of stairs toward the first floor, he suddenly heard screams coming from the direction of the lobby. Jumping three stairs at a time, he descended until he reached the first floor landing. With Glock in hand, for the second time that morning he rounded the corner into the lobby, this time expecting the worse. What he saw was the front door of the building standing wide open. He knew it had been closed the first time he'd seen it, so with some alarm he rushed up to the door with the intention of closing and locking it. He immediately witnessed a horde of zombies encircling the two idiots whom he'd found alive in Apartment 67 only a short time ago. The fools had obviously decided to make a run for it, but had only made it as far as the curb before being engulfed by a mass of what had once been their neighbors and possibly friends. Miss Brat was screaming, while Mr. PITA was trying to fight his way out of the mass, but both were all too quickly overpowered and ripped to shreds. Their screams were abruptly cut off as if someone had flipped a switch. Harry watched the massacre for only a moment before slamming and locking the heavy oak door.

He had told them he would be back, to stay inside and not come out until he told them it was okay. Although they had the deer-in-the-headlights expression when he'd said those words, he'd thought they would listen. The immense guilt that suddenly washed over Harry was almost too much to bear. Not only for the two people he'd watched die, but for the others he had killed. "I'm getting too old for this shit," he said as he slowly walked down the hall toward his apartment.

4

Through the haze of his emotional rollercoaster he knew he was in shock, and just wanted to crawl into bed, pulling the covers over his head, and let the world self-destruct on its own accord. Walking into his apartment, he once again closed and locked the door. Making his way into the bedroom, he placed the Glock and extra mags on the desk, got into bed, and fell into a heavy, dreamless sleep. Outside the now empty apartment building, the City of San Francisco did, in fact, continue to self-destruct.

After a twenty-five-year career in law enforcement, Harry had made the decision to retire, taking his pension along with a decent investment portfolio, and had planned to enjoy a less stress-infused life. He had never married, had no kids, and had only just reconnected with a family he'd had little contact with over the years. That had been the most life-altering event he had ever experienced. He had not spent money frivolously, nor on many material items other than what he needed to live comfortably, so he'd invested and those investments had been doing rather well. Still young enough to start another career before "permanent retirement", his strategy had been to start a security firm with two other retirees who were close friends, specializing in low threat dignitary and celebrity protection. Nothing had been set in stone, but that was the direction they had been leaning.

Harry had worked a radio car his entire career, never seeking promotions. He had truly enjoyed street level policing, and the community interaction that came with it; he didn't want to sit behind a desk dealing with the political bullshit that rank frequently required. He was a no-nonsense cop who didn't take shit; his was one of the first cars en route if back up was needed, yet he was even tempered, had a reassuring and calming demeanor, and always had a soft stuffed animal in the car trunk for a kid.

He was respected by the rank and file because they knew he could be counted on to have their backs. His outspoken bluntness however, generally pertaining to bullshit, didn't endear him to certain elements of the command staff, but even those he pissed off at times grudgingly respected Officer Harold Lancaster. At some point he had even earned the handle "Dirty Harry" when a couple of his buddies had conveniently let it be known that his favorite movies were Clint Eastwood's *Dirty Harry* series; all five of them.

Harry never really got that though. He didn't think he was anything like Harry Callahan. Yeah, okay, so he did happen to own a Smith and Wesson Model 29, with an 8 & 3/8" barrel chambered in .44 mag, with accompanying speed loaders, but he hadn't carried a wheel gun since the mid-1980's. Which had been a Colt Python .357 in those days. Now, with bad guys having access to automatic assault weapons, cops carried autoloaders. However, he had made an impression on the target range with that .44 many times, usually putting six out of six in the center consistently.

Nor had he once, in his entire career, run through the streets of San Francisco, jumping over cars, shooting "punks" one-handed with that cannon. He didn't consider having his wrist broken the most practical way in which to end a pursuit, with all the reports that had to be written, while delivering iconic catchphrases such as *"this is a .44 Magnum, the most powerful handgun in the world, and would blow your head clean off; you've got to ask yourself one question: "Do I feel lucky? Well do ya, punk?"*

After some good-natured ribbing and friendly pressure from colleagues he had worked with over the years and who had been promoted up through the ranks, he finally relented and accepted an FTO position the last few years before retirement. Being able to work the day shift, after fifteen years fluctuating between graveyard and swing, was one of the carrots that led him to finally promote up at least one small rung. As a Field Training Officer he was able to pass along experiences and real world techniques to the young men and women just starting their own careers – experiences that the academy could never hope to teach.

The "Dirty Harry" handle, and highly overstated reputation, had followed him to day watch. He had overheard rookies several times saying things like, "I heard Lancaster is kind of scary but a great FTO, and they say he gets all the most exciting calls! I really hope I get assigned to 'Dirty Harry'." Usually a couple of his buddies were in the vicinity, turning shades of purple to keep from laughing theirs asses off, while looking everywhere but in his direction.

"Yeah, they had nothing to do with this shit," Harry always said, chuckling. But that was great because if the rookies respected him, or even feared him a bit, they would listen to what he had to say, and hopefully the experience they gained from his critiques would help them throughout their careers.

He remembered his own FTOs that first year, and how vital that portion of the training had been in developing his own career. As a rookie, which seemed like a hundred years ago, he'd trained with some of the most dedicated and qualified police officers he'd ever met. That was why, in part, he had enjoyed such a long, successful career and had developed into a decent cop himself. *I hope to God some of those young men and women I helped train survived this zombie thing*, Harry had thought sadly several times over the past few hours.

All retirement plans went in the toilet with the 2008 financial downturn when Harold Lancaster lost his entire investment portfolio. Like millions across the nation, he found himself scrambling to make decisions pertaining to his future. With only his retirement pension to live on, and Social Security still too far down the road to even consider, his plans were completely and totally fucked. His two buddies who were to partner with him also lost everything they had.

The apartment building Harry had lived at for the past several years was quiet with a fairly good group of tenants, and was located in Nob Hill, one of the most desirable areas in the City. He had gotten to know the owners of the property fairly well, so when the previous building manager retired, Harry was approached to take the job.

"All you have to do is collect rents, call a plumber when needed, and rent vacant units when they come up," the owners had said during an impromptu hallway meeting.

"I've handled domestic violence calls, rapes, robberies, and shootings for years, how hard could it be! This'll be a piece a cake," Harry had concluded after that conversation.

With the allure of a free apartment and utilities, he'd accepted the position. It would be an easy way to eliminate one major expense from his tight monthly budget. It rapidly became apparent that the role of resident manager was anything but *a piece of cake*. The plumber could not be reached most times, tenants paid their rent late for all manner of reasons, and renting overpriced apartments, in one of the most expensive cities on the west coast, was like selling used cars at times.

Just eight months after taking the manager position, the owners had sold the building to an investor group, who could have cared less what happened, as long as the apartments were rented for the highest price possible. "We'll get back to you," was the general reply for anything else. Pest control was a foreign concept completely, and "Yeah, just send us an email and we'll look into that," quickly became their response for maintenance issues. Referencing back to his *outspoken bluntness generally pertaining to bullshit*, it was clear Harry's bullshit limit was close to being achieved with these folks.

5

Along with his quickly growing angst with property management, and his retirement plans no longer conceivable, Harry came to the realization that he missed his former *stress-infused life* more than he had expected, which led him back to the department as a Level 1 Reserve Officer. A Reserve Officer is an unpaid POST, *Police Officer Standards and Training*, certified peace officer, who must maintain the same stringent POST standards and training as regular full-time sworn cops.

Reserve Officers have full police powers while on duty and in uniform, and must volunteer at least sixteen hours of their time per month, although they usually put in many more hours than the minimum. They patrol in vehicles, on bikes, on foot, and in some cases on marine craft. Most recently they were deployed to assist in all of the Occupy demonstrations in the Financial District.

Although a bit long in the tooth to become a Reserve at his age, Harry had ultimately been accepted after demonstrating he was still in great physical condition, passing the oral interviews along with the updated background investigations, and completing a recertification POST program.

It also did not hurt that Harry still knew many of the department command staff, including the chief, but those relationships only gained him a foot in the door. He still had to prove he could do the job, and would have had it no other way. This was not like becoming a security guard at the San Francisco Centre keeping homeless out of Bloomingdales or looking for a lost kid.

He remembered feeling his *long-toothed* age with all the young men and women enrolled in the POST program he had attended to obtain his recertification, but there had been an immense sense of relief that none of those young folks knew anything about *Dirty Harry Lancaster*. He had specifically approached the POST instructors, who would have known he was a retired cop, to request that they not refer to his former career.

Harry actually thought he saw some disappointment at the time, as he was certain they had some training scenarios planned around his experiences. He had no intention of reliving his FTO days, nor of imparting pearls of wisdom from the *dinosaur age*. He had found that had been a most liberating decision, and thus actually enjoyed the program immensely.

Although the physical conditioning required just about did him in. "Those fucking instructors are offering up some pay back for not letting them use me as a visual aid," he had said after one particularly grueling day of hand-to-hand demonstrations in which they used Harry as the assailant, of course, and generally kicked his ass.

What was ironic was that after years of resistance, he had also accepted the rank of Reserve Sergeant just eight months after being sworn into the Reserve Unit.

"It's about time you finally took on some responsibility for a change, *old man*," Captain Lester Tomey, who supervised the Reserve Officer Unit, had said with a huge grin while handing Harry a star with the word SERGEANT engraved on the upper rocker, with the word RESERVES directly below.

"Screw you very much, *sir,*" Harry had replied good naturedly as he had accepted the star from his friend of many years.

Lester Tomey and Harold Lancaster had gone through the academy together and even worked a car together several years later until Les had been promoted to sergeant.

"Who the hell names their kid *Lester?*" Harry remembered kidding with him when they'd first met and been teamed up for take-down drills.

"They were probably the same kind of folks who would name their kid *Harold*," Les had immediately replied, laughing and then adding, "Let's get pizza later." Harry knew they would be friends.

Les promoted up through the ranks to captain, and the word had been he was in line for the next commander position. Those positions rarely opened up, but Les was patient, and he had made it clear on more than one occasion that he would retire only when they dragged him out "kicking and screaming and tossing my ass through the door."

Harry unfortunately had not spent much time with him over the past several years, as life goes on and all, but he had always wished him well and much success. He hoped Les had survived the April 1st onslaught, or that he had at least died quickly and was not a zombie somewhere.

After the promotion, which really only meant Harry got a new star with a different word on it, he began to work a higher than average of twenty-five to thirty unpaid hours per month. Normally assigned security at special events or demonstrations for crowd control, he had also been utilized many times in regular street patrol. That had thrilled him, and although his reserve status did nothing to increase his pension, or pay him an additional salary, he nonetheless felt that old sense of fulfillment he had missed after retirement.

Harry's thoughts at the time, finding himself back in police work, had run along the lines of *the more things change, the more they stay the same*, but as it turned out the decision to enter the Reserve Unit had ultimately saved his life. Being a Level I Reserve came along with a California PC 832 peace officer status, allowing him to carry, keep, and maintain firearms much more easily than as a retired cop, especially in the City and County of San Francisco with its progressive anti-gun laws. Harry *clearly* understood now what being *truly screwed* would have meant on April 1st when the madness began.

6

Pulling his thoughts back to the present, Harry stood up from the bed and walked the few short steps to the heavily curtained window. He had installed the curtains several years ago to block light from entering the bedroom when he had still worked the graveyard shift. It had been hard enough to get use to sleeping during the day without sunlight flooding the room, reminding him what a normal nine-to-five working person should be used to.

Now the curtains kept any light from the battery-powered lantern he had been using, not to mention the laptop and small television he had brought into the bedroom, from escaping the apartment and announcing his presence. Carefully pulling back a small section of the curtain, he looked upon a scene straight out of a horror movie. He said with a smirk, "Wonder what the new owners will do about a little zombie infestation."

Nothing in his twenty-five years of dealing with the worst humanity had to offer could have prepared him for what he had been witness to since this all began. There were at least fifty of those *things* directly below in the street. They were going in and out of buildings, which were obviously breached, pounding on doors of those they could not get into, all the while emitting that incessant moaning.

It was also apparent that the screaming he heard this morning had been from more survivors being found. Zs were pouring into the building across the street. Harry clearly saw, even in the dim morning light, fresh blood on the steps and sidewalk of the building that had not been there the day before. The bodies of the permanently dead kind lay everywhere, in every conceivable position, most mutilated beyond recognition.

Between the dead bodies and the zombies, the smell was horrendous, even through the closed window. Harry had come to know that odor intimately while responding to welfare checks on the elderly or the home bound left forgotten. The odor was of death personified; it permeated clothing, and assailed the senses almost to the point where you could taste it. Clothes could be cleaned, but that indescribable stench would linger in the nose for days. This was what once again assaulted Harry but a hundred fold; that, and an underlying trace of smoke.

Looking up slightly at the skyline above the buildings with concern and a real sense of dread, he saw the glow of the city burning. "This must've been how the folks felt who witnessed the '06 fire," he said, closing and sealing the curtain.

Although the fire might possibly destroy the City, he was fairly confident that it would do so at a much slower rate due to the automated fire suppression built into buildings along with fire retardant construction materials required by the vastly improved building and planning codes since the 1906 earthquake, and the resulting fire that had destroyed the majority of San Francisco east of Van Ness Avenue to the Bay.

"The City will surely die, but at least it will take out a large percentage of those fucks as she does," Harry thought. The spread appeared to be moving from the south side north, and although still south of Market Street, he knew his time frame to remain in the building was quickly closing.

"And I hate packing!" he said sarcastically.

It had only taken two days before the local TV stations went off the air and Internet service began to fail. But during those two days, there had been all manner of speculation as to what had happened. A virus, "Maybe." Terrorist act, "Probably." Some super-secret government experiment gone wrong? "Who knows?" Every religious zealot known seemed to be crawling out of the woodwork spouting, *"End of Days has arrived; repent as God's wrathful judgment is at hand."*

Then 'respected government experts' began describing medical reasons to explain why they were seeing *"people suddenly becoming extremely aggressive, attacking and appearing to bite and consume their victims, with many of the victims then getting up and joining the hordes of infected"*— and something about a mutated form of *"Super Rabies"*?

The local TV stations had field reporters in every part of the City, all with endless rhetoric about the events unfolding, although much of their descriptive had just been superfluous information. The old adage *"a picture is worth a thousand words"* was never a more true observation based on what was transmitted through the camera lens those first couple of days. Crowds of people, either pursuing or being pursued, running through the streets or pouring from buildings, with the infected indiscriminately attacking anyone they could get their hands on.

During all this, on a banner scrolling at the bottom of the screen from the San Francisco Office of Emergency Management, instructions were being relayed that all citizens should evacuate to one of the listed "established safe zones". Other officials from the police department were encouraging citizens to remain wherever they happened to be, to lock all doors and windows, and that "help would be dispatched to your location as soon as possible". Too many mixed messages to effectively save anyone.

Hastily assembled police skirmish lines, replete with officers uniformed in complete riot gear, were unable to hold back the hordes of people they had sworn to protect. Verbal commands were useless, as was the use of non-lethal weapons such as batons, pepper spray, or tear gas. Even less than lethal weapons – shotguns with rubber composite rounds – proved ineffective. At the point somebody decided to finally use lethal force it was obviously too late. The infected overwhelmed the lines in mere moments.

The officers surviving an onslaught at one particular line were seen regrouping to establish a new line, until there was simply nobody left as they finally succumbed to the massive size of the zombie horde. Most of the mauled cops, like many other victims of the zombies, were seen standing up, with all manner of horrendous injuries, to join the exponentially growing ranks of the infected.

Harry knew that even if he had been able to respond to the call out he had received on April 1st he would have also been killed, or worse yet, become one of the infected. That fact did little to ease the sense of deep loss for friends and the horrific way in which he'd watched them die live on television.

Every part of the City, from the Financial District, Russian Hill, Telegraph Hill, the Avenues, South of Market and all other districts, were in complete chaos. Harry watched as those "established safe zones" that had been set up in Golden Gate Park, AT&T Park, and a couple of other centralized locations were overrun by the infected.

The local TV channels showed the same horror until the field reporters either abandoned their cameras as the hordes were closing in on their locations, or were ripped apart waiting too long to join their fleeing colleagues. More than one reporter was heard screaming just off camera, while surely realizing their dream of a Pulitzer for their "career changing exposés" had been flushed. "Let's get the fuck out of here!" A few made it, but most did not. Finally, the stations just stopped broadcasting.

7

Thanks to the large water storage tank still used on the roof to service the apartment building, there was enough backpressure to shower. Although the water was cold and the pressure low, Harry did not care. Standing under the weak and frigid water, the events of the past several days inundated his thoughts.

In particular, he thought back to an interview he had seen on GNN, which was the only network still broadcasting by that particular time, just about a week after it all began. Fortunately, right before the batteries in his small portable 10" television had drained out completely. An interview that helped wake him to the stark realities of life in this new evolving world, and motivated him to do the one thing he had not given much consideration to until that moment. Survive!

There had been a GNN helicopter flying in the Southern California area, between Los Angeles and San Diego he thought, apparently reporting on conditions as seen from the air. Harry had no real interest in what was happening some four hundred miles from his own Hell, but something caught his attention. He saw a large helicopter rising up to hover next to the GNN chopper. Turning up the volume, he listened intently to the exchange.

**"*Yes, Fox, the helicopter on that strange ship has taken off and is climbing towards me now. I am unsure of their intentions, but I will wait here to see if they are friendly. Wait a moment. It looks like I'm receiving a radio message on the emergency frequency. Hold on while I patch you all into the conversation ... Yes, this is Chet in the GNN news helicopter over the Port of Long Beach, who is calling me?"*

"Hello there, Chet, this is Commodore Allen of the Sovereign Spirit, flag ship of the Survival Flotilla. I've been watching your

broadcast and thought it would be a good idea to come up and meet you. Maybe we can set the record straight before you and Mr. Rusher jump to any wrong conclusions. I'm flying the helicopter moving into position next to you and I'd like to invite you down to conduct an interview, if you're interested."

"Yes, Commodore, we at GNN are very interested in interviewing you. But can you tell me and our viewers something about what you are doing right now? We are broadcasting live, so you can consider this an interview if you like."

"Sure, Chet, we can do an interview over the radio if you like. It shouldn't take too long. Go ahead and ask your questions."

"Thank you, Commodore. Can you start by telling us who you are and what you're doing here? Who are all the people with you? And all these ships and boats? What are your plans? And how have you survived the zombie apocalypse?"

"Those are a lot of questions to handle at once, Chet, but I'll give it a shot. My name is Scott Allen. I'm in command of this Survival Flotilla by authority of the CDC, FEMA, and the Department of Homeland Security, with assistance from the Coast Guard and the U.S. Marine Corps. My current mission is to assist survivors on boats and ships along the coast of Southern California and to establish coastal safe havens for as many survivors as possible in the aftermath of what you are calling Z-Day, or the Zombie Apocalypse.

"My ship is called the Sovereign Spirit. She is a former cruise ship and ferry, converted into an expedition yacht before this crisis. Now she's the Flag Ship of the Flotilla and serves as our command center and mother ship for amphibious rescue and recovery operations. As for the other boats with us, we've collected a growing number of what we call boat people who survived the zombie outbreak by going to sea. They have become my primary responsibility. What we're doing here is securing a source of supplies to keep the people with us alive."

"We've isolated a small area in this port as a safe haven for the Flotilla and we're loading cargo that will help us establish more safe havens on islands and isolated anchorages along the coast. So, for the people listening, if you are on a boat right now and need assistance, you can come here to get it, or wait for us to come to you. But there is no way to get here by land anymore, unless you can fight your way through tens of thousands of zombies surrounding us.

"And even then you wouldn't be able to get past the barriers we have built to keep the zombies out. In the future we hope to be able to open some sort of supply line to survivors inland too. But that isn't possible right now. So, at least for now, only those who have access to a boat or a helicopter can come here for supplies. Otherwise, you won't be able to get here, so don't even try."

"That seems a little unfair, Commodore Allen. What about all of the people trapped in their homes? Don't you have any plans to help them too?"

"I'd like to be able to help everyone who's listening to me now, Chet, everywhere. But you know I can't do that. What I can do is tell them how to survive on their own, or preferably with the help of other survivors near them. There are a few critical things that we've learned since Z-Day. First, zombies don't swim and are afraid of water. Use that knowledge to your advantage.

"Secondly, zombies prefer to walk down hill, unless they get attracted to something up hill. If you can get to high ground and avoid attracting attention, your chances may improve. Hilltop strongholds are a good place to organize a defensive community; not as good as an island or a boat perhaps, but much better than a house in a city or suburb.

"Third, and perhaps most obvious, we need to eliminate as many zombies as possible and the best way we know to do that is to shoot them in the brain. If you don't have a gun, try to get one, or improvise a weapon to defend yourself. However, if our Flotilla is the only organized resistance force in this area, then Los Angeles is doomed. So get it together people!

"Don't wait for the police, or the government, or the military to come and rescue you. They won't. They can't. The closest organized military resistance is in San Diego, and the only thing they can do for civilians right now is put them into crowded refugee camps on Coronado Island. So don't expect help to show up here any time soon."

There was more to the interview but it related to what was currently happening around their specific area in Southern California. Harry had understood though, very clearly, the basic concepts that Commodore Allen had been trying to get across. This was not a local, regional, or even national crisis. This was on a world-wide scale, and there was no assistance imminent for anyone. Except maybe those lucky enough to be in close proximity to this *Survival Flotilla.*

But the interview had given Harry optimism, and at least the initial building blocks of a plan. But, more importantly, it had given him a reason to live. All was not lost, as he had initially thought, and there were other people out there. Now those survivors needed to act, to help themselves and others when possible, or they would simply *not* continue surviving. Humanity was being pushed toward an extinction level event, and it needed to start pushing back if anyone was to survive this madness.

Okay Commodore Allen, I may not be able to get to your flotilla or your stronghold, Harry had thought with passion, *but I have a very large bay, my own marina with boats, and several islands in the middle of that bay. Let's just see what we can do about setting up our own survivor stronghold.*

8

Stepping from the shower, clearing those thoughts, he looked in the wall mirror of the dimly lit bathroom, two small candles being the only light source. At fifty-four years old, soon to reach yet another birthday, his 6'6" frame was still in decent shape thanks to regular gym visits, eating well-balanced meals, and, as he had always said, "just plain ole good Midwestern genes."

He still maintained a fairly youthful appearance, with piercing hazel eyes, which had most people thinking him at least ten years younger. He had started going grey by age twenty-five, which he had felt gave him an air of maturity. Now, looking at the short-cut, mostly grey head of hair, he thought it gave him an air of just being *old*. "Still, all things considered, not too bad, but *am* I really too old for this shit?" Harry asked his reflection, then turned away and headed toward the bedroom to dress.

He pulled on jeans, a well-worn and broken-in pair of tactical boots, and a heavy, long-sleeved shirt. From the closet he took out a lightweight leather jacket, along with a pair of Kevlar-lined leather gloves. Foregoing the much heavier, and bulkier, duty belt he had routinely worn while in uniform, he selected a lightweight nylon tactical belt.

To that belt he added the respective lightweight nylon cases containing an expandable baton, Streamlight high lumen LED flashlight, and four polymer magazines loaded with .45 caliber 230-grain brass-jacketed hollow point rounds, and finally a high rise break front holster. The final piece of equipment, and undoubtedly the most important, sat on the desk in front of him – a Glock, Gen4 G21, .45-caliber autoloader that held a thirteen-round magazine.

Over the years he had found the Glock 21 to be one of the most reliable and durable service sidearms he had owned. The stopping power of this weapon was impressive, and it had a manageable weight and reasonable recoil. Picking the gun up, he pulled the slide back to chamber a round. Holstering the Glock, and locking it in, he thought, *you're a beauty, but I am going to need more than just you.*

Harry had a total of sixty-five rounds loaded in magazines, thirteen per mag with four of those on his belt and one in the Glock, and only fifteen boxes of twenty to reload from. He knew that more fire power needed to be located if he was to have a chance at surviving for any length of time. Refilling the magazines was a bit time consuming, even though the springs in the five mags he had were fairly well broken in, allowing rounds to slide in a bit faster. But with zombies trying to bite his ass he had to increase the amount of firepower he carried. "I know just the place to get it, too," he said with a slight smile.

The last items he picked up were his badge, a seven-point star he had already attached to a belt clip, and his wallet. The only difference between an active duty officer's star and a Reserve's were the small letters spelling out the word RESERVES just above the center badge number. He slipped the clip with the badge on his belt in a location designed to hold it securely.

Opening the wallet briefly, he saw the familiar police credentials, both with his picture on them, showing through behind opposite compartments covered in clear plastic. One was his active reserve officer ID and the other a regular police ID with the word RETIRED stamped on it. *These just might come in handy at some point,* he thought, closing and placing the wallet in a rear pocket on his jeans.

Turning to the laptop on the desk, with the intention of placing it in a backpack to take with him, Harry had a spur of the moment idea. Sitting down, he brought up Internet Explorer and then the Google search page, which loaded extremely slowly. Once the search page finally loaded, he typed in *Scott Allen* and *Sovereign Spirit,* then pressed the enter key. After staring at the screen for almost a full five minutes, watching the little *working arrow* spin indicating a search was in progress, he started to think the Internet had finally failed.

Just as he was reaching to turn the laptop off to conserve what battery was left, he was shocked to see search hits suddenly pop onto the screen. There was only one site that even remotely matched what he thought he was looking for, and that was *sovereignspirit.net.* He clicked on the website and impatiently waited while the server once again attempted to connect, his anticipation growing by the second.

To his relief, the website finally downloaded and opened. The homepage indicated it was originating directly from the ship *Sovereign Spirit,* and that they had their own web server with direct satellite link. Looking over the page, Harry located another link on the site that he clicked on. That brought him to a blog page, with the current date, inviting survivors to post information on their particular locations and what was happening!

Excitedly scrolling down the page, he read post after post from people across the nation detailing what was currently happening in their areas. Several seemed desperate, others seemed to have things under control for the time being, but what struck Harry was that he saw only one other post from San Francisco. This concerned him a great deal, and he wondered if maybe there had just not been that many people who had survived the zombies in the Bay Area.

Reading further, he saw that the posts were being answered by Billy Allen, onboard the Sovereign Spirit, who apparently was Scott Allen's son. His replies were supportive but it was clear that the Sovereign Spirit would be unable to help most of those who posted or needed help. They were inland and Scott Allen had made it clear in his GNN interview that his focus was on the western coastal areas for now.

Harry decided to add to the blog the limited amount of information he had gained since the infection had hit, what he had observed in San Francisco, and what his plan was. *For all the good it will do*, he thought as he sat typing. "If nothing else, it will let them know there *are* survivors in this area, and they may decide it worth the effort to reach us at some point," he muttered to himself.

My name is Harold Lancaster and I am in San Francisco. I have watched as the City has been flooded with the infected. Seemingly hundreds have died right before my eyes as a result of that ever-rising horde or whatever these things are. People have been torn apart in the streets and devoured. Or worse, have risen from attacks with horrific injuries to join the ranks of the infected. It has been like watching piranhas in a feeding frenzy or the worst horror movie ever made! There has been no sign of military assets anywhere in the City, and the police that initially attempted to control the storming masses of infected were quickly decimated.

All the established 'safe zones' set up by the local government have been completely destroyed. There must be other survivors, I am certain, but I have no idea of the numbers or their locations. Unfortunately, I know for a fact that weapons, guns of any type, are almost impossible to locate with this City's strict anti-gun laws. I doubt folks were able to react quickly enough with other forms of weapons to defend themselves before being overwhelmed.

I listened to the rather unorthodox interview between Commodore Allen and GNN. Because of what he had to say, I am taking responsibility for my survival. It is my sincere hope that other survivors in the City were able to hear that interview and act accordingly. Our local city officials have accomplished little in helping San Franciscans and, as typical, many mixed messages were sent out about what to do. That included instructions to shelter in place, which I believe caused the direct death of many more people.

I am a retired cop and have weapons in my possession. Not the level of firepower to do much at this point, but enough I believe to help accomplish a plan I have been roughing out. Upon completing this email I am headed to the closest police station from my location which is about ten blocks away. If I am able to breach the station I will attempt to locate additional firepower which will greatly aid my ability to get through the City.

I plan to attempt securing water transportation of some sort from our marina and head out to one of the Bay islands. Alcatraz is the closest to the marina and that seems the logical choice. I will be keeping an eye out for survivors that I may be able to help, but at this point I am not sure what I would be able to do in that regard.

The information you passed along about water and hills is extremely helpful. As you may know, San Francisco is famous for steep in-city hills. I believe that it might be possible to avoid some encounters with the infected by using stealth, staying quiet, and using some of the steep streets to my advantage. Although that may just be wishful thinking from what I have seen. However, the City is also burning, so I will have little choice but to move soon. I also observed something happen near or on the Bay Bridge. Looked like several large explosions but I have no idea what that was about at this point.

There is something else very important that I need to pass along in the event this could prove helpful to others. I had begun to notice a peculiar behavioral pattern developing in the infected the second day after the infection hit. In the late afternoon, always at about the same time, they seemed to start to move in what I can only describe as a migration pattern. I spent a couple of days watching them but the reason for this behavior eluded me. That was until I saw the GNN interview with the Commodore! The infected are afraid of water and the realization of what was causing this strange movement hit me! It's the fog! They are trying to get away from our heavy moisture-laden fog!

Although I realize the Flotilla cannot help us here, we can nonetheless take the example of what you have done. Humanity stands at the doorstep of an extinction level event but we certainly do not have to go quietly into the night. San Francisco is dead but the Bay may offer hope. I know it will offer at least a chance rather than waiting here to either burn to death or be consumed by these spawns of hell. I will write more if, and when, I am able. Luck to us all!

9

After completing the blog entry, which he also copied and pasted into an email to the *Sovereign Spirit,* Harry powered down the laptop and slipped it into the backpack sitting by the desk. This pack contained the boxed ammunition, several energy bars and a few bottles of water, a small first aid kit, and a change of clothes. "Thank God for earthquake preparedness," he said, shaking his head. "If the Big One could only have been the least of our worries."

Taking one final look around the apartment, realizing he might not see it again, he walked toward the front door, slipping on his leather jacket, pulling on the thin Kevlar-lined tactical gloves and shouldering the backpack. He looked at several mementos, photos with friends, several framed commendations, art he had collected over the years, and several other items that once held sentimental value for him. Each item now seemed different, void of anything meaningful somehow.

What he had once seen in those objects was now gone. "There's no more room for *stuff* other than what can keep me alive," Harry said to himself. He knew the old life was dead, and it was time to move forward with the plan he had formulated after finally realizing he had an unexpected ally of sorts; an ally that had almost gone completely unnoticed.

Harry had been watching the infected closely from his apartment windows since the first day. He'd watched the growing horror unfold; the survivor population was quickly being decimated, with more zombies than people left on the streets. That was when he began to notice what he'd thought was a pattern of behavior, but with the stress of everything, his brain wasn't getting what his eyes were seeing.

At around 5 p.m. or so every day, the zombies all seemed to start heading south. After the first couple of days, Harry went up to the roof; from there, he had a fairly decent view of the surrounding area. Being six stories up, he was not too concerned about being seen from the street, but he was nonetheless careful in remaining hidden.

His job had required him to be observant, to notice every nuance of his environment – searching for evidence, interviewing victims and suspects alike, noticing what was being worn, bulges in a coat that could represent a weapon. It had become second nature to take in a scene at first glance, and although Harry did not have a photographic memory, he had developed a method in which he cataloged what he saw and was able to bring it to mind fairly well when needed.

But this zombie pattern, if a pattern at all, was eluding him. He knew they moved in the late afternoon, at about the same time, and usually in the same direction. In a moment of complete frustration he remembered his first FTO, Shane O'Connor, the stereotypical *Good Irish Cop*, who had once told him, "You better get your fuckin' head out your ass there, boy! You want to be a good cop someday? You keep your mouth shut, your eyes open, and you damn well better pay attention to what's going on around you at all times!"

O'Connor's pearls of wisdom, along with a hot, heavy, spit flying, all in your face ass chewing, had occurred after an area search on a robbery investigation; Harry had walked right past the weapon that had been used in the crime. It had been thrown in some bushes, and not easily seen, but O'Connor had found it by double-checking the rookie's initial search.

For the rest of Harry's tour assignment with this FTO, he was constantly challenged on his observation skills, along with a thousand other things FTOs threw at rookies. O'Connor's favorite exercise was to allow Harry to inspect the squad car, as was normal procedure prior to going in service.

The car needed to be swept to ensure nothing illegal had been dropped by suspects, to confirm all equipment was present, that the radios worked, as did the lights and siren, and any puke had to be cleaned up. That was every rookie's job: cleaning up puke, urine, and all matter of disgusting things left behind by the previous shift.

O'Connor would plant objects in the car, and if Harry did not find them he was privileged to spend the first couple hours of the shift listening to the shortcomings of all rookies, and *"why they had believed their mommas when they told them they could be cops,"* along with references to Harry's inbred ancestry resulting in his level of intelligence being equal to pond slime.

Harry had been surprised to get one of the highest evaluations O'Connor had ever written, according to the division captain. O'Connor had retired a year after Harry had passed probation, and he had been invited to his going away party at a seedy Irish pub in the middle of the Tenderloin, of course. He remembered O'Connor coming up to him, grasping his hand firmly, and saying it had been an honor to work with him.

Harry had not only deeply respected Shane O'Connor, but during his own time as an FTO had utilized much of the training techniques O'Connor had. Not as much yelling, screaming, ancestry references or ass chewing, but nonetheless very similar. Rookies still got to clean out the puke, but that was a rite of passage – one other thing O'Connor took great pleasure imparting on many occasions. Harry had even been convinced at one point that Shane O'Connor was somehow related to R. Lee Ermey. That salty, bushy-eyebrowed, sadistic old drill sergeant turned actor, *of sorts.*

So he continued to watch for that elusive pattern the zombies were demonstrating. He knew it was there; he just needed to *keep his mouth shut, his eyes open, and needed to damn well pay attention to what was going on around him.*

Looking down from three various locations on the roof, he observed many of the infected moving south at about the same time each day, almost like they were migrating. Three things he was certain of was the time of day this apparent migration occurred, that they all headed in a southerly direction, and that there seemed to be slightly less of them in the areas surrounding his location.

Their numbers were relative, of course. There were still seemingly dozens spread out in the area, but less of them than in the beginning. Something was definitely odd about their behavior, other than the obvious fact they were *zombies,* but he just couldn't put his finger on it. He could see down Stockton Street, a fairly steep hill, past Union Square, toward a section of Market Street that appeared to be packed with the infected. "Why are you all down there?" Harry pondered several times.

On the second and final day of his zombie stakeout, another event occurred that would ultimately help Harry. As he was just getting ready to open the roof door to descend down the stairs back to his apartment, he heard what could only have been the report of a very large weapon from the direction of the Bay Bridge, which was southeast of his building. It was very similar to something heard during fireworks shows just before the huge shell blanks exploded overhead.

As he turned toward the sound, a section of the Bay Bridge was clearly in view. The next thing he heard was a huge explosion followed immediately by thick black smoke rising from the bridge section nearest Treasure Island. Harry had just said "What the fuck!" when he heard three more shots in fairly rapid succession and, with the corresponding explosions, more black smoke rising but in different sections of the upper deck. All in very close proximity to the Treasure Island connector.

Harry had no idea what was happening, but the effect the noise had on the zombies was immediate. They all started walking, running, or crawling in the direction of the bridge and the noise, clearing yet more of them from his area. In addition, they were headed right for the burning section of the City, so it became Harry's fervent hope that the fire would also take out some of them along the way.

The elusive zombie behavior had finally become very clear to Harry, the realization hitting him like a ton of bricks, as he was watching the interview on GNN "… *zombies don't swim and are afraid of water,*" and "*zombies prefer to walk downhill, unless they get attracted to something up hill.*" Harry had sat bolt upright in the chair when he heard that. "Could it be that simple?"

"It's the fog!" Harry had shouted. "They're trying to get away from the heavy fog, forcing them downhill!" That was when the gears started turning in formulating the plan he was going to attempt. But he needed to be sure. The City was continuing to burn, and his time was running out to remain in the building much longer, so whatever he was going to do, he needed to do it soon. Being burned to death or ripped apart by zombies were options Harry preferred to avoid.

10

The late spring and summer months were generally the time of year that the fog was the heaviest in San Francisco; it was very thick and rolled into the Bay past the Golden Gate to ultimately blanket a good portion of the City. This fog brought along with it a heavy mist, almost like a light rain drizzle, sometimes covering everything like dew. *"The coldest winter I ever spent was a summer in San Francisco,"* was a saying that had become a San Francisco cliché. Although this was supposed to have been something Mark Twain had said, it had turned out to be an invention of unknown origin. But never truer words were spoken. This time of year San Francisco was the *foggiest*.

Going back onto the roof, Harry spent a couple days, just to be certain, never leaving and only dozing for an hour or two at a time, observing the zombies and their behavior. Unfortunately he was forced to witness things he would have rather not: survivors apparently trying to make a break for safety, wherever they had thought that might be, and either on foot or in vehicles. The ones on foot were usually brought down almost immediately, being set upon and consumed. Harry had been an avid NatGeo fan. Now he had center seat to an all-new series for them. *The feeding habits of the anything-BUT-elusive Super Rabies Infected Zombie.* "See mutilation and death in 3D, high definition," he'd said to himself sarcastically. "Thank God we don't have smell-a-vision."

The survivors in cars, vans, or trucks fared only slightly better, which meant they just lived a little longer than those who tried running on foot. The sheer number of Zs that would surround a vehicle would bog it down to a complete halt. The vehicle took out portions of the horde, smashing them into bloody masses of flesh and bone, but never enough to really do much good.

The infected would quickly surround vehicles, bringing them to a halt as their tires could simply find no traction on the inches-thick gore that covered the street. Once the vehicles were stopped, the zombies made short work of breaking the windows and dragging the survivors out, kicking and screaming, to be lost in the middle of yet another feeding frenzy. There was never much left of the bodies when the zombies were finished with them other than scattered bloody bones and pieces of shredded clothing.

But Harry was able to confirm that the zombies did, in fact, move away from the fog. Harry spent those two days on the roof watching the thick grayish fog slowly roll in like a specter arriving to consume all in its path. It was fascinating to see the zombies' reaction to the fog. Once the moisture touched them, they became as frenzied in their need to move away from it as during their wholesale slaughter of survivors. Whether these things felt fear was unknown, but they definitely had *issues* with what Mother Nature brought to their doorstep each evening. Harry was now ready to put his plan in action.

With one final glance, Harry left his apartment, feeling the need to lock the door to what would surely become nothing more than a dusty time capsule. Or more likely it would be completely consumed by fire. He then made his way down the main hallway to the building's front entrance and approached one of the side windows next to the door.

Carefully looking through the small window, he was satisfied that at least for the moment the immediate area in front of the building was clear enough for him to slip out. The Zs appeared to still be distracted by whatever they had found in the building across the street, or whatever zombies did in their spare time, and it was time to move. Glancing out one last time to make certain the coast was still clear, Harry quickly exited the building and made his way down the street, using the many stalled vehicles for cover as much as possible.

Harry's first destination was the closest police station to the Bay, which was Central Station located on Vallejo Street. He knew that he needed to reach the Bay, the marina specifically, to work his plan, but along the way he wanted to follow Commodore Allen's suggestion of eliminating as many zombies as possible.

To accomplish that, he reminded himself once again that more firepower was needed. He had been assigned to Central right before retirement, and usually reported there when he was on reserve duty, so knew the layout very well. But the most important thing Harry knew was that this station housed one of the SWAT units, which meant there could be some interesting items still in the armory. Whether anything was left after the heavy April 1st response was unknown, but he needed to start somewhere. Harry figured that not enough officers had been able to make it to the station to have taken all of the equipment and weapons.

When Harry left the apartment building, dawn had just began to break, giving just enough light to see the otherwise darkened streets. He immediately saw it was the typical San Francisco morning he had needed, cold and with a heavy high fog. This was not the typical fog most people recognized, covering everything; rather it was a higher, swirling type.

It was maybe a hundred and fifty feet up from the ground, but with a mist that left a heavy layer of moisture on everything. Exactly the kind he had hoped for. This was the type of morning Harry had worked into his plan, and would use for cover while making his way to the police station.

Harry knew that from his current location on Pine Street, he would need to go west one block and then turn north onto Powell. If he were lucky, he would be able to take Powell the ten or so blocks to where it intersected with Vallejo Street. Then he would turn east on Vallejo, as Central Station was located about half a block down on the left-hand side. Seemed simple enough at first glance, but he knew things were never "that simple".

As he slipped through the streets, he begin to see zombies roaming the area directly in from of him, although the heavy moisture in the air seemed to be affecting them. They were stumbling around, seemingly disoriented and in a rage, clawing at themselves as if on fire. There were probably thirty to forty that he could make out in the dim morning light.

Thankfully, they were spread out, with the closest one to him being almost two hundred yards away. He was sure there had to be more, but he had to focus on what he could see for now. He knew this was going to become a running battle, and he hoped his alliance with Mother Nature would help him out or it was going to be a very short campaign.

With a sardonic smile, he knew it was time for *Dirty Harry Lancaster* to start kicking zombie ass and screw taking the names part. It would only be a matter of moments before Harry Lancaster would embark on an all-new form of police work. He was still serving and protecting, but now he would be doing it with a shoot-first-and-ask-questions-later mentality.

With one fluid motion, he withdrew his Glock from the breakfront on his right side, pulling back the first trigger safety, and took aim at the nearest zombie. A famous line that *Harry Callahan* had said from *Sudden Impact* popped to mind: *"To me you're nothin' but dog shit, you understand? And a lot of things can happen to dog shit. It can be scraped up with a shovel off the ground. It can dry up and blow away in the wind. Or it can be stepped on and squashed. So take my advice and be careful where the dog shits."* With that thought, he completed the finger pull on the trigger and blew the top of the first zombie's head off.

The Glock is not the easiest weapon to use in an extended firefight due to the safety features built into the trigger pull, and it took practice to master any real accuracy, but once mastered it produced some awesome results. Results Harry was appreciating greatly at the moment.

He continued to fire while steadily moving forward, stopping briefly to aim, watching the zombies approach while trying to zero in on his location, and then falling under the impact of the heavy .45 caliber hollow point slug. Advance, aim, discharge the weapon; advance, aim, discharge the weapon. Drop the empty magazine; place the empty in the left rear pocket of the jeans. Insert a fresh mag, pull the slide, sweep the area for the next threat, aim, and discharge the weapon. A smoothly controlled, automatic process with accurate results.

Several of his shots went low but Harry was close enough that even though the shots to center mass did not kill the zombies, it was enough to put them down, and they were slower to recover. Harry took macabre satisfaction in seeing chests explode, legs and arms blown off, and in many cases, spines shattering. The zombies, paralyzed with those wounds, could then only stare at him while he passed.

It dawned on Harry, as he kept up his steady progress down Powell Street that he did not have to achieve kill shots on every target. Although many of the rounds he discharged were effective in removing large portions of zombie heads, he just needed to inflict severe enough damage to slow them down. The .45 caliber hollow point round obliged very nicely toward that end. Harry began to target center mass along with the pelvis area, which would take the legs right out from under them.

11

Harry was making headway, and had gotten maybe six blocks when, as he feared, more zombies began to appear from some of the buildings; they were drawn, he was certain, by the noise from firing the gun. As he had already seen, they knew he was there, somewhere, but they still could not focus enough to get his precise location. He even watched, to his horror, a group of at least eight of them start running in his direction as he was changing out magazines. "Fuck me!" was all Harry could say. But to his surprise they ran right by him.

The zombies knew he was there because they stopped just a few yards past him, moaning and growling in apparent frustration, arms extended with hands almost claw-like, turning their heads as if on a pivot to look for him. It appeared as if the moisture in the heavy fog caused some serious sight distortion in their unblinking eyes.

Harry didn't waste time in contemplating the reasons; he just got his ass in gear and took advantage of this newly confirmed information. He was not going to stick around to find out how keen their sense of smell might be.

Harry had been able to put some distance between him and the last grouping of Zs. Realizing they were probably being drawn more to the sound of the gun discharging than actually seeing him, he decided to try a slightly different tactic. Down to two full mags, twenty-six rounds, there was little choice.

He did not think he could call a time out to reload the three empty mags that were in his back pocket. Reloading the rather bulky .45 round into spring-loaded mags, even ones well broken in, could be a bitch in the best of times, let alone when there were zombies trying to eat one's face off.

Making sure there was a fresh mag inserted, Harry holstered the gun and deployed his ASP expandable baton that was located on the left side of his belt. He cross drew it across the front with the dominant right hand for greater control. He had carried several different forms of batons over the years, which were striking weapons to force compliance, and were very effective in most cases.

With all the shit a cop had to carry on a duty belt, the reduced size and comfort of an expandable baton soon outweighed some of the downsides. Also, an expandable was always on the belt, so during the adrenaline rush of a pursuit or hot response an officer no longer had to worry about forgetting to grab their baton as they exited the car. This tended to happen more frequently than one would think.

Harry flicked his wrist, extending and locking the baton to its full 26" length. The ASP had been touted as the more reliable and effective baton on the market. It was made from 4140 steel tubing, and had been purported to be twenty-five percent stronger than the standard steel shaft competitors, with a much higher tensile strength. Having used the ASP many times over the years, training extensively on the proper methods of body strikes to effectively force compliance, Harry had never considered, nor attempted, to use it as a lethal weapon.

But circumstances certainly dictated thinking outside the box right now. "Let's just see if the sales hype was *all that*," he said as he advanced on the nearest zombie. Swinging the baton with a standard side sweeping blow to complete a peroneal nerve strike, hitting the area roughly a hand span above the knee towards the back of the leg, brought no results from the zombie. Normally, this strike would have taken down a person almost instantly; now all it did was assist the infected to hone in on Harry's precise location.

"Well that's not going to work," Harry said aloud while immediately changing his stance and bringing the full force of the next strike directly across the side of the zombie's head. The thing went down and Harry instantly delivered an obviously fatal blow to the thing's forehead, caving it in with a wet, cracking sound. The zombie remained motionless, apparently truly dead. *One down, a few hundred thousand to go*, Harry thought dismally.

12

He began to jog the rest of the way down Powell, reciting a cadence of "I'm getting too old for this shit, I'm getting too old for this shit, I'm getting too old for this shit," punctuating the words as each foot made contact with the street. He would momentarily stop to deliver his newfound striking technique to the head of any zombie in his path, and then continued his advance, finally reaching Vallejo Street. Rounding the corner, he nearly collided into possibly the largest woman he thought he had ever seen except on maybe a vintage Russian exercise film.

Harry had been fairly close to many of the zombies he had taken out, but had never really looked at them in his haste to keep moving. This time, however, he noticed every detailed feature of this particular zombie who was preparing to rip him apart. The eyes were like those of a corpse, yet at the same time appeared feral. The ever-moving mouth, like it was chewing on something, contained a bloody, white frothy discharge around broken and blackened teeth, those having all manner of obscene sinew stuck between them.

There were chucks of skin and muscle missing from the Z's cheek and both arms. Its clothing hung mostly in torn rags. One foot was missing a shoe and was at an impossibly wrong anatomical angle. The long hair was matted, with a large section missing on the right side revealing the ivory skull below. There were streaks running down the inner thighs but Harry did not even want to consider what might have been the source. With each exhalation of breath as it emitted the ever present moaning, the putrid odor that emanated from it engulfed Harry's personal space, gagging him and bringing tears to his eyes.

The huge Amazonian zombie began to close the very short distance that separated it from Harry. It was too close to execute an effective blow with the baton, so Harry brought the ASP up and simply shoved it into the gaping mouth with enough force to collapse it completely back into the ready position. If a zombie could look surprised, this monstrosity certainly did. It stumbled back a step, clawing at the piece of metal shaft protruding from its mouth, not seemingly aware enough to grasp and pull it out.

Taking advantage of the momentary distraction, Harry pulled the Glock and put a round into the zombie's face point blank, which blew most of the head from its shoulders, and unfortunately taking the ASP with it.

"Asshole! I really liked that stick! " Harry said, looking back at the headless body as he continued to jog to the station which was now just a few yards in front of him.

Central Station was a bulky four-story over lobby building, very linear, fortress-like and blockish, with a façade mostly of concrete. Built in the 1960's, the style of the building was referred to as Brutalist, or Modernist, architecture. This style came about for government buildings, low-rent housing and shopping centers in order to create functional structures at a low cost. This certainly described the visual appearance of Central Station. Being one of the oldest district stations in the City, and closest to the Bay and the consistent sea air, it needed constant maintenance on its façade to repair cracks.

There were four entrances into the station: a garage level and the main entrance on the Vallejo Street side, and a garage and prisoner entrance on the Emery Lane side, which was just a narrow alleyway on the east side of the building. Harry saw immediately that the Vallejo garage roll door was down, so he assumed the main entrance would be secured. He continued to jog around the building onto Emery Lane. He hoped that he could somehow gain entrance on that side.

As he got closer to the doors which were toward the end of the building, he slowed to a walk, scanning the area for any threats. Emery was a very narrow alley so there was only police vehicle parking allowed, and at the moment he only saw two radio cars alongside the building. One of them looked very clean, as if it had been recently detailed. The other, however, looked as if it had just been driven down Main Street in Hell. It was covered in what appeared to be drying blood, along with bits and pieces of flesh and hair. The left side windows were all completely broken out, and as he passed the front he saw both headlights were gone. Both the front and rear ends were severely damaged, but what really caught Harry's attention was the arm protruding from between the front push bar and the grill. He could only imagine what had happened to this car.

13

Continuing past the cars, he cautiously approached the prisoner entrance and pulled on the door, which was normally electrically locked and could only be opened from inside the station. To his surprise, the door easily pulled open. Apparently the backup generator for the building was down; even though the electricity in this part of the City had been out for several days, this door should not have been unsecured. He entered, closing the door quietly, then turned the inside manual lock to secure it.

The area in which he stood now was like a sally port in a jail. There was the exterior door, which he had just locked, and then another door directly in front of him which allowed entry into the booking area. This sally port controlled access to the station proper. Harry approached the second door and also found it unlocked. He began to think the building had been abandoned, because this door also had a manual lock that obviously had not been used.

When he entered the booking area, he was surprised to find the emergency lighting on, which meant the generator was in fact operational; otherwise, he would have walked into pitch blackness. The feeling of not being alone in this building instantly hit Harry. He immediately drew his Glock, crouched down, and listened.

Satisfied that there were no imminent threats, Harry moved toward the hallway with his weapon locked forward while looking down the sights. The direction he looked was where the weapon was pointed. Entering the hallway, where doors on either side led to various offices, conference rooms, and storage rooms, he slowly and quietly walked to the end, then turned to his right.

This took him to another short hallway, with only one door at the end, and he immediately walked up to that door and put an ear against it. He couldn't hear anything from the other side, so he grasped the doorknob and turned it; once again, to his surprise and dismay, he found it unlocked. This door led into the station armory, and finding it unlocked was not a good sign.

As he entered the brightly lit room, he saw empty racks where weapons should have been. There were still several shotguns, but what brought an immediate smile to Harry's face were the three Colt AR-15A3 tactical rifles in the furthest rack at the rear of the room. That was his reason for coming to the station. This was the heavy firepower he was looking for, although without ammunition for the ARs they were just pieces of aluminum alloy and synthetic materials.

Turning to his right, he walked up to the large steel reinforced door of the ammo locker. This was actually a medium-sized room that contained the live ammunition, less-than-lethal rounds for the shotguns, a few riot shields, and other pieces of equipment. What he needed to find was the 5.56 mm ammo for the ARs. He quickly discovered that the door was locked.

Okay, I knew it wouldn't be that easy, so now I ... Harry didn't get to finish that thought as a shout from directly behind him interrupted it.

"FREEZE, POLICE! SHOW ME HANDS! DO IT NOW!" This command appeared to come from someone very young. The shaky male voice cracked a bit, like a kid just going through puberty. It was obvious whoever Squeaky Voice might be, he was at the armory door, and he was scared.

"I'm a police officer," Harry replied, beginning to turn. "My ID is in my pocket, so if you'll allow me ..."

"I SAID DON'T FUCKING MOVE AND SHOW ME YOUR HANDS GODDAMN IT OR YOU'RE DONE!" Squeaky Voice said.

Harry had raised his hands immediately with the first command, but this second command actually made him laugh. "Are you serious? Who says *'or you're done'* for Christ-sake!" Harry said to the person behind him. He knew this was a dangerous situation, but he couldn't control the outburst. He realized it probably hadn't helped.

"Listen," Harry continued in a calm voice as he tried to defuse the situation. "As you can see, my weapon is holstered, and if you will allow me to remove my ID from my right rear pocket we can step this all down a bit."

"NO YOU LISTEN! I GAVE YOU A LAWFUL ORDER AND I EXPECT YOU TO COMPLY!" Squeaky Voice was beginning to piss Harry off.

"Okay Slick, a little lesson here. If you are going to order a suspect to 'comply', have a fucking idea what compliance you are seeking! You ordered me to *'freeze'* – done. You ordered me to *'show you my hands'* – done. NOW WHAT THE FUCK DO WE DO NEXT?" Harry finally shouted the last in frustration as he remained facing the door with his hands up at shoulder level.

"I DON'T KNOW WHO YOU ARE BUT THIS IS A POLICE STATION! HOW THE FUCK DID YOU GET INTO A POLICE STATION AND INTO A SECURED WEAPONS ARMORY?" Squeaky continued, still shouting.

Harry's angst was growing by the second with this bullshit. "I have identified myself as a police officer, so that should answer both of your questions, and since you are seriously beginning to piss me off, I think this little chat is over!"

Just as he finished speaking, Squeaky racked a shell into what was obviously a shotgun. Harry's sphincter constricted so tightly at that sound he thought he would only be able to shit rabbit pellets for a month. That is, if he didn't get his head blown off first by this twit. He was certain this guy would shoot any moment and he needed to respond quickly.

Just as Harry was deciding if he could pull his weapon and dive for cover, a second voice joined the conversation. A slow, deliberate, commanding voice that you would always remember once heard; a unique deep bass of a voice.

"Yeah, that old man isn't a real cop anymore. He had to retire because of his advanced age and because the department wouldn't allow him afternoon naps. I also heard working interfered with his evening programming of Wheel of Fortune and Jeopardy. Oh, he plays at it on the weekends, but that doesn't really count, does it, *old man?*" That last bit was directed at Harry.

"But I'd make a suggestion here, Rook. I'd probably lower that Rem you are holding on that *old man* before he takes it away from you and shoves it so far up your ass that your tonsils become the barrel sight. While you're at it, you might want to keep your damn voice down!" Deep Voice said this time directly at Squeaky.

But Harry knew that voice. Dropping his head slightly and experiencing relief so profound he almost sobbed, he said, "Yeah, well, you'd better remember that due to my advanced age, sudden shock could cause me to have a heart attack. I sure as hell don't want your ugly mug giving me mouth to mouth!"

Turning, Harry watched his friend Derrick Washington, wearing the black jumpsuit with the muted-color sleeve patches and sewn-on cloth star that identified him as a SWAT officer, enter the room and approach, closing the short distance between them. Harry grasped Derrick's outstretched hand, pulling him in for a quick one-armed hug.

"Jesus Derry, it's really damn good to see you, man," he said with no small amount of emotion.

14

The first time he had met Derrick Washington was when a group of new rookies had been assigned FTOs, Derrick being assigned to Harry. It was not often that Harry was at eye level with someone, but this mountain of a man not only could look him straight in the eyes, he could probably bench press him with little effort. This huge African American guy who approached him on that first day of assignment stood 6'5", and was 240 pounds of solid muscle. With his smoothly shaven head, at first glance he reminded Harry very much of a younger version of the actor Ving Rhames, and that deep bass voice only confirmed the impression.

Derrick Washington was a natural as a police officer, and every FTO he rotated through during his first several weeks in the department, including Harry, gave him the highest of reviews. He was a natural on the streets and developed a good reputation within the neighborhoods he worked. He had a firm knowledge of police procedures almost from the first day, as if he had been working the streets for years. His size also beguiled a hidden talent that more than once had surprised a few folks who thought they could outrun this hulk of a man. Derrick was fast!

Harry had witnessed several foot chases in which a suspect would suddenly bolt like a bat out of hell with Derrick hot on their heels, surely thinking that they were home free, only to be suddenly tackled and taken down. Harry had to chuckle at times seeing the expressions of pure astonishment on a suspect's face, as they tried to figure how this huge man had caught them.

Derrick was one the most intelligent and qualified people Harry had ever met; he was also a genuinely nice guy with a heart as huge as one of his biceps – at first glance, those biceps seemingly the size of a normal average man's thigh. He completed a Masters in criminology, had graduated top of his academy class, and had recently enrolled in Golden Gate University's law program. Derrick had always talked about becoming an attorney but maintained that any lawyer, whether defense or prosecution, should spend time as a street cop to understand all levels of the judicial process.

Derrick Washington had been accepted into the SWAT program five years prior, becoming a sniper who could put a round downrange with awesome accuracy, although most of the squad wanted him to remain on the breaching team. "Hell, we don't even need the Stinger Ram with Derry since he just busts doors open with a fist," his team had jokingly agreed when he was offered the sniper position, one of the most essential positions in this highly specialized police unit. Although the center of many jokes about his size, Derrick was highly respected by the squad when it came to doing the job. Each member felt a sense of safety knowing Derrick had their backs.

Looking past Derrick, Harry said, "Who's the kid?" referring to the young man that could easily pass for eighteen years old, but since he was in a full police uniform, albeit torn in several places, he had to have been at least twenty-one.

"This is Officer Frank Lewis. April 1st was his very first day on the streets with an FTO, and he had just gone 10-8 when the calls began about the zombies. Or whatever the hell these things are. He's been through some shit, Harry, but he's alright," Derrick replied.

"Frank, I would like to introduce you to a very good friend of mine," Derrick said, turning slightly toward the rookie who was still holding the Remington Model 870P shotgun, but now had it pointed toward the floor and slightly to the left. "This is Harold Lancaster. One of the best cops this city ever had, and the guy who taught me a great deal when I was a rook like you."

Jerking his head up abruptly, wearing what Harry swore was a look of sheer terror, Frank said, "You mean like *THE* Harry Lancaster? Jesus, I heard about you in the academy!" With obvious mortification he continued. "I'm really sorry about all this Mr. Lancaster, I just didn't know who you were, and …"

"Don't sweat it, kid," Harry interrupted in an even tone, giving Derrick a quick glance of *'been talking shit again, haven't you'*. Derrick just chuckled and turned to look at something on the ceiling that had suddenly become extremely interesting.

"We've all been through more than any human being should the past few days, and that's bound to make a guy a little nervous." But Harry respected the fact that even though this kid was under a huge amount of stress, he had remained in control, specifically in not immediately shooting him, and that spoke volumes for this rookie's potential. "Thanks Mr. Lancaster," Frank responded, obviously relieved. "It's been crazy out there. My FTO and I had just gone in service when everything went crazy. There were high priority dispatches flooding the radio, assigning units to riots breaking out all over the City. The car laptop actually crashed with the amount of information being sent out on it." Frank took a breath, looking at some distant point unseen. Harry and Derrick remained silent and let him collect his thoughts.

Frank Lewis had grown up in Florida, in a family of cops, and for as long as he could remember, becoming a police officer was all he'd wanted to do. His grandfather, father, and an uncle all served with distinction. At twenty-two years old, just after graduating from San Francisco State, he had entered the academy to carry on the tradition. Being very youthful in appearance, and standing only 5'8", he had put up with a lot of good-natured ribbing from instructors and some of the other cadets. He had heard on more than one occasion the comical references to the SFPD starting a *Jump Street Squad*, with Frank being their very own version of Johnny Depp.

But he had done extremely well in his academy class, had garnered the respect of all through hard work and determination, and was looking forward to beginning his career. His friends had kidded him about April Fool's Day maybe not the best day to start that career, but he had laughingly shrugged that off at the time. He had found himself thinking about that suggestion many times over the past few days, and wondered if any of those friends were still alive.

"We were dispatched to Market and Van Ness to back up several other units. When we arrived there were five or six units on scene with the officers trying to push back maybe twenty or thirty people that seemed like they had gone crazy. By the time we got out of the car those people had taken down all those cops and were tearing into them with their hands and teeth! Both Baker and I shot into the crowd, putting a bunch of them down, but all that really seemed to accomplish was to draw their attention to us!" Frank pleadingly looked from Harry, to Derrick, and back again, with tears forming. "They didn't fucking care that we were dropping people all around them! Baker finally yelled at me to get back into the car, but before he could make it to his side a mass of those people just swarmed him!"

Harry had known Jim Baker; he had been an FTO for several years. Baker knew what he was doing, was a good cop, and Frank could not have had a better example for his first few weeks. Harry was saddened at yet another person perishing at the hands, or claws, of the infected. But what Frank said next reminded him yet again that there were worse things now than death.

"I dove in my side and crawled over the center computer swivel to get behind the wheel. It took me a couple seconds to get my set of keys off the ring and into the ignition, but by that time those things were at the left side of the car pounding on the windows. The right side was blocked with all them on top of Baker. I got the car started and tried to back up, but there were too many of them around the car by that time." Frank again paused to collect himself.

"I began to shove the transmission into drive and reverse repeatedly, knocking down whatever was at the front and back of the car. Seemed like this went on for hours. I know it was probably only a few minutes, but I was just about free. That's when the right side window finally exploded inward and I saw Baker trying to crawl through!" Frank's voice rose at the memory of the event that was most assuredly seared into his mind forever.

"Baker's face was almost completely gone!" Frank continued with a haunted look on his face. "No nose, his lips ripped off, and one eye hanging out of the socket. He had his mangled arm and head in the car. I raised my weapon and blew his head off! After that I threw the car in drive and pushed the accelerator pedal as far as it would go. The car finally broke through those fucks and I tore out of there." That clarified what had happened to the car Harry had seen parked at the side of the building.

"I didn't know what else to do," Frank said pleadingly to both Harry and Derrick. "I know I should have done more for Baker, but my God, I didn't know what more to do ..." Frank finally broke into wracking sobs but quickly recovered. "I just didn't know what else to do."

Harry clearly heard not only what Frank said, but how he said it, as if he had now given up entirely. Harry and Derrick exchanged quick glances, then Harry said to Frank, "Listen to me kid, I knew Jim Baker fairly well and he was a good cop. But there were two good cops in that car in a situation none of us could ever hope to understand, that none of us were trained to handle. You did the best thing possible given the circumstances, and thanks to keeping your head, one of those two good cops made it! You made it and that's all that matters right now. We will all have time to grieve our losses at some point, but now is not that time.

"The three of us have survived so we know others must have. I served this city and its citizens for twenty-five years, and I for one will not allow this fucked-up shit to destroy what might be left out there! We are going to keep our emotions in check, take all the crap we've seen and had to do, and we are going to use that as our motivation. We are going to use the loss of friends and family, of brothers and sisters in the department, the people we never met, and we are not going to give up. We are going to remain professional and do our jobs; do whatever it takes to survive this! Do you hear me Frank?" Frank continued to stare at the floor until Harry said again a bit more forcefully, "Do you read me, Officer Lewis!"

That seemed to snap Frank out of it. He looked up at Harry, and with a bit more steel in his voice, said, "Yes sir, Mr. Lancaster, I read you, whatever it takes to survive. But I don't think you could understand what it's like. Having to kill your partner?"

Harry slowly nodded, keeping his eyes locked onto Frank's, and said, "Kid, I know exactly what it's like to deal with these things, and let me be real clear, that *thing* that looked like Jim Baker was not your partner when you shot it. Jim Baker was dead the moment those things swarmed him, and nothing you did or did not do would have changed that.

"I've seen and dealt with the same shit over the past several days, young man, on a scale you couldn't begin to understand, and I know there is no escape once they swarm a living person. You didn't kill your partner, Frank; you killed a mindless, crazed zombie, a *thing* that would have ripped you apart without hesitation! I have killed dozens of these things and I know it isn't easy to live with …" Harry was suddenly flung back to the first day of the infection, and his first experience with the infected.

Pushing the memories of what had happened in the apartment building and his little trip to the station back into the recesses of his mind, Harry, who had continued to look into Frank's eyes while briefly reliving the horror of his first day, said, "Yes Frank, we *will* do whatever it takes to survive," while placing a reassuring hand on the young rookie's shoulder.

Frank nodded slightly and repeated, "Whatever it takes, and you can count on me, sir."

15

"You didn't mention how we hooked up, Rook," Derrick said with a slight smile, obviously trying to break the tension.

"Oh, that?" Frank replied. "Well, I was headed up Van Ness thinking I should get back to the station. I had just crossed Geary when I saw Officer Washington running down the sidewalk ahead of about twenty zombies. It was pretty awesome, too. He had that big Remington 700P rifle strapped around his shoulder and was really booking it. I pulled up about a half block in front of him thinking he would get in the passenger side door, but instead he jumped on the roof and just yelled '*Go, go, go!*' Guess he hung onto the light bar. I thought I lost him a couple times before we got here, too."

Harry had to laugh at the image of Derrick Washington running ahead of a bunch of zombies, with a rather large sniper rifle strapped on a shoulder, and then jumping onto a police car's roof and hanging on for dear life from a light bar. He was probably cussing every inch of the way, too.

"Damn, Derry," Harry said through a stifled laugh, "why didn't you just get in the car?"

"Yeah, well, so I wasn't thinking so clear at the time. With zombies trying to eat my ass and all, you know!" Derrick responded with a comical expression on his face, which included crossing his eyes for effect. Harry, and even Frank, had to cover their mouths to hide the growing smiles at that. "Okay, okay, back to current events here, guys," Derrick said. "So what's our next move?"

Harry related the interview he had seen on GNN and what Scott Allen had said. He also told them about how the zombies were affected by the fog and about the Sovereign Spirit's website and what he had read on their blog.

"So I'm thinking that we follow the Commodore's example. We get supplies and we get to the marina. Once we secure a couple of boats, I'm thinking we head out to Alcatraz. But we still need a way to do all this, and that's the reason I came here in the first place. Our handguns are not going to cut it out there and I was hoping the station still had long guns and ammo. But we are going to need more than those three AR15s back in the corner. The shotguns are good, too, but we need to be able to put some serious firepower down range," Harry said, looking around the nearly empty room that had once stocked a sizable amount of various weapons. "We're also going to need to figure out a safe way to get around."

Derrick smiled, saying, "I think we can help you out with that. Have a look in the ammo closet." He tossed Harry a set of keys.

The ammo closet was not a closet at all, but rather a room attached to the main armory and accessible through a steel reinforced door. Harry took the keys, unlocked the door and flipped on the light switch. Stepping into the room, he said with a great deal of satisfaction, "Okay, now we're talking here." He saw box after box of ammunition for rifles, shotguns, and pistols. There were at least a dozen AC4 riot shields, several AM2 full body riot shields, and cases of tear gas grenades, flash bangs and full body riot gear. It was everything Harry had hoped to find and more.

Derrick and Frank had followed Harry into the room, and Derrick began an inventory assessment. "Harry, you know that Central is the main SWAT Division location with ammo being dispersed throughout the City from here. We had just received a new shipment of ammunition on March 29th. When the Rook and I got in, we made a quick count. We've got at least eighty thousand rounds of NATO 5.56; thirty-five thousand rounds of .45 and 9mm; forty thousand rounds of '00' and twenty thousand less-than-lethal polys for the shotguns; five hundred tear gas grenades and about eight hundred flash bangs. There's at least a thousand PMAG 30-round magazines for the ARs, too."

Harry just stared at Derrick for a moment with a look of pure amazement. "Dude, this is fantastic! Now all we need is more weapons and a way to transport it all. I have an idea but I don't think we'll find what I have in mind here."

"Well, now that you mention it, there is more," Derrick replied, smiling. "The Rook and I found twelve of the ARs in the armory and have already taken them down to the garage. We were on our way back up to start taking boxes of the ammo down when we ran into you."

"Okay," Harry said, "that's great. Do you know where they parked one of the Bearcats? If we could get our hands on one of those, we'd be golden."

Derrick cocked his head to the side slightly, smiled and said, "Well, if a brand new right-out-of-the-box BCRC will work for ya, there's one parked in the garage right now. Probably still has that 'new car' smell."

Harry was astonished. "When did the department get a Riot Bear? More interesting question, *why* did the department get a Riot Bear?"

The BearCat Riot Control Vehicle is designed mostly for international police forces operating in hostile urban environments. The BCRC is equipped with a heavy-duty hydraulic forward-facing V-shaped ram, capable of moving cars, barriers, and other debris. That also included making its way through crowds of people. With a ten-person seating capacity, two in the front and eight in the back, along with equipment storage for each of those people, this vehicle would be perfect for moving around a city full of zombies. Especially with all the ballistic glass and body protection these vehicles came with. God only knew why the police department bureaucrats felt as though a vehicle like that was needed in San Francisco. Maybe they thought it would come in handy during the monthly bicyclists Critical Mass or the annual Pride Parade.

Shaking his head in disbelief, Harry continued. "I don't understand why they would spend close to a half million dollars on something like that, but they have unknowingly helped us a great deal. Now if we can find the keys …" Harry did not finish as Derrick raised his left hand and jingled a small set of keys.

"Okay Harry, have any more questions?" Derrick laughed. Harry could only smile in response.

"You're the man, Derry," Harry said absently as he suddenly walked toward the door leading out of the armory. Something had occurred to him that he should have thought of the moment he entered the station.

"If you guys can start loading up the Bear, I'll help you in a few minutes," Harry said to both men, continuing to quickly make his way into the hallway and turning left toward the station's dispatch room. "I just realized that since the generators are still operating we might be able to use the radios! I need to check it out."

Derrick had followed Harry to the door at his sudden departure from the room and shouted to Harry's retreating back, "Great idea, but what do you think we should take?"

Turning his head slightly so Derrick could hear him, as he continued down the hall at a fast pace Harry said loudly, "We take it all! Everything not nailed down. Take all the ammo, the equipment, shields, flash bangs, and *anything* else we can find and will fit in that vehicle."

"Okay," Derrick replied a bit dubiously. He did not fully understand why Harry would want that much ammo and equipment, but shrugged a shoulder in acceptance. "Guess he knows what he's doing," he said, turning to Frank. "Grab that dolly and let's get moving, Rook."

16

Harry entered the dispatch center that housed the state-of-the-art communications equipment for the station. Suspended from the ceiling were two large LCD screens that he knew normally would have contained vital information on car locations and their status, pending calls at a glance in order of priority, and other pertinent information – if Dispatch had been operational. Now the screens were just a bright solid blue, but that at least told Harry there was, in fact, power to the center. Walking over to a desk, which looked more like something NASA used in their Mission Control, he gazed down, taking in the vast controls. *Thank God I've operated this stuff before*, he thought.

Harry had pulled many shifts in dispatch as a Reserve assignment, and had received basic training on the operation of the communications equipment. Although San Francisco had a multi-million-dollar 911 Emergency Communications Center, each district station could dispatch and track routine calls – although there really was no such thing as a routine call for a cop, and Harry knew full well a "routine" call could become a full alert SWAT call out within minutes. But the general idea of the station dispatch was to free up the understaffed 911 Center to handle imminent life-threatening calls for police or medical aid.

All the equipment seemed to be powered up and operational. Harry picked up the earpiece with the thin boom mic from the desk and attached it to his left ear. He then sat down in front of the communications monitor and typed in his access code on the keyboard. The system could not be used until the operator was signed on, thus allowing it to track all dispatches coming in and going out by that operator. Harry's ID was accepted, giving him full access to the system.

Reaching up and to the right of the monitor, he then activated several switches to engage his earpiece and to select the appropriate frequency he wished to transmit over. Harry activated the button labeled "Citywide Broadcast", allowing him to be heard by anyone within any of the police, fire, or emergency city services departments who still had access to a radio.

Depressing the in line button on the cord attached to the earpiece which would activate the boom mic, he said, "Three Edward Six at Central Station, any unit please respond." Having stated his department unit call sign along with his current location, he waited for a few moments. Only silence met his first call. "Three Edward Six to any unit, can anyone hear me?" Leaning back in the chair, frustrated, he glanced up to the button labeled "DEM". The Department of Emergency Management was only fully staffed during catastrophic emergencies such as earthquakes or other severe citywide emergencies. "Guess they will have to add zombies to the list," he said sarcastically, knowing they had activated the DEM on April 1st when the infected first started to ravage the City.

Sitting back up in the chair, Harry reached up, activating the DEM switch, and repeated his call. "Three Edward Six at Central Station, does anyone copy?" After a few moments of silence, he was rewarded with a response!

"Hello? Can you hear me? Oh God, can you hear me?" came a female voice through Harry's earpiece.

"Yes I can hear you!" Harry said excitedly. "This is Harold Lancaster. Who is this?"

"Sarah Shoemaker," the voice responded. "I'm one of the mayor's aides, and we're at the DEM. We've been stuck here for several days and can't seem to reach anyone. We really need help. Just a minute, Officer …"

A new voice came over the radio. "Officer, this is Mayor Jarvis. You need to get us out of here right now! I have to get back to City Hall!" Harry was preparing to respond when Derrick and Frank came into the room, so he flipped another switch to activate an external speaker so they could follow the conversation.

"We're loaded up and good to go, Harry. We also found a few other things that will help," Derrick said. Looking up, Harry nodded his reply, realizing he had been sitting at the console longer than he had thought.

Focusing back on the radio, Harry said, "Mr. Mayor, I'm glad that you're alright. You need to remain at the DEM for now. I'm with two other officers and we are preparing to relocate to the marina to secure a couple of boats. Once that's done we will try to reach your location, but for now you need to remain calm and keep everyone else the same way."

Harry knew the DEM was one of several distribution centers for the city's emergency supplies. As long as they kept the building secure, which they obviously had since he was talking to them, they would have food and water for weeks.

Once Harry released the transmit button, he was somewhat startled to hear the mayor screaming, all pretense at self-control gone. "What the fuck are you talking about? We can't stay here! Those things are pounding on every goddamn door to the building. Now you listen to me Officer, I gave you a direct order to pick us up and I mean right now! You are an employee of this fair city, and being the Mayor you work for me, so I expect to see you as soon as you can get your ass moving! There are also several board supervisors here so if you want to keep your fucking job I'd strongly urge you to follow those instructions! Oh, and if you're unclear, please understand those are orders and not a request! Do I make myself clear?"

Mayor Edgar Jarvis was a career politician who had served in several elected positions in the city throughout his career, finally being appointed interim mayor after the position had been vacated due to the then-mayor winning a state government election and moving to Sacramento.

Interim Mayor Jarvis had said he would only serve out the year remaining before the next election and that he would then step down. Many had listened to that hype and knew it for what it was.

This had been the position Jarvis coveted for years, and everyone knew he would not give it up easily. Sure enough, ignoring his initial statements pertaining to not running for the office in the regular election, Jarvis submitted his name, and, with the help of his many big business political allies, won by a very narrow margin. Unfortunately, Edgar Jarvis tended to bend whichever way the political wind happened to be blowing, so it was generally felt his agenda was anything *but* for the good of the City. The already out-of-control fiscal deficit the City had been in during his year as interim mayor continued to spiral out of control after his election.

Looking up at Derrick and Frank incredulously, Harry's anger was clearly evident. After a couple of deep breaths, he activated the mic button and said condescendingly, "Now you listen to me, *Mr. Mayor*, there are only three of us here and we are on the other side of the City. Obviously we are having some serious issues with the citizenry of this *fair city* right now, so getting to your location would prove somewhat problematic, and for the record I most certainly *do not* work for you as I'm retired. Since I do not foresee pension benefits direct deposited into my bank account any time in the near future, that factoid definitely reinforces that particular point at least for me. I'm a Reserve, and in case that position eludes your understanding, you pompous ass, that means I *volunteer* my time, at my pleasure and the department's, not yours! Now stay off the fucking radio and let me talk to one of your security detail!" Harry was referring to the police officers assigned as mayoral protection.

As soon as Harry released the transmit button he heard Jarvis still screaming. "Pompous ass? How dare you call me a pompous ass? And for your information, I placed my brave officers at the doors while they were being secured to prevent those poor unfortunates outside from gaining entrance into our facility. Unlike you they died doing their jobs! YOU'RE FIRED YOU ARROGANT SON OF A BITCH! Put one of those other officers on right now!" Jarvis' voice had steadily risen until it was an almost unintelligible screech.

Angrily pulling the earpiece from his ear, Harry held it toward Derrick and Frank. "You heard what that piece of shit said? I'm *fired!*"

"Nope, not me, I don't want to talk to that idiot," Derrick said, backing up half a step from the console and shaking his hands in front of him.

The normally reserved and quiet Frank, looking at Harry, said with a confused expression on his face, "Does he know what the word volunteer actually means? Geez, that guy really is a dumbass!"

With that being said, the tension was instantly broken and both Harry and Derrick began to laugh. Not so much at what Frank had said, but how.

"What?" Frank responded to their laughter.

Derrick reached over and clapped Frank on the back and said, "You're a rookie, kid, but no truer words have ever been spoken by one so young!" Frank cracked a small smile, but still did not seem to understand what was so funny. He genuinely thought Jarvis had lost his mind.

17

Sobering, Harry stood, leaning forward slightly and placing his hands on the top of the console desk. "Listen guys, Jarvis may be a twit but his bullshit just brought something home to me.

"You do realize I am in fact retired, right?" he said, looking first to Derrick then to Frank. "I really don't hold any more authority than the average citizen now, and you both know that. Somebody will get this mess under control at some point, and I sure as hell don't want either one of you to be in the shit because of me." Looking to Derrick, Harry continued. "I really think you should take this, Derry. You're the most senior officer on scene, so the responsibility really does fall to you. Besides, you of all people know I don't play well with others when there's too much bullshit involved. Right now I feel like I'm up to my ass in it." Harry let out a deep sigh, then turned his back to the desk and leaned his butt onto the edge, crossing both arms across his chest. "I'm just getting too old for this shit."

Derrick was silent for a moment, obviously in deep thought. He then turned toward Frank and said, "I'm not sure exactly what you may have heard about Harold Lancaster, but let me give you a little insight on the man," speaking as if Harry were not in the room.

"This isn't the time, Derry," Harry began, but was immediately cut off.

Raising a hand toward Harry, but still looking directly at Frank, Derrick said, "Not finished here.

"As I started to say," Derrick resumed, "not sure what you heard about Harold Lancaster, but you should know that he is among the most respected officers in the department.

Not only by those who served with him but also by the folks we are all sworn to serve. Hell, I think even the bad guys he busted respected him! He has received so many departmental commendations that it would take a librarian to catalog them all. I don't even want to try to count the times he has received a Medal of Valor. I know there were a half dozen Bronze, Silver, and at least four Gold medals pinned on him.

"One of those Gold medals was awarded for a little action he and a couple others carried out when there were hostages taken at the Ritz Carlton. One of those folks held hostage just happened to be the head of Her Majesty's Inspectorates of Constabulary. He was a seriously important British dignitary, who also happened to be attending an international law enforcement conference here in San Francisco. Harry would have you believe that he was just at the right place at the right time, just doing his job, and the other officers played a more vital role – as he said during the awards ceremony. What happened was they dressed as waiters, gained access through a side window in the basement, and worked their way up to the area where the hostages were held.

"But it was later revealed by the other officers who had gone in with him that day that Harry planned the whole action, spur of the moment, and actually took out four of the six bad guys himself before SWAT had even gotten the call out. Yes, it was a team action for sure, but Harold Lancaster led that team and because of their actions saved a room full of people." Derrick took a breath and turned, looking directly at Harry, but continuing as if still talking to Frank.

"If he hadn't turned down so many promotions over the years he would have been at least a captain, or hell, maybe even chief. But he thought if he promoted up he would lose what he loved the most in the department and would become what he liked the least. What he didn't realize, Frank, is that by remaining a street cop he helped develop a whole new generation of caring, well-trained and professional police officers, men and women, by his example and leadership. Not to mention the countless citizens he touched on a daily basis that came to know and respect him deeply. He's told me, and others, dozens of times over the years that he didn't need strips of gold on his collar to do his job. His very clear gratification was just being a cop and doing the job that was his life's love," Derrick finished with another deep breath.

Then walking up to Harry, Derrick said, "Now you listen to me, Harry. I don't give a rat's ass what that ID you carry has stamped across it. Retired or not, *you* are the most senior officer on scene and you *will* take command of this little operation whether you like it or not. You served this city for two and a half decades, then came back to give more on your own dime. So, until a 'bar' or better shows up, you're it. I, for one, would follow you through the streets of Hell, my friend, and if those streets happen to be full of zombies then so be it! Get over the 'too old for this shit' pity party you're at and lay out what we're doing here!" Derrick concluded, folding his massive arms across his chest, mimicking Harry's current posture and giving him a defiant look.

"What the hell does that mean?" Frank asked. "A *bar or better?*"

Clearing a rather large lump in his throat, Harry said, "What my friend is trying to say, Frank, is that until someone with rank – a sergeant or lieutenant – is on scene, the senior officer remains in command of an incident."

"Oh, never heard that term in the academy, but did hear it in a war movie once. But I believe the term was *butter bar*," Frank said.

Derrick seemed a bit hurt that the wind under his speech had been taken away a bit. "Whatever, I know I heard somebody say that once on scene," he said defensively.

Frank actually produced a full smile as he then turned to Harry. "I want you to know, Mr. Lancaster, that I couldn't agree more with Officer Washington. I trust your experience and judgment explicitly and I also consider you senior officer on scene."

Harry nodded solemnly then, taking a deep breath, he took charge. "Obviously with the weapons and ammo we have now, not to mention the Bearcat and a few other supplies, we could easily secure the marina. But I want you to know that once we get set up somewhere I'm coming back into the City to look for more survivors."

"Yeah, we'll do just that," Derrick said without hesitation, looking toward Frank who nodded in agreement.

Harry looked at both men for a moment. "You do realize how dangerous that will be. I'd feel more comfortable if you guys stayed at the stronghold as security."

"Well, I can see your point there, Harry," Derrick replied as he feigned deep thought, "but I'm thinking a better idea might be if I come along and maybe cover your ass. I know you're *Dirty Harry* and all, but you can't have all the fun!"

Frank added, "I think I'd like to drive that Bearcat around the City, too. Since I'm from the Deep South, well, Florida if you count that, I always did think about maybe becoming a NASCAR driver someday. Here's my chance to live out that boyhood fantasy. Wow, a redneck with a badge behind the wheel of a big truck: scary stuff!"

"Great, that's all we need, another redneck in the world," Derrick said with a smile. Frank shrugged his shoulders in reply.

Harry walked back to the console desk and sat down. "Okay, we'll discuss that when the time comes. Let's see what we can find out here for a few more minutes, then we move out."

Harry replaced the earpiece. He could still hear Jarvis screaming, but he was suddenly cut off.

"Edward Six, do you copy?" a female voice intoned over the radio, albeit in a slightly exasperated manner.

After a few moments of consideration Harry pressed the transmit button and simply replied, "Edward Six."

"Mr. Lancaster, this is Julie Roth, part of Jarvis' security detail. Jarvis has been taken out of communications and escorted to a rear office. He has been *encouraged* to relax and allow us to work through this. I'm done with his bullshit. He's already gotten two officers killed and he's not going to kill the rest of us." Harry picked up a great deal of emotion in her voice, which included very clear anger.

Harry glanced up at Derrick. "Do you know her?"

"Yeah, she's a tough one and a very competent police officer," Derrick replied. "She was scheduled to take the SWAT placement exam this summer. She probably knocked the crap out of that little asshole while *encouraging him to relax.*"

Harry nodded, than responded to Roth. "Officer Roth, I know you appreciate the current situation we're all in. As I was trying to explain to Jarvis, since you are in a secure location, and have supplies, we are going to carry out our initial plan on this end. Once we have secured a location, which will be on one of the Bay Islands, we will come back for you and the others as soon as possible." Harry then spent a few minutes outlining those plans to Roth in more detail, once again including everything he had seen and learned.

"I understand Mr. Lancaster and I completely agree. We are good for supplies including water and food, plus our location is secure here. It is a bit noisy with those things constantly pounding on the doors, but it would be nearly impossible for them to breach," Roth said without hesitation.

"Good, then I will leave that location in your capable hands and we will see you in a day or two," Harry said, silently praying that would be the case.

"10-4, Edward Six, One Charlie Fourteen is 10-10." With that, Roth concluded the radio transmission, letting Harry know she was actually the supervising officer and would be standing by.

Flipping the citywide switch once again, Harry tried the call out several more times. "Three Edward Six at Central Station to any units, do you copy? Does anyone hear me?" He tried a half-dozen more times, waiting several seconds between calls, then finally pulled the earpiece out again, laying it on the desk. Sadly he said, "Guess that's it for now. I'm not convinced there aren't people out there though. Batteries could be dead or a whole host of other reasons nobody is replying." Harry did not want to entertain the alternative, that there just was not anyone left alive to answer.

Standing up and turning toward Derrick and Frank, he said, "Okay guys, time to roll. Has the building been cleared?"

Frank spoke up, saying, "Only this floor, since this is where most of the supplies were located, and of course the armory. We really didn't think it necessary, or wise, to search the entire building, although we did ride the elevator to each floor. Listened to see if there might have been any sound or movement, and even called out several times when we thought the floors were clear of those things. Guess everyone evacuated or were on calls because we didn't get responses, so we locked the elevator off on this level. The stairways use one-way access doors and those are secure."

Derrick added, "We also cleared the two garage levels below. Didn't find anything except the Bear and a Ford truck. It looks like everyone bugged out or were already on calls like Frank said."

"What about the locker rooms?" Harry asked. "I want to change out of these civvies and put on a jumpsuit. I keep a couple in a locker back there, and guess I should look more the part. I also think Frank should change out of his standards. It's going to get interesting out there so we all should be as comfortable as possible."

"Yeah, the locker room is clear," Derrick replied. "I think Frank should be able to find one that will fit in our ready room. Jessup was about his size." Jessup had been on the SWAT team with Derrick, and Harry picked up that Derrick had not elaborated on Jessup's fate.

"Thanks," Frank replied.

"Okay then, let's get to it", Harry said as he walked out of Dispatch and headed down the hall toward the locker room, Frank right behind him.

"I'll meet you guys in the garage," Derrick said as he followed them out, then took off in the opposite direction down the hallway.

"See you in about fifteen, Derry," Harry replied.

18

Harry took Frank to the SWAT ready room located just before the general locker rooms and told him to go in and find a jump that fit. Harry continued to walk the short distance to the main locker room and entered. Continuing to the rear of the room, then turning left, he came to the dozen or so lockers that were utilized by reserve officers. Nothing was locked here as the only things in the lockers were uniforms, and this was a police station after all.

Stopping in from of Locker 27 and opening the door, Harry found the two very familiar jumpsuits just as he had left them. The standards he wore, which referred to the regular uniform most prevalently seen worn by police officers, he kept at home. Pulling out the one dark navy blue jump, he noted the name LANCASTER embroidered on a cloth patch attached just above the right hand pocket, with a silver cloth star sewn on just above the left with the words SAN FRANCISCO on the top rocker and POLICE on the lower rocker. In the center was his star number.

Unlike Derrick Washington's black SWAT jump with muted-color shoulder patches,

the ones on Harry Lancaster's had a bright blue background, trimmed in gold, with the image of the Phoenix in the center and the words SAN FRANCISCO POLICE in gold lettering above the bird. The words 'ORO EN PAZ - FIERRO EN GUERRA' were on a banner clutched by the bird's talons, which translates "Gold in Peace, Iron in War". This was the motto of both the City and the County of San Francisco, as well as the Police Department's. Above each of the shoulder patches was a blue rocker with the word RESERVES. On each side of the jump's collar, just above the collar points, was a silver three-chevron pin denoting the rank of sergeant.

The final items not an original part of the jump were sewn on the lower left sleeve. Those items being the five blue "years of service" half-chevrons outlined in white, each chevron denoting five years of service. "Where did the time go?" Harry asked himself. Sighing, he laid the jumpsuit out on the floor bench that ran the length of the lockers and started to remove his equipment.

Happening to glance down the end of the section of lockers he suddenly stumbled back a couple of steps, drawing the Glock and aiming at a zombie that had unexpectedly appeared at the end of the row!

What kept Harry from firing was that this zombie was also aiming a gun at him. It took him a few seconds to process, but he finally realized who his new friend was. After his heart stopped trying to pound its way out of his chest, he walked the short distance to the end of the locker row and gazed at the image in the full length mirror that was attached to the wall. "Shit, no wonder the kid was going to blow my head off," Harry said with an astonished look on his face, which was also reflected back in the mirror.

His clothes were covered in dried blood and all manner of bits, pieces, and chunks of flesh and sinew and Lord only knew what else, with some of the stuff even in his hair. He looked exactly like one of those things outside, which did nothing to quell the rising bile in the back of his throat.

Grabbing the jump off the bench, Harry walked straight to the shower area, stripped out of his civilian clothes and turned on the water to the hottest temperature he could tolerate without peeling skin. Soaping up and rinsing off, he was horrified to see the water going down the drain was a pinkish color, replete with the aforementioned bits, pieces, and chucks swirling down the drain with that rancid water.

He soaped and rinsed five or six more times until the water remained a nice clear soapy mixture and his skin felt nearly raw. Then Harry just stood under the spray of water for a few minutes in an attempt at washing away some of the stress that had built up since he'd left the apartment building. That helped a little, but only by a varying degree. "Note to self," Harry said aloud, "if I haven't mentioned this before, I'm really, *really* getting too old for this shit."

Finally turning the water off, Harry grabbed a couple of towels from the stack just outside the shower stalls. Drying off, he quickly dressed, transferring the items he had been carrying into the various pockets of the jump, slipped into his TAC boots, pulling the side zippers up to close them, then snapped the nylon duty belt around his waist. Finally he placed the Glock in the high rise break front holster. With a slight twist of the belt to adjust how the weight of the gun was riding at his waist, Harry was ready.

He glanced at the pile of bloody street clothes he had changed out of and quickly stepped over them on his way to the main door to exit. As he turned the corner of the final row of lockers, he saw Frank sitting on one of the floor benches. Frank immediately stood up when he saw Harry approach.

"Hey Frank, sorry it took a little longer than I thought. Needed to clean up a bit," Harry said with a look of repugnance on his face. He saw that Frank had also changed, but into what appeared to be a brand new jump. It had the muted shoulder patches of SWAT, but bore no name or star patches and it had several package creases. Frank had simply placed his metal star and nameplate in the appropriate positions on the front of it. Harry also noticed he had swapped out his leather duty belt for a nylon one.

"No problem, Mr. Lancaster. I sort of figured you might want to do that," Frank replied with that crooked smile.

"Listen kid, I really appreciate the fact you didn't shoot first and ask questions later when we first met. I didn't realize how bad I looked or what you must have thought when you saw me," Harry said with all sincerity. "And please, call me Harry, okay?"

"Okay, Harry, but only if you stop calling me kid," Frank said as he looked down toward the service chevrons on Harry's jump sleeve. "Wow, I just realized you've been a cop longer than I've been alive. What a trip!"

Harry took a deep breath, shook his head slightly, and said exasperatedly while walking past Frank, "I really am getting too old for this shit. Let's go, *kid*, we need to get this circus on the road."

"Sure thing, Mr. Lancaster …" Frank began, but Harry, walking away, immediately cut him off with a hand raised and a finger pointing up. "I mean *Harry*, let's go," Frank finished.

They headed down the hallway toward the main lobby area of the station, which would lead them to the garage entrances, when Derrick called out.

"Hey guys, up here."

Looking up, Harry saw Derrick on the small balcony that slightly overhung the lobby. It really served no other purpose than some sort of architectural design as it did not go anywhere. But it did offer a view of the front of the building and the street. Harry immediately changed direction, with Frank right behind him, and ascended the small sweeping staircase that led up to where Derrick stood.

"Well, you both look much better," Derrick said as Harry approached and mumbled an acknowledgment. Leaning against the four-foot-high frosted glass wall, trimmed with heavy stainless steel on the balcony's top edge, Harry noticed two AR15s with multi-point black nylon tactical slings already attached. These particular weapon slings were one of the best made; they wore comfortably due to the nylon shoulder pad and adjusted easily to anyone's height. Derrick nodded toward the ARs and said, "Thought you might want one of those."

"Hell yes!" Frank replied, picking up one of the weapons.

Harry picked up the other weapon and with practiced ease quickly brought his left arm through the sling, slipped it over his head, and adjusted the shoulder pad to a comfortable position on the right side of his neck, allowing the AR to dangle in front of his chest. He made a minor adjustment to the strap that connected the weapon to the upper part of the sling to allow for his size and height, and to enable him to easily bring the weapon up into a firing position.

Harry then used the AR's sliding butt stock to extend it to its full position, again to allow for his size and arm reach, then briefly brought the weapon up to a firing position, pointing it over the balcony, to ensure a good fit. Satisfied with that, he used his right hand to release the 30-round magazine, allowing it to drop down and catching it with the same hand. He used his right thumb to push down on the top of the rounds in the mag a couple of times to ensure they were seated properly, then replaced the mag back into the weapon.

He then positioned his left hand under the area just forward of the clip and used his thumb to depress the bolt catch. With his right hand he pulled the charging handle back and released the bolt catch, which freed the charging handle in a back unlocked position. This would allow him to inspect the magazine feed. Glancing inside the feed area through the ejection port, which was located on the right hand side of the AR and just above the mag, he was satisfied the feed was good. Turning the weapon with his right hand on the grip, he used the heel of his left hand to slap the upper part of the bolt catch. This sent the firing bolt back into battery and ready to fire. Harry pushed the safety and once again allowed the AR to dangle on his chest. The whole procedure took less than sixty seconds.

The department did not normally use iron sights on their AR-15A3 tactical carbines. Instead, each was equipped with EOTech holographic optical sights attached to the upper mid rail of the weapon, which was much better suited for urban use. These electronic sights were extremely accurate once sighted in and utilized a red dot to line up targets. Harry reached down to the lower portion of the sight, pressing the power button and activating it. Bringing the weapon into firing position, he sighted the red dot on a computer terminal sitting upon a desk just below the balcony. He glanced over to Derrick who had been watching him go through the weapons ready procedure and raised an eyebrow.

"They're sighted in, and the batteries are fully charged. If you can believe the sales hype, the charge should be good for up to eleven hundred hours, but of course we've never had to use them that long," Derrick said, anticipating Harry's upcoming questions.

"Great, was just going to ask. Are all the ARs you located ready to go?" Harry asked with a slight smile, knowing his friend knew him pretty well.

"Including the three we have there are five more I can guarantee. Frank and I secured the eight of these from the SWAT backups. The rest I can't be sure of. There's a mix with EOTechs but also several with the old style-iron sights which probably means they just haven't been converted yet."

Harry nodded in reply, then glanced over to Frank who was just finishing up his weapon check. He stared with amazement as Frank fairly flew through the procedure.

"Damn kid, looks like you've done that one or twice," Harry said, a bit surprised thinking he had always been fairly fast.

Finishing up with his own left-handed slap to lock in the firing bolt and then letting his AR dangle on the sling, Frank looked up and said, "Many times actually. My Dad was a prepper before prepping was cool, I guess. I've been around and fired ARs, in several different variations, since I was eleven." He glanced between Harry and Derrick, continuing, "He wasn't a fanatic or anything, but after twenty years with the Florida State Highway Patrol, and then another ten years in our County Sheriff's Department, he'd concluded that humanity was headed down a path of self-destruction. Guess he just wanted us to be prepared for that eventuality. Mom was never completely on board with the whole 'end of the world thing' but she loved my dad so she went along. Dad had my brother and me shooting several types of weapons by our teenage years and we were pretty good at using them, too. Not sure if Daddy thought the end of civilization would be from a zombie outbreak though." Frank had lowered his voice, trailing off almost to a whisper, looking at the floor and obviously thinking about something aside from the current topic.

"Listen, Frank," Derrick began, "I'm really sorry about your family. I wish there was some way we could get you in touch with them."

Frank looked back up to Derrick and said, "Oh, it's cool, Officer Washington. My parents were killed in an auto accident when I was seventeen, and my brother and I drifted apart; we really didn't have any other relatives. My brother, unlike my dad, became a nutcase fanatic about prepping and spent a ton of money on it. His wife finally left him and the last I heard he'd tried to set up a bunker system in the swamps somewhere. He was even featured on that National Geographic prepper show I think."

"I saw that episode! The guy who bought those semi-trailers and buried them in the middle of the Everglades, right! Too bad he was arrested for trespassing on federal property. I think he was charged with something like destruction of federal lands. I thought the idea was really good though!" Harry excitedly responded. Both Derrick and Frank gave him a sideways look. "What! NatGeo just happens to have some very intelligent and interesting programing, I'll have you both know!" he said defensively. "You should hear my idea on a new reality show I have in mind for them on this zombie thing!"

"Okay Harry, take it easy there, we understand. It's kind of like a Wheel of Fortune or Jeopardy thing again, right? I realize one has to have reached a certain age to appreciate such fine programing. See Frank, what'd I say earlier about senior citizens?" Derrick laughed, with Frank trying, rather unsuccessfully, to maintain a professional demeanor but quickly losing that battle.

"Yeah, whatever," Harry mumbled defensively, more to himself. "No wonder the younger generation is going to shit. Can't even appreciate good television programming."

With that, both Derrick and Frank lost it completely, erupting into laughter. Harry just watched them go on for a few moments, finally saying, and "Okay, that's enough from the peanut gallery. Shall we get on with this please?"

Wiping tears from his eyes, Derrick said, "Yeah, sure, but we have another little problem Harry. Take a look out front."

Harry walked over to the portion of the balcony that had the best window view of the street and looked out. "Oh my God," was his instant response, which was not due to the beautiful, nearly perfect San Francisco day he saw for a split second, with only a slight smoke haze hanging in the air to detract from the otherwise flawless weather. A day that should normally have been reserved for enticing people out to shop or visit their favorite cafes. No, what had prompted Harry's response, what had immediately grabbed and held his attention, were the dozens of zombies, at least fifty of them he was certain, just milling around on the street in front of the station.

"Guess I must have attracted some attention getting here," Harry said in complete amazement.

"The biggest problem though," Derrick began, "is that the garage roll up door opens directly onto Vallejo, as you know. The Bearcat is parked on the lower level, so that means we have to drive up the ramp to get out. That thing is powerful, but not sure we could get enough momentum to push through that many bodies and make the turn we will need to make. Not to mention we are going to have a bunch of those things pour through that roll up door once it's open."

Harry nodded his head and stood looking out of the window in thought. After a few minutes he said, "I think I have an idea that might thin them out a bit. When I came in through the side doors I noticed the two radio cars parked out there. The one Frank drove in is trashed and too close to the front of the building. The other one, however, is parked almost next to the side doors. You and Frank go down and get the Bear ready to roll. I'm going to go back out and turn on the lights and siren of the unit, which should draw a bunch of those things to it and hopefully clear us a path in front."

"I'll do it," Frank blurted. Harry started to argue the point when Frank interrupted, "Look, no offense or anything, but I *am* younger than you and probably a bit faster." Frank could see the indecision on Harry's face. "Really, I got this, Harry."

"He's right, Harry," Derrick said. "We'll get the Bear up to the ramp, then radio him when we're in position."

Looking at Frank for several moments, Harry reluctantly agreed with a sigh. "Okay Frank, move to the first set of doors and the sally port. Not sure how much attention that big diesel will create when we start it, but I don't want you to move until we've brought the Bearcat to the bottom of the ramp and shut it down. Once we're in position, I'll give you the go ahead. You carry your ass to that car, light it up, and then haul that same ass back in and to the inside garage stairway entrance. I'm coming back up once we get the Bear in position to hold the door open for you, and if I don't hear the pitter patter of your little feet booking it down the hall I'm coming after you. You copy that, Officer Lewis?"

With a crooked smile, Frank just repeated, "I got this, Harry."

"We need to go back to Dispatch and pull radios ..." Harry said, but stopped as Derrick picked up a nylon ready bag, reached in and handed him and Frank an HT 1000 Motorola hand radio with belt holsters, ear pieces, and corded speaker mics already attached.

Derrick then pulled out another radio for himself, attaching a third radio to his duty belt. He pulled the speaker mic up and around his left shoulder, attaching that to the radio mic tab sewn onto his jump, then said, "While you two were freshening up a bit I got all the hand helds and chargers out of Dispatch. Put all but these three in the Bear. There were nine fully charged and thought they might come in handy."

Harry looked at Derrick and said, "I'm going to kiss you right on the mouth, Derry."

Putting both large hands in front of him, palms out, Derrick replied, "You stay the fuck away from this pretty face you freak. I got standards here!"

All three men laughed at that.

"Okay, so before we get this party on the road, here's the route to the marina I think we need to take. We'll exit the garage and turn left on Vallejo and then take a left on Columbus. We'll go left on Columbus to Bay, taking that all the way to Marina Boulevard and to the entrance of the harbor. We don't stop for anything and we'll take alternate routes if necessary, but I want that big beast moving hard. Once we get to the marina, we're going to look for something to get us onto the Bay waters and then we head for Alcatraz. All copy?" Harry looked at the two of them. Both Derrick and Frank indicated that they understood.

Harry looked toward Frank and said, "I don't suppose living in Florida and all you know anything about boats, do you kid?"

"As a matter of fact, we had a couple large ..." Frank began, but Harry waved him silent.

"That's what I thought," Harry said, smiling. "You keep this up and you're going to be waived through the field training part of your training, Rookie." Sobering, Harry looked at each of the men and said, "This is going to get serious real fast so we go professional, we go hot, and we reach our goal – and that goal is to survive. This group of people in Southern California has made it, so we have a shot at doing the same. We know there are others in the City we might be able to help, but we will only be able to do that if we get ourselves set up first. Okay, everyone on Channel 3. Unless there's questions or comments, let's get this done."

19

Neither Derrick nor Frank said anything, and after making certain they all had their radios set on Channel 3, Harry and Derrick headed toward the garage while Frank continued to the side entrance to put their escape plan in action.

Derrick led Harry down four flights of stairs before they reached the lower garage. Harry saw the two vehicles Derrick had mentioned parked in the lower garage area as they entered. One was a white Ford pickup, probably belonging to an officer, and the other was the BearCat Riot Control vehicle. The huge vehicle reminded Harry of an armored car on steroids. It was painted a matte black bearing vehicle logos of a blue seven-point star, outlined in gold, with the letters SFPD in the center also in gold. Those logos were on both the driver and passenger doors as well as on the left-hand side of the double rear cargo doors. What really caught Harry's attention was the front ram assembly that he knew could be raised and lowered from the cab of the vehicle. "Wow, that'll do for sure, I think," Harry said aloud to no one in particular.

"If you think the outside is pretty, wait until you see the inside," Derrick said as he walked up to the rear double doors, inserting a key and swinging them open. Harry walked to the open doors and could only stare in astonishment at the neatly stacked boxes of ammo, various supplies, and the weapons that had been secured to racks on the inside walls of the Bearcat. He also noticed at least a dozen cases of MREs lining one area of the compartment. Seeing Harry looking at those, Derrick said, "Oh, we found the MREs in the supply room along with about thirty gallons of water before you showed up at our back door. We'd thought maybe those would also come in handy, so the Rook and I loaded it all."

"Derrick, not only am I going to kiss you, I might even give you some tongue!" Harry said with a huge grin, still looking into the compartment.

"Dude, seriously! I already spoke to you about this pretty face and all!" Derrick replied, chuckling.

Harry stepped up into the compartment and, although a bit tight with all the items Derrick and Frank had loaded, there was still plenty of room to move comfortably. Harry looked at the center roof hatch then, reaching up, he tried to unlatch and push it open but it would not budge.

"No, you open like this," Derrick said, stepping into the rear compartment and showing Harry a toggle switch just to the left of the hatch. Harry flipped the toggle forward and was a bit surprised to see the hatch rise approximately five inches, then slide back toward the rear of the vehicle.

Derrick then reached toward a recessed lever on the right side of the compartment wall, pulling it outward. Harry heard what reminded him of air brakes as they released pressure and then watched as a small platform rose from the floor just under the ceiling hatch. It stopped after reaching a height of about two feet.

"That's awesome." Harry said as he excitedly stepped up on the platform to look out the hatch.

"Careful, Harry," Derrick said, knowing his warning was too late.

Harry stepped up, put his upper body through the open hatch, and immediately banged the top of his head on a ceiling light fixture that was hanging above the Bearcat. Ducking back down, rubbing the top of his head while spewing several verbal metaphors, he looked at Derrick as if he had set him up.

"Told you to be careful. We only have about a ten-inch ceiling clearance here," Derrick replied, shrugging at Harry's accusatory gaze.

"Whatever," Harry replied, stepping off the platform and exiting the rear of the vehicle still rubbing the top of his head. "Let's just get this done. Damn that hurts!"

"I'll kiss your boo-boo later," Derrick responded as he went to the driver's door and got in. Harry gave Derrick's back a one-fingered salute and closed the two rear doors.

Walking up to Derrick's door, Harry said, "Go ahead and move it to the bottom of the ramp. When I hear you shut it back down I'll go up and radio the kid, then wait for him at the stairway door."

Derrick gave him thumbs up and started the BCRC. Harry was pleased at how quiet the big V-8 turbo turned out to be. It was not as loud as he had first feared, and he knew that would be to their benefit. He watched for a moment as Derrick maneuvered the big vehicle down the garage and toward the ramp, then turned and ascended the stairs, going back to the first floor entrance.

As soon as he reached the stairway door and opened it he radioed, "Frank, it's Harry, you ready?"

Frank instantly replied back and said, "I picked up the unit's keys from the intake desk and am looking out of the street door now. Looks clear so I'm ready when you are."

"Okay, just remember the plan, kid. Out the door, start the car; activate the lights and siren, then book it back in. You even think there's danger you abort and head back here. Got it?" Harry said with growing anxiety, and then muttered, "I should have gone myself."

"Don't worry, *Dad*," Frank responded with what Harry thought for sure was some form of teenage angst. "I've got this, okay. Ready?"

Harry had been listening to the Bearcat while he spoke to Frank, the rumble of its engine quite clear in the quiet and empty garage. After a couple of minutes he heard the engine go quiet, indicating that Derrick must be in position and had turned the truck off.

"Do it," Harry said into the radio mic. From Harry's location he would not be able to hear anything other than the siren if all went according to plan. He would give it a slow count of ten, then he would run to Frank's position. He knew if anything did go wrong he would be far too late to help by then. He cursed again, second-guessing himself.

Harry had not even reached the count of eight when the wail of an electronic siren became very evident from outside.

"Frank, you okay? FRANK!" Harry shouted into the radio mic as he rushed out the stairway and into the main floor.

"On … the … way …" Frank finally replied, obviously running and speaking between breaths. "There … in … a … few …"

Harry let out his own breath that he had been holding while relief washed over him. He had already started toward the inner hall that led to the side doors when he reached a count of four. Knowing that Frank was headed back in one piece, Harry immediately veered his direction and took the stairs onto the balcony proper. Once he reached the balcony, he looked out of the windows onto the street in front of the station. He was relieved to see the Zs making their way toward the side of the building and the sound of the siren. Some ran like Olympic athletes, while other shambled slowly like they didn't have a care in the world. A few, he noticed to his complete disgust, were dragging themselves along with what appeared to have been broken and mangled legs, but they still moved with dogged determination. "It's working," he said to himself as he descended the stairs to wait for Frank. He didn't have to wait long.

As Harry reached the bottom stair, he saw Frank run around the corner into the lobby. He was clutching his AR to his chest, and sweat was pouring down his face. Stooping in front of Harry, leaning over and placing his hands on his knees, Frank gasped, "That was intense."

"You okay, kid?" Harry asked while placing his hand on Frank's shoulder.

Not looking up but taking in deep breaths, Frank said, "Yeah I'm good. Just got the lights and siren going and was headed back in when I looked up and saw a shitload of those things coming around the other side of alley. They saw me, too. I was able to get the outer door closed and locked before they hit it. Boy did they hit it! Locked the inner door and booked it back here." Frank was then able to stand and it looked as if his breathing was returning to normal. The next thing he said caused Harry great concern, but he kept that hidden from his expression. "You know both of those doors open inward and I'm not sure how long they're going to hold. I know they are normally pretty sturdy but the electronic locks are not engaging for some reason. The only thing securing them is a deadbolt."

Harry nodded his understanding and said, "Doesn't matter, we'll be gone before they get through the first one." As if on cue, however, both men heard what sounded like a muted explosion coming from the direction from where Frank had just come: the double security doors at the side of the building.

"Let's go!" Harry said while looking in the direction of those doors. "Let's go *now*." With that, they immediately ran for the stairway leading down to the garage.

20

Once they descended the stairs to the lower garage, Harry turned to Frank while pointing to the white Ford pickup truck and said, "See if you can gain entry into that truck and let's get it ass-ended against this door," indicating the door to the stairway they had just come through. Frank nodded once and ran to the truck; within moments Harry heard glass break. Glancing over, he saw Frank open the driver side door, shattered glass on the concrete floor around his boots, then lean down below the steering column. *Daddy must have taught him how to hotwire a car I guess.*

As he was walking toward the ramp where the Bearcat was parked, Harry heard the pickup truck start from behind him. The engine revved just a bit, and after a moment there was a slight screeching of tires as Frank put it in reverse, then a minor metal-on-metal bump confirming he had backed the rear end of the truck against the inward-opening stairway door, thus securing it. Within another couple of seconds, the truck was shut down, and before Harry was within fifteen feet of the Bearcat, Frank trotted up beside him.

"I'm not even going to ask," Harry said with a grin while glancing sideways toward Frank. Looking straight ahead, Frank shrugged his shoulders. Harry clapped him on the back and they both continued to approach the big monster truck waiting at the ramp entrance.

As they approached the Bearcat, Harry saw Derrick sitting on the rear ramp, with the back doors open, thumbing 5.56 rounds into magazines. Harry walked over to Derrick, while Frank continued around to the driver side door, and asked, "How many mags good to go?"

Derrick glanced up without breaking his loading rhythm and said, "I think maybe two hundred and fifty 30-round mags for the ARs, and one hundred 13- round mags for our Glocks. The Rook carries a Glock 17 9mm so he's got seventeen in the handle and I saw four mag cases on his belt. I didn't load all these mags, of course. They must have been done at some point while there were still other officers left in the station." Harry simply nodded in reply but was suddenly troubled, knowing that from what he had seen so far, and the sheer number of those things running around, they could burn through seventy-five hundred rounds of 5.56 and thirteen hundred rounds of .45 caliber very quickly. Frank's sixty-eight rounds would be gone before they could go a city block.

"Damn Derry, how come you guys couldn't have a couple SAWs lying around?" Harry asked rhetorically. He was referring to a Squad Automatic Weapon machine gun that fired a heavy belt-fed 7.62mm round at almost eight hundred rounds per minute. "With a couple of those we could have just taken a leisurely stroll down to the marina."

"Seriously dude? You do remember our SWAT operates in San Francisco and not Afghanistan, right?" Derrick said with a chuckle.

"Yeah I know, I'm just saying," Harry muttered. Taking a deep breath he said, "Let's button up and get ready." Climbing into the rear of the Bearcat, Harry made his way to the front, stepping over the center console and sitting down in the passenger side seat. This was the first time that he'd been in the front section, and he was amazed at all the buttons, switches, and monitors on the dash, ceiling, and center console. Glancing over at Frank who was sitting behind the wheel, Harry swore he was doing what looked like some sort of preflight checklist.

"Now I suppose you are going to tell me your dad had one of these things, too?" Harry asked Frank.

"Naw, I glanced over the owner's manual," Frank replied, not looking away from some sort of display screen in front of him. He briefly gestured toward what appeared to be a four-inch-thick full-sized binder sitting on top of a closed mobile laptop attached to the center console.

"Seriously, you know how to operate this thing by *glancing* at a copy of what looks to be a book out of an encyclopedia set?" Harry said while picking up the heavy, thick volume that Frank claimed was an *owner's manual*.

"It's all just basic operational stuff, but man, is it cool! State of the art GPS, satellite uplinks probably for faster NCRC and Interpol connections. This radio system is more advanced than anything I've ever seen," Frank said excitedly, looking and acting more like the eighteen-year-old kid Harry had thought he was when they'd first met in the armory. That only being about three hours prior. Harry felt the weight of responsibility hit him full force once again. He had to do this right. He had to help this kid, his close friend in the back, and anyone else he could to survive. There were no other options for Harry to consider; no other course available.

Taking a deep breath to clear his thoughts and get his head back in the game, Harry said jokingly to Frank, "Okay then Number One, activate the cloaking device and arm forward phasers. Prepare to engage."

Frank quickly looked over to Harry with a huge grin on his face and said, "Actually, I was just thinking how awesome it would be if this thing was a Transformer! Not just any ordinary Transformer, but a Prime! It would transform into *Bear Prime* with twenty-four-inch talons on one hand and a mini gun on the other! With rockets that would fire from his shoulder! *Bear Prime* could seriously kick some zombie ass!"

Harry knew exactly what Frank was referring to. He had really enjoyed the three Transformer movies and knew that a Prime was a leader, the most powerful and advanced Transformer from Cybertron. Harry actually laughed and said to Frank, "That *would* be totally awesome!"

Derrick had been leaning between the rear compartment and front during Frank and Harry's exchange and finally said, "Okay kiddies, not to interrupt your interplanetary strategy session or anything, but if you're ready to rejoin adulthood we're buttoned up back here and ready to roll."

Frank and Harry exchanged glances like two kids caught doing something they shouldn't. Harry fired back to Derrick in a whiney voice, while pointing at Frank, "Yeah, but HE brought all that stuff up! I was just trying to do my homework, Dad!" Both Harry and Frank burst out laughing at the dumbstruck expression on Derrick's face.

"Geez, children; one just out of diapers and one getting ready to wear them." That was the best Derrick could get out before he joined the other two men in laughter.

Turning serious, Harry said, "Let's give it ten to fifteen minutes for the siren to draw as many as possible. They know somebody's in the building now, and it sounded like they broke through at least one set of doors downstairs. Hopefully a bunch of them will pile in looking for us, clearing more from the street out front."

Frank had also reverted back into the professionally trained police officer that he was and said, "I know they saw me, and from what you relayed from GNN and the other reports they should continue to look for a while before losing interest. That truck should keep the door secured if they get this far down."

Derrick nodded in agreement and asked, "Maybe we should try that super keen radio while we wait?"

"Do you think we could get anything down here? I know we used to have to be on street level before our cars could transmit," Harry asked Frank.

Looking up from the manual he had opened as soon as Derrick had suggested the radio, Frank said, "This vehicle has a microwave transmitter array built into the roof which is necessary to utilize the type of satellite connections it can use. Most of our radio systems we use standardly operate on an 800-megahertz bandwidth which has a much weaker power range compared to microwave transmission. That's why those radios lose signal when blocked by heavy or thick obstructions. The radio equipment in the Bearcat is almost military grade so I don't think the building would be a problem. I don't understand it all completely, not yet at least, but I'm confident it has transmitting and receiving capabilities far more powerful than our main central dispatch, let alone the station equipment or our cars."

"Okay, so I think he just said it's a pretty good radio. So unless I need a lead cup to protect the jewels from those microwaves, I say we fire that sucker up. Let's see if we can talk to Finland or maybe the International Space Station," Derrick said with a chuckle.

Harry was too engrossed with what Frank had said for Derrick's comment to register and said, "Hope it's been programmed with at least the local channels but let's find out." Frank flipped three different switches on the dash and instantly, in what seemed like quadraphonic surround sound, they heard radio traffic!

There were units calling in from various locations reporting their situations, and a calm female voice responding back to each call. The radio traffic sounded almost normal but everyone in the BCRC knew it was anything but. The thing that hit Harry hard was the actual lack of traffic. There should have been more units transmitting than he was hearing.

Harry pulled the hand mic from the dash clip and said, "Three Edward Six, Central Station." The response was immediate from the calm female voice.

"All units, 10-3, all units 10-3 unless emergency traffic." The calm female voice had just directed all units on air to stop transmitting. "Three Edward Six, please advise current status. One Adam is standing by."

"You're in deep shit now, Harry. The chief wants to talk to you!" Derrick retorted with a snicker.

21

One Adam was the Chief of Police's radio call sign. Harry was almost too excited to reply, but finally said, "Edward Six, with two other officers and secure at Central Station. We will be mobile in about fifteen in the Bearcat."

"Edward Six, Adam One, 10-6 to channel ..." Harry heard the voice of Chief Greg Ekers, someone he had known during his entire twenty-five-year career, directing him to change radio channels. Glancing over to Frank, Harry nodded once and Frank immediately started programming in the new channel on the Bearcat's radio system.

Greg Ekers was a thirty-year career cop who had worked his way up the ladder in the department and was highly respected by the rank and file. He was a no-nonsense police officer and a very effective commander and administrator. Ekers spent as much time in the field with the officers as he did sitting behind a desk. He was able to work and interact very well with the many diverse groups of people who lived and worked in San Francisco. The most surprising attribute Ekers had mastered was the ability to work well with city government which, in and of itself, amazed most people who knew him.

When Frank acknowledged that the new channel was programmed, Harry said into the mic, "Greg, can you hear me?"

"I hear you Harry, and you don't know how happy I am you're alright! Please bring me up to date," Chief Ekers said in a calm, professional tone.

Harry took a couple of seconds to gather his thoughts, then responded, "Well Chief, looks like we have a bit of a situation in the City. Seems as if some folks want to eat other folks and they are being damn persistent about it. I'm with Officers Derrick Washington and Frank Lewis. We've been able to secure the armory at Central and transferred what was left into the Bear. We have created a distraction and are now waiting for Vallejo to clear, then we're headed out. What are your orders, Greg? How can we help?" Harry was praying to be relieved of this responsibility and was eager to have the command staff give him direction. Any direction.

The chief, chuckling through the radio speaker, said, "Yeah, citizens don't seem to be showing much respect for each other right now, that's for sure." Harry heard him take a deep breath, then continue, "I know Washington, he's a damn fine officer and I would stand with him any time. Did you know that Officer Lewis there is a near genius, Harry? His IQ is higher than us two old beat cops combined."

Harry glanced at Frank, who was thumbing through the BCRC owner's manual and who was now beet red. "That certainly answers a couple of questions, now doesn't it?"

"I knew this rook was smart!" Derrick added, patting Frank on the head, attempting to cover his own embarrassment at the lofty accolade the chief had just paid him.

"What are your plans then, Harry?" Chief Ekers asked

With that question posed, Harry spent several minutes outlining what he had observed since April 1st from his building, including the information he had been able to gather from GNN. He laid out his initial plan to secure the marina and head into the Bay. "But that was all just 'shooting from the hip' ideas," Harry concluded, releasing the transmit button.

There were several moments of silence, to the point that Harry said into the mic, "Greg, did you copy?"

"I copied Harry, stand by one," Ekers replied.

After several moments with Harry beginning to wonder if they had lost radio contact, the chief was back on the radio. "Harry, continue with your plan. We are currently barricaded at the Hall and secure for now."

Harry knew that the Hall of Justice at 850 Bryant was a safe location and could easily be secured, although it was on the other side of the city from Central Station. Regardless, he was not going to just leave his friend and whoever else was there stranded.

"Wait a minute Greg, we can help you! Those *things* are everywhere," Harry said with growing concern plainly evident in his voice.

"I know they're everywhere, Harry," Ekers calmly replied. "There are hundreds of those things congregated right outside our windows. I'm looking at a mass of bodies so thick I can't see the street or sidewalk surfaces in either direction. There is nothing you can do for us for the time being. Now listen carefully; we've been in direct contact with the Coast Guard and I'd like you to meet face-to-face with them if at all possible to act as the Department's liaison. The USCG Cutter Tern, and her Captain William Overton, has operational command right now of the military assets in the Bay. There is also a contingent of National Guard on Treasure Island, also under Overton's command, that set up a refugee center for those who were able to make it there. Unfortunately as the survivors were streaming onto the island from both the Oakland and San Francisco sides, they had more of those zombie things chasing them than the Guard had bullets. The decision was made to blow both Bay Bridge entrances to Treasure Island, effectively sealing it off. Can't say as I disagree with that decision entirely, but that cut any chances of survivors reaching TI from the bridge. Overton did mention, however, that almost a thousand people got onto the island before they sealed it off," Chief Ekers finally concluded, weariness evident in his voice.

Frank stared out of the windshield as Derrick leaned against the center console, both in silent consideration of what they had heard. Harry was also trying to digest everything Ekers had said. At least he now knew what the explosions had been that he'd heard that night on the apartment building roof. But what his thoughts centered on were the hundreds of people that had been cut off from Treasure Island. He had seen too many times what happened to those pursued by the infected, and it was apparent what had probably happened to those survivors.

"There's something else you need to know, and this is going to directly affect your immediate plans." Ekers picked up when he received no reply from Harry. "Captain Overton told us that there are at least a couple dozen boats in the Marina Harbor with survivors aboard each one. That's great news, of course, but unfortunately there also seems to be a couple hundred infected along the marina docks. The fencing that had been erected is keeping those things from getting at the boats and people, but you only have one way to get in. You worked security at a couple of the initial events at the Golden Gate Yacht Club, so you know what I am talking about."

As with many areas in San Francisco, the term 'marina' was a fairly generic reference, but Harry knew the area to which Ekers was referring: the oldest recreational marina operating in San Francisco and perhaps the greater Bay Area. Vessels had been berthed in the harbor's original basin, now known as the West Harbor, since before the 1906 earthquake. The original marina was expanded in the mid-1960's and was now approximately thirty-five acres in size. The entire facility had almost seven hundred berths, ten end ties for guest berthing vessels up to a hundred feet in length, free pump out stations and a commercial fuel dock. The West Harbor marina area included the St. Francis and the Golden Gate Yacht Clubs, the Harbormaster's Building, and the park area known as Marina Green. The large harbor was in the shape of a near perfect 'U' but squared off at the bottom. The squared-off west side of the harbor was closest to Yacht Road, which was accessed off Marina Boulevard, and led to the north side of the 'U'. This was the bayside of the harbor which also served as the breakwater wall for the boat slips and where the yacht clubs were located.

Harry also knew that the heavy fencing had been installed as a security measure around the docks for the America's Cup that had been scheduled to be raced in the Bay later that year – a race that would probably never be run again, at least in his lifetime. At ten feet high, the security fence spanned from the west end of the Marina Green, running the full length of the harbor's south side. There was also a similar section along the western section of the 'U' that ran across Yacht Road to the edge of the causeway and the Bay water. In the middle of this section, a large double gate had been installed to allow controlled access to the moored boats and the two club houses.

"Oh shit, there goes the neighborhood," Derrick said uneasily.

Frank added with slight panic in his voice, "What're we going to do now?"

"Easy guys, let's take this a step at a time," Harry replied, trying to ease tensions. Taking a deep breath then releasing it, he responded to Ekers, "This is a lot to take in Greg, any more good news for us?" he asked mordantly.

"Yeah, maybe," Ekers began, ignoring Harry's tone. "Overton said he had received several distress calls from some of the boats tied up at the docks, so he sent a Defender Class boat to render assistance. However, the Coasties were unable to do much other than fire their mounted deck gun into the crowd of those zombie things around the fence. Because of the size of their boat they were unable to get it into the harbor proper.

"Overton said they took dozens of the damn things out, but with every one that was put down two more took their place. He did mention that with the amount of fire the Defender had poured into the area they had destroyed most of the fencing and many of the unoccupied boats nearest the shore side. The infected didn't enter the water where the fencing had been, so guess there's a buffer zone of sorts between the horde and the remaining boats on that side."

"I can see that," Derrick commented from behind Harry. "The patrol boat would have a .50 caliber mounted on it and those rounds would have devastated anything they hit. Probably took out two or three of those things with each round and would have simply disintegrated the chain-link fence material."

Harry nodded in agreement as Ekers resumed. "Overton wasn't able to render direct aid to the people left on the boats. They did not seem to be organized, and after rounds being shot literally over their heads they became quite wary of that Coast Guard boat. He said they would not answer their hails. The crew on the Defender did launch a small life raft with some survival rations, but he doesn't know if it was picked up by anyone.

"One other thing to mention here is that the Tern has also been in contact with their counterparts in Southern California. Not sure what the pecking order is between the military in SoCal and up here, but Overton has ordered all his available assets to secure the Oakland Ports. Seems to think there might be valuable supplies there. Here's the thing though, I got the distinct impression Overton was feeling us out. Maybe as to whether we could offer any assistance from the land side. I told him we were pinned where we are and wouldn't be able to do much for the time being. Hell, at the time I couldn't offer him a cup of coffee." Ekers stopped transmitting for a moment. Harry remained quiet because he knew there was more coming.

After another minute, Ekers said, "What I am trying to make very clear is that you will be on your own out there, Harry. The Coast Guard has already pulled back to the Oakland Ports. The last transmission we heard was their units had landed ashore. Apparently the port area is crawling with the infected, and from what we gathered from their transmissions it was dicey as to whether they could do anything to secure it. What is left of the National Guard on TI is in effect stranded there with both bridge accesses destroyed. You need to think very carefully before leaving

Central, Harry. If you decide to remain, nobody will judge that decision…" Ekers trailed off and stopped transmitting.

Harry was just beginning to reply when Ekers' voice came through the speakers once again. "But I know you, Harry, and I know you could sooner remain out of this than I could if I had the chance and thought I could make it out. You asked for my orders, so here they are. I want you and your team to attempt to make contact with any survivors, offering whatever assistance possible. Attempt to make contact with Captain Overton and let him know what you have in mind. I don't think he will stand in your way, but don't expect any help from him. Be very careful in that contact though. They are edgy as hell right now. I recommend you make radio contact before approaching them. Do you copy that?"

"We copy and that's reasonable. I will not put us in undue danger, but you're right that I can't just sit here and do nothing," Harry said into the mic. "Anything else, Chief?"

"So, yeah, that, umm, does bring me to something else I need to take care of here," Ekers said cryptically.

"That would be?" Harry responded after almost two full minutes of dead air over the radio.

"As you already know, the nation is under martial law," Ekers began again. "However, it is pretty clear by what we've seen and heard that everybody is really on their own. Therefore, I am issuing an emergency departmental directive that reinstates you, Harold Lancaster, as a full-time sworn police officer for the City and County of San Francisco, effective immediately. Do you copy that, Harry?"

22

Harry stared at the radio mic as if it were a radioactive alien artifact that had just fallen from the sky and into his hands. He was, however, finally able to torpidly say through that radioactive artifact, "Copy ..."

Ekers then said with evident relish, "There's one more thing, but before I lay that on you I am ordering both Officers Washington and Lewis, I know you guys can hear me, to take all action necessary in preventing Lancaster from shooting the radio with what I have to say next. That includes handcuffing him if necessary, gentlemen. Now then, Harry, in addition to being reinstated to full-time status, you are hereby promoted to the rank of Lieutenant and ordered to oversee all field operations such as they are right now."

Harry lost it with that announcement. "ARE YOU OUT OF YOUR FUCKING MIND GREG? I'M TOO OLD FOR THIS SHIT AND YOU KNOW IT! THIS ISN'T THE DAMN ARMY! YOU CAN'T JUST DRAFT ME FOR CHRISSAKE!" he bellowed into the mic. What followed was a 'hot and heavy, spit flying, all in your face ass chewing' directed at Chief Greg Ekers, albeit delivered over the radio. It would have made Harry's old FTO, Shane O'Connor, immensely proud.

"Harry, let go of the mic," Derrick said, reaching over Harry's shoulder and trying to pry his friend's hands from the small piece of plastic that was in imminent danger of imploding from the death grip that had been placed upon it.

"You better get that away from him before he breaks it or blows out the circuits," Frank urged, but made no attempt to assist Derrick.

"I'm working on it here, Rook. Harry, damn it, LET GO OF THE MIC!" Derrick yelled.

Harry kept his harangue flowing until Derrick decided to take drastic action. Leaning forward and bringing his face close to Harry's, he licked him; licked him from jaw to hairline.

Instantaneously snapping out of his one-sided scream fest, Harry turned to Derrick with a shocked expression. "What the hell, Derry! Did you just lick me! DID YOU JUST LICK MY DAMN FACE?" At that Harry let the mic drop to the floor, opened the passenger side door and jumped out, vigorously rubbing the side of his face with the sleeve of his jump. Derrick moved into the passenger seat and hurriedly closed the door, engaging the lock.

Harry was now directing his full ire on Derrick, attempting to establish a logical reason for this last course of action. "Listen you big ox, open that damn door 'cause I am going to kick your ass all over this garage! You LICKED ME!" Harry was shouting but it was muffled because of the armor and bullet-resistant glass.

"Wasn't he going to kiss you not too long ago?" Frank asked, looking past Derrick to Harry who was still articulating his immense displeasure.

"Yeah, he said it again when he saw all the stuff we loaded in the Bearcat, too. Even said he'd use tongue. But older folks who miss their afternoon naps can get a bit cranky," Derrick answered.

"Well, guess we don't have to wait for your 'bar or better' now," Frank said, continuing to watch Harry's antics.

"Nope, we're good now," Derrick replied.

Harry walked over to the Bearcat and yelled again, "Get out of the damn truck!" With that he pounded on the up-armored door twice, very hard, using the side of a closed fist. His next action was to immediately step back, look at his hand like it was yet another alien artifact, then cradle it as if said artifact was a very delicate item.

"Bet that hurt," Frank commented.

"Sure looked like it did," Derrick said.

"Think he'll try to shoot you through the door?" Frank asked.

"I don't think so, but what's the rating on this glass again?" Derrick replied with amusement.

"Harry, are you there?" Chief Ekers' voice came over the radio.

Picking up the mic, Derrick said, "Chief, it's Washington. Umm, Harry seems to be having some transitional issues with his recent promotion at the moment."

"Yeah, I'll just bet he is, Derrick," the chief replied with a chuckle. "Please inform *Lieutenant* Lancaster to grab his balls, suck it up, and get back on the damn radio."

"Yes sir. Stand by one," Derrick replied.

By this time Harry had ceased his rant and was staring fixedly at Derrick. Unlocking the door and opening it just enough to be heard, Derrick said, "You okay now Harry? The chief wants to talk to you." It was taking everything he had to keep from falling out of the door with laughter.

"I. Am. Fine," Harry replied, emphasizing each word.

Swinging the door open fully as Harry approached, and before Harry could say anything, Derrick said into the mic, "Chief, *Lieutenant* Lancaster is right here, just a moment." With that, he pushed the mic toward Harry.

Grabbing the mic, Harry said, "Don't think you're getting off that easily, *Officer* Washington. Payback's a nasty bitch and I just happen to know she has been having very bad days here recently." Derrick groaned, realizing he was waist deep in fecal matter, but still could not wipe the grin from his face.

"Go ahead Greg, I'm listening," Harry said sarcastically into the mic, still glaring at Derrick.

"Harry, I know you would rather walk over hot coals than accept what I've just laid on you, but we need you to step up. Out of our original twenty-two hundred officers and command staff, I might be lucky to have two to three hundred left, and we can't even confirm that count." Harry was stunned at that information. He knew it had to be bad for the department after what he had seen on the televised broadcasts, but he had not realized just how bad until that moment.

Ekers continued. "Most of the ones we can confirm alive are barricaded in one of the stations, at City Hall, DEM, or anywhere else they could secure themselves. There are probably others, but right now you are the only unit that even remotely has the chance of being mobile. I need you to do what you can out there. Once you get set up somewhere we'll work out a plan to find the rest of our people and see what we can do for the City."

"What about the fires?" Harry asked, realizing that further resistance served no purpose other than to vent his own angst. Personal feelings were just not high in the greater scheme of things, and he felt a bit of embarrassment at his initial reaction.

"It appears they are burning themselves out," Ekers replied. "The fire chief is here and she thinks because of the new building codes and the lack of heavy winds to aid the spread, we just might have a City to reclaim. Although I have no idea what we will have left to reclaim other *than* buildings. Anyway, it's a good thing because we have also been unable to contact any SFFD personnel. Other than a few personnel here with us, every fire station has gone silent."

Harry had lowered his head and was leaning against the door with one foot on the side running board. "Okay Chief, copy that. At least some sort of good news I guess. I'll do what I can, for now, but I am not guaranteeing anything past some sort of resolution to this mess or until someone else can take over out here."

Although Harry would not simply abandon the City or his friends, he had already decided that he was going to head east once he had the chance. His family was in Indiana and he was determined to reunite with them. His fifteen-year-old nephew, Eric, had been able to get an email out several days after the outbreak, letting Harry know that they were being relocated to a safe zone. Eric had not given many details other than they were scared but safe and that he wanted Harry to come home. Eric had closed that email with, "Mom is being cool but dad is a bit freaked out. I'm really scared but I'm remembering all the things we have talked about. Please stay safe and find us soon. I love you!"

Harry and Eric were very close. Along with the many other things they had shared together over the years, they had spent many hours talking about what to do in the event of an emergency. That included everything from dealing with bullies to people coming into school with guns. Harry tried to impart as much of his experience as a fifteen-year-old could absorb. Eric always asked relevant questions considering each answer before repeating it back to his uncle, demonstrating his understanding.

With everything that was happening, Harry had been forced to remain focused on staying alive. As the days had passed, his growing concern for his family was making it extremely difficult to maintain that focus and remain in San Francisco. He had no idea how he would make the nearly twenty-three-hundred-mile trek across country, but he was determined to do just that. If humanity was to fall, then he would be with the people that mattered most in his life when it did. With this new 'promotion', and the overwhelming responsibility that was sure to come with it, he had the growing fear he would not reach them in time.

"That's fair enough," Ekers said, interrupting Harry's thoughts.

Harry quickly shook off the depression that was threatening to creep into his soul. He had no choice right now. If he was to reunite with his family he had to continue to keep his head in the game. If he did not, he was going to get himself killed or the two men sitting in the truck that now looked to him for direction. Pushing back the thoughts of his family for the time being, he looked up and realized his longtime friend was looking back fixedly.

Derrick could read people well and Harry was no exception. Derrick had met Harry's family many times, and Eric was quite enamored with this large black man. Although Eric had no desire to become a cop, much to Harry's immense relief, he was still a kid who was easily impressed with authority figures.

As Derrick was a very easy person to like, it came as no surprise that he and Eric had hit it off so well. Both huge sports fans which quickly gave them common ground. A good-natured debate was often heard between the two in regard to Derrick's San Francisco Giants and Eric's New York Yankees. Having no family of his own, Derrick had adopted Eric as a surrogate nephew and would do anything for that kid. Including laying down his life to protect him or the rest of Harry's family without a moment's hesitation.

"You'll see them again, Harry," Derrick said to him. "Just remember that when you go, I go with you."

Harry was taken by surprise at this statement, but what caught him off guard the most was the intensity with which Derrick made those two simple statements. All Harry could do was to nod once to Derrick in reply.

"Go where?" Frank asked, looking to Derrick, then Harry.

"Not now, Frank," Derrick replied. "We've got work to get done here and we need to concentrate on that for the time being."

Frank didn't offer any further comments but it was clear by the expression on his face he had questions. Harry had to take things down a notch as his emotions were threatening to overcome him. In his usual fashion, he quickly formulated a plan to do just that in the manner he fell back on in situation like this.

"I do have one request, Chief," he finally said into the radio mic, looking squarely at Derrick with a slight grin playing around the corners of his mouth.

The look on Derrick Washington's face was as if someone had walked over his grave.

"Now wait just a minute, Harry! I know what you doing and I suggest you don't go there damn it! I'm serious here, brother!"

Ignoring Derrick, Harry continued, "Chief, I need a sergeant and I would like to recommend Derrick Washington for immediate promotion." Harry knew that Derrick's aversion to promotion was as strongly felt as his own. Derrick was using the experience in law enforcement as part of his career goals, and those goals did not include rank.

Looking over to Frank, Harry said with all sincerity, "No offense kid, you understand?"

"Absolutely none taken! I have no problem with any of this. I'm just happy to be with you guys!" Frank replied enthusiastically.

"Harry, you are *such* a prick, you know that, right!" Derrick said in a flustered tone. Harry just stood by the door smiling with what could only be described as a Cheshire cat grin.

"Oh, and by the way, even though you may feel the need at some point very soon, I would strongly urge that you not to punch the Bear, Derry. It's rather unyielding I recently discovered," Harry offered with quiet laughter and to further pick at Derrick's crestfallen demeanor.

"I have no problem with that at all, Harry. Consider it done as of right now. Congratulations, Sergeant Washington," Ekers said, responding to Harry's request.

"Thanks Chief. I'm sure I speak for *Sergeant* Washington when I say it is an honor to serve the City." Derrick threw double-digit finger salutes in Harry's face with that.

"Okay guys, get to it. Although I really can't offer you more information at the moment, I have the utmost confidence in your abilities. I'll update Captain Overton on your status and that you will be in contact with him at some point. Here's the radio frequency the Tern is operating on …" While Ekers relayed the frequency, Frank quickly jotted it down to program into the radio. "Contact me when you can but keep on task, gentlemen, and God speed. One Adam clear." With that, Chief Greg Ekers signed off.

"Three Edward Six," Harry acknowledged, then leaned up and across Derrick, placing the mic back in the dash clip. As he did so he caught his image reflected in the window glass of the door. Without a moment's consideration, he reached up to his jumpsuit's collar and removed the set of silver chevrons, handing them toward Derrick. "Put them on, *Sergeant* Washington."

"Blow me, *Lieutenant* Lancaster." Derrick dejectedly attempted to sink his large frame as far into the seat as possible, crossing his arms like a pouting child.

"Now Sergeant Washington, this is quite unbecoming a person of your rank, especially in front of Officer Lewis here," Harry said, mustering all the self-control he could to maintain a straight face.

"You love this shit, don't you," Derrick retorted.

"Well, since you asked, more than you could possibly imagine right about now," Harry said, no longer being able to hide his grin while still holding out his hand, palm up, with the two silver chevron pins lying in the center.

"Okay, so I put them on, payback's done, right?" Derrick asked suspiciously.

"Yep, we'd be good; for the most part," Harry replied, laughing.

"Fine, give me the damn things," Derrick said in a defeated manner, pinning the chevrons on his collar. "Satisfied?"

During this exchange, Frank had buried his face in the Bearcat's operations manual, closing both sides of the thick book against his cheeks in an attempt to avert the fits of laughter that threatened to overtake him.

"Oh quite, thank you, *Sergeant*," Harry said, mischievously adding a very sloppy salute. Sobering, he looked past Derrick and said to Frank, "Okay kid, time to roll, and paraphrasing somebody way smarter than me, we have promises to keep, and miles to go before we sleep."

"I really like Frost. He's one of my favorite poets," Frank responded absently while finishing his 'preflight check'.

Harry chuckled while glancing at his wristwatch. He was a bit surprised to realize that less than forty minutes had elapsed since they'd first entered the garage. It felt like several hours had passed.

23

While Derrick moved into the rear compartment of the Bearcat, Harry stepped up and pulled himself into the passenger seat, closing the heavy door with a thud. Frank turned the ignition key and the big truck started instantly, emitting a soft rumble from the powerful diesel engine. Harry was again astonished at how quiet the Bearcat was considering the engine's size.

The dash of the Bearcat illuminated with an array of various lights in a subdued orange glow obviously designed to assist those in the front compartment with maintaining night vision when necessary. Reaching to a lever which looked somewhat like a gearshift arm, just to the left of the steering column, Frank pushed down slightly which raised the V-ram on the front of the truck.

Harry could see this action transpire on a monitor in the center of the dash, the image obviously being sent from a camera built into the front section of the vehicle. It made sense to him to have a forward-facing camera; otherwise, because of the limited view from inside, it would be impossible to know what position the ram was in at any particular time. The monitor screen was actually split into two views, with the lower image from a camera positioned above the rear double doors of the Bearcat.

Once Frank had the ram up, he moved the gearshift selector lever, located to the right of the steering column, putting it into the drive position and engaging the automatic transmission. With his left foot slightly on the brake, he applied a slight pressure on the accelerator with his right, giving the big truck torque and moving it slowly forward. The garage area was flooded with light so Frank did not bother turning on the headlights.

The ramp leading up from the lower garage into the next level was sizeable, but because of the width of the Bearcat it was still a tight fit. Especially with the curve of the up ramp. Unfortunately, Frank misjudged the clearance between the side of the truck and the wall. He slightly scraped the right rear bumper as he drove up the ramp. It wasn't a hard hit but enough to be heard inside the vehicle.

"Hey! Watch it there Frank!" Derrick cried out from his position between the front and rear compartments. He was leaning slightly forward, enabling him to see through the windshield. "This thing is brand new! You better not wreck it!"

"Shit, sorry guys!" Frank exclaimed in response.

Harry knew 'wrecking' the heavy behemoth would be almost impossible, but replied over his shoulder with a laugh, "Don't worry Derry, a few scraps and dings will give it some character."

"Yeah, well just be careful," Derrick replied.

"I'm thinking it'll get some more *character* before we're done with this ride," Frank said, with nervousness evident in his voice.

Frank continued ascending to the upper garage, then drove to the bottom of the final ramp that would take them out of the building and stopped. Harry opened the passenger side door, stepping down, then jogged over to the roll up door control. Looking back toward Frank, who gave him the thumbs up through the front windshield confirming that he was ready, Harry pressed the upper green button labeled 'open'. While the roll up door began to rise, he rushed back to the Bearcat, resuming his position in the passenger seat and slamming the door closed. He watched as the roll up door opened painfully slowly.

"*Go … go … go!*" Harry urged when he saw the door almost fully up.

By the time Frank drove up the ramp the door was fully open. He made an immediate left on Vallejo Street toward Columbus which was only half block down. Frank also instantly collided with at least a dozen of the infected that still milled around on the street in front of the station. They had obviously been attracted to the sound of the roll up door, not to mention the siren that could still be plainly heard in the background. Frank kept the vehicle's momentum powering forward and had no difficulty plowing through the mass of bodies. That did nothing to ease the revulsion each man felt seeing the destruction the heavy Bearcat delivered to the soft bodies in its path.

The big truck flung the infected to both sides as if they were rag dolls as the ram served its intended purpose of wedging a path. Because the ram was raised to its highest position, many of the bodies were being caught under the front wheels, creating a noticeable thumping sensation felt through the flooring, quickly followed by one set of the double rear tires finishing the job of grinding what was left into the street surface. Harry was very much aware of the blood and gore that erupted outward each time one of the heavy front tires rolled over and crushed a body.

"Lower the ram a bit, Frank. We don't want to get anything caught in the undercarriage," Harry said, not taking his eyes from the horrific scene unfolding in front of them and being displayed in all-too-living-color on the cab monitor. The Bearcat was powerful, but he still had concerns that if enough bodies got caught under the vehicle at once it might high center them and they could lose traction. He did not want to take any chances being stranded in what he was observing.

As Frank operated the lever, Harry continued to watch the monitor with the front camera view; he saw the ram slowly lower to about ten inches off the street surface. Just enough room to keep it from gouging the surface if they happened to hit a depression or rise in the street.

"That's good," Harry said, satisfied with the new position.

The Bearcat continued to clear the infected that flung themselves in its path while they travelled the short distance to the intersection. Frank made the left turn onto Columbus, then stepped hard on the brakes, bringing the big truck to an immediate halt. Looking down Columbus, all three men could only stare in total disbelief at what they saw.

Trash and litter was slung everywhere, with dead and mutilated bodies lying amongst the debris. The men could see many of the infected still kneeling by the bodies, tearing them apart. In some cases as many as six of them on one body. For some reason the scene brought to mind the movie *I Am Legend*. Harry fervently wished the infected currently roaming San Francisco shunned the light of day like those in the movie. But the scene before him told of an entirely different plot as he watched a rather large group of infected quickly moving in their direction.

"Back it up and go to Powell. We'll try to get onto Columbus further up," Harry said urgently.

Frank quickly put the Bearcat in reverse, backing up a few feet, then steered onto Vallejo again. There were more of the infected on the block between Vallejo and Powell in front of the station. It was obvious that the noise from the Bearcat had attracted a few more to the area, but not as many as Harry had feared. A *few* were too many but more tolerable to the psyche than the dozens that were making their way toward the men on Columbus.

Harry glanced over at Frank, pleased to see that although he was white-knuckling the steering wheel and sweating bullets from the adrenalin that was assuredly coursing through his system, he seemed to be in control.

"We've doing just fine, kid," Harry said calmly in an attempt to reassure Frank, who simply nodded his reply.

"Yeah, but we're going to need a car wash real soon," Derrick added disgustedly.

"Frank, I want to you to drive to the next intersection and stop if possible. We need to see what it looks like before we get in the middle of more of those things," Harry directed.

Frank closed the distance very quickly, once again knocking aside anything that was in the truck's path, bringing the Bearcat to a halt about halfway into the intersection of Powell. Harry looked out his side door window and down the street to the north. Although he still saw the infected milling about, he noted that there were not as many compared to what they had just seen on Columbus. Also, there weren't as many vehicles blocking the street in this direction. Harry took that all in within sixty seconds.

"Okay, looks like we've got some cars down there but we should be able to either go around or push through them. Of course some of our infected friends are milling about, but we should be able to clear them. Frank, you do whatever you have to but, get us through and back onto Columbus. Take that to Bay Street and hang a left. Go to Fillmore which should give us a clear shot right into the marina. You know how to get there as well as I do. Stay flexible though, and detour if you feel it necessary. Copy that?" Harry asked, knowing his directions were redundant. Frank would know the easiest route to take but Harry felt better voicing the directions.

Frank glanced over and replied, "Copy that, LT."

Over his shoulder Harry then said, "Derry, we need to ride cover in the hatch. We'll try to thin out those things as much as possible. I know this truck is badass but, I don't want to take the chance of getting bogged down somewhere."

"I'm on it," Derrick replied as he turned to open the roof hatch and raise the platform under it.

Harry gave Frank a quick pat on the shoulder as he climbed over the center console and into the rear compartment to join Derrick. As soon as Harry cleared the console, Frank put the truck in reverse and backed up just enough to make room for the right turn onto Powell. Just as he put the truck into drive, a throng of infected caught up with them and started hammering on the rear of the truck. It was obvious to the men that it was part of the horde from Columbus Street.

Moving the short distance to the platform, Harry saw that Derrick had already stepped up and was in position through the open roof hatch. He also noticed that there were two small field bags attached to the hatch edge. Derrick glanced down, seeing Harry looking at the bags, and said, "Magazines."

Harry nodded while stepping up on the platform. He unslung his AR, bringing it up and out of the hatch opening first so it was in position. At only about four feet in diameter, the roof opening was going to be tight with both men filling it, but they would manage. Disengaging the safety on his AR, Harry was ready to rock.

Both men were back-to-back, Harry facing forward and Derrick facing the rear. The moaning and pounding from the infected on the Bearcat made normal conversation almost impossible. Harry shouted, "Derry, take three to nine and I'll focus on nine to three. Let's take out what we can but keep it single-round-fire to conserve ammo. We just need to keep the Bearcat clear enough to move. Headshots kill but shooting out a hip or center mass for spinal damage will at least put them down. Let's execute this with extreme prejudice." Harry had not intended a pun but grimly thought it appropriate for the situation.

"Copy that," Derrick replied and immediately fired his first round as he began clearing his sector.

Harry brought his own rifle into firing position and aligned the EOTech electronic sight on the first infected: a woman who might have been beautiful before the outbreak. The right side of her face was a smooth, creamy-soft complexion. Long, reddish-blonde hair fell slightly over her right eye, obscuring what Harry momentarily envisioned as an iris of ice blue. That image of beauty was instantly broken as she turned and he took in the left side of her face. Skin, hair, and muscle were ripped from the skull, and a yellowish white eyeball dangled against her cheek by the optic nerve, swinging from side to side as the woman shuffled toward the truck. "Head in the game here, Harry," he muttered as he pulled the trigger, sending a round through her head and obliterating it from the body. Quickly taking a deep breath, he realigned on the next target as the Bearcat began to move slowly through the mass of infected.

24

Harry found his rhythm moving from target to target, blocking any thought that the rancid things surrounding the Bearcat had once been human beings. Now they were just an impediment to his goal. Putting the red dot on the next target he fired, reacquired a new target and fired again, continuing through this process and his first 30-round mag. When the bolt locked back on his rifle, he ejected the empty mag, grabbed a new one, and kept shooting.

Derrick was going through the same process. They were both in their zones. He desperately tried to ignore the horrific stench from the putrid near-dead carcasses that ran, walked, or crawled toward the Bearcat. Any lingering doubts that Harry might have had in regard to what the infected were, or more specifically were not, had finally been laid to rest.

With what he had been forced to do in the apartment building and during his excursion to the police station, he had still held onto a fine thread of hope that these people, these things, were salvageable. A cure could be found and the infection reversed. What he was witnessing now, however, clearly delivered the indisputable truth that these things were nothing more than monsters made real. These mangled, mutilated, and rotting near-dead things that infested the City, the world, would not be cured by some miracle vaccine or divine intervention. It was far too late for that possibility, and the only thing left for Harry to do was survive.

The infected could not be reasoned with, only pitied momentarily for their lost humanity. Destroying them, completely eradicating them from the face of the Earth, was the only logical path to take. Harry now fully accepted that they were nothing more than blight, a horrendous scourge that had to be pushed into oblivion if the rest of what remained of mankind were to survive. He had a long way to travel and knew if he did not keep that fact clearly in mind his family, his friends, and others he might encounter would perish. This final acceptance drove steel into Harry's very being as he continued to fire relentlessly into the horde surrounding the Bearcat.

Frank kept the truck moving down Powell Street, maneuvering around obstacles when possible or pushing them from the Bearcat's path with the ram. The infected were converging on the moving truck in ever-increasing numbers, and he knew he could not slow the progress being made. Up to this point Frank had tried to avoid hitting as many of those things as possible, but he felt the truck slowing under the onslaught. If the truck lost forward momentum the men would be in serious trouble, so Frank applied pressure to the gas pedal and started plowing straight through them. The Bearcat's matte-black finish had become slick with all manner of gore. He had to use the windshield wipers several times to clear the blood and unidentifiable bits and pieces of body parts that flew over the front of the truck as he drove through groups of the infected.

Finally reaching Columbus, Frank made a hard left-hand turn and accelerated down the surprisingly obstacle-free street. The infected were still evident, but he was able to push the Bearcat up to almost thirty miles per hour. He slowed at intersections but did not stop, and fortunately was only required to go around a few vehicles that had been abandoned on the street.

Frank reached the Bay Street intersection within minutes, then made a sharp left turn, knowing they were at about the half way mark to the marina. Although vigilant, he continued to push the speed as much as possible given the current conditions.

Bay Street remained relatively clear until the Bearcat reached the intersection at Fillmore where Frank needed to make a right turn for the final leg of the trip. The intersection was blocked by two ladder trucks from the San Francisco Fire Department, a bus, and several cars. Quickly determining that he could not get the Bearcat around that mess, Frank brought the truck to a complete stop, put it into reverse and floored the gas pedal to back the truck up to Webster. The quick stop and reversing of the truck tossed both Harry and Derrick around in the open roof hatch.

"Hey! What the hell's going on?" Derrick yelled in annoyance.

Frank could not hear Derrick's protest nor would he have bothered responding since he was intently watching the cab monitor view from the rear-mounted camera. He saw the truck collide with a mass of ten or twelve infected with jarring results. He braked once he had backed up just past Webster, moved the gear shift selector to drive, then turned right and raced down the street.

"Damn it, Rookie! If you can't drive this fuckin' thing, pull over and let someone who can!" Derrick bellowed after being thrown into Harry for the second time.

Harry leaned back, pushing Derrick off and said, "You know he can't hear you, right?"

"Yeah, I know. Makes me feel better to vent though," Derrick replied while bringing his rifle up and sighting in on another small group of infected converging on the truck from behind. "I hate rollercoasters and this is what it feels like!" With that he fired, bringing down six of his targets with as many shots.

Harry and Derrick continued to fire their weapons until the Bearcat was about three blocks from making the left turn onto Marina Boulevard which would take them to their destination – the marina entrance. Harry began to notice that the infected had thinned considerably. Stepping down and off the platform, Harry tapped Derrick on the leg, waving him in. Derrick nodded his reply and also stepped down, then pushed the switch next to the hatch to close it.

Harry made his way back to the passenger seat while looking intently through the windshield. Frank asked, "Left on Marina Boulevard?"

"Yeah, then drive over to the Green so we can get a closer look at the docks," Harry replied. The Marina Green was a strip of grassy land used for flying kites, jogging, football, picnics and other general public use.

Frank followed Harry's instructions, making the turn and bringing the truck up to a good clip down Marina Boulevard. They covered the short distance to the eastern edge of the Marina Green very quickly. As he rounded the slight curve of the street, however, he stomped on the brakes before he reached the beginning of the Green proper, throwing Derrick into the center console.

Derrick had to pull himself off the center console and prepared to remind Frank that he still had a long way to go before receiving his NASCAR license. As he looked up through the front windshield he changed his mind. "Oh my God!" was all he could manage. What had once been a beautiful green oasis in a city otherwise covered in asphalt had been transformed. It could best be described as a vision of Dante's epic poem, Divine Comedy; what Dante surely would have seen on his journey through Hell.

"Frank, shut us down now!" Harry commanded, and Frank immediately turned off the Bearcat.

There were several things that stood out very clearly for Harry, all of which he took in at the same time. The first was the dead bodies, and as many body parts, carpeting the area with what appeared to be dozens of all-too-active infected milling around. Several creatures at the rear edge of the horde had noticed the Bearcat's arrival, turning toward it. Fortunately they seemed to be more interested in what was in front of them, and quickly turned away once the truck stopped moving. Harry was also interested in what held their attention.

The Marina Green was rectangular in shape, with Marina Boulevard on its south side and Marina Green Drive on the north, closest to the edge of the Bay waters. The infected appeared to be moving toward the marina harbor area which lay to the west side of the Green.

"Frank, get us moving and head toward the harbor entrance but go slowly. Let's not attract any more attention than we have to," Harry said while gazing at the scene before him.

Frank started the truck and drove slowly toward Yacht Road, which would take them to the main entrance of the Marina Harbor and the docks where the boats were berthed. The truck drew some attention from the throngs of infected, with a few closest to the outer edges breaking off to investigate, but for the most part the truck was not what held the horde's interest. Although moving fairly slowly, Frank was able to outdistance any curiosity seekers from getting too close.

Once the truck had travelled about halfway between the Green and Yacht Road, Harry said, "Pull us over here, Frank. Let's see what has these things so interested."

Frank brought the truck to a stop and shut down the engine. Looking out of the passenger door window, Harry had a fairly clear view of the area. This side of the harbor ran parallel to the shoreline and was where the heaviest concentration of the infected appeared to be amassing. Because the truck sat high, he not only could see the infected that were lining the shore facing the dock, he could also see just about all of the boat slips.

Approximately thirty feet from the water's edge were several dozen boats of various types; Harry could just make out from his vantage point that many of those boats had live survivors aboard each. They were staring back at the crowd of infected as if some divine intervention would bestow itself upon the situation to save them from the horde. Some sat on the edge of their boats with feet casually dangling over the sides. Others paced back and forth with blunt weapons in hand – everything from bats to hammers – as if they were waiting for the infected to commence their assault on this small flotilla. Harry could only make out a few of the details.

The last thing that Harry noticed was sitting just to the east of the remaining docks and boats: the SFFD Fireboat Phoenix II. He knew the boat immediately, as he had been invited to the christening of this awesome vessel. He was also privileged to have been among a few to tour the fire department's newest addition to their fleet that day. The particular boat that Harry now saw sitting in the Bay waters had replaced another bearing the same name. The original Phoenix had been constructed in the mid 1950's, and had been instrumental in saving the Marina District in the aftermath of the 1989 earthquake when the entire area lost water pressure. The old boat was able to pump water from the Bay, charging fire hoses and refilling tankers which helped to save many structures. After much debate it was determined that the Phoenix had serviced the department well, but with age came deterioration. The cost of hull repairs and the needed modifications to update the electronics of the old boat was nearly as much as the cost of a new one. It was finally decided to retire the Phoenix. Realizing the boat's vital contribution, the fire department spent millions of dollars on what was then christened the Phoenix II.

At nearly ninety feet long and twenty-five feet wide, painted bright red with white trimming, the Phoenix II was very impressive. It had six fire monitors, sometimes referred to as water cannon, and twenty-six manifold valves used to connect hose line. With massive onboard pumping capabilities, it could deliver more than sixteen thousand gallons of water per minute with enough pressure to put water on target from a distance of over three hundred feet.

Boasting a steel hull with a main deck and forward-positioned pilothouse, it could accommodate three crewmembers, four firefighters, and up to sixty rescue victims. It also had forward-looking infrared (FLIR) to aid with search and rescue, along with a fuel capacity that allowed the boat to remain on scene and pumping water for up to thirty-six hours without refueling.

Harry could not understand why the Phoenix II was sitting idle and not attempting to assist the people on the other boats. He could detect movement but it was too far away to see anything clearly; he hoped the movement he saw was a good sign.

"Frank, can you get the fire department frequency on the radio and see who answers the phone?"

"You're on, LT," Frank replied almost immediately, having anticipated Harry's request.

Pulling the radio mic from the dash clip, Harry said, "Phoenix II, do you copy this frequency?" Waiting a few moments without a reply he tried again, "Fireboat Phoenix II, this is the San Francisco Police Department unit off your port, do you copy?" There was still no reply from the radio, but there did seem to be increased activity. "Did we pack long eyes with the toothbrushes?" Harry asked.

"Try these," Derrick said, handing him a pair of tactical binoculars.

"Okay, let's see what these guys are doing," Harry muttered as he focused in on the boat. What he saw made him sit up in the seat. Without taking his eyes from what he was observing, he said, "Derry, time to go to work; get eyes on that boat."

"On it Harry," Derrick responded without question, turning back to the rear compartment to retrieve his Remington 700P sniper rifle from the wall rack. After hitting the switch which opened the roof hatch, he stepped up on the platform. Glancing around the truck to make certain there were no unwelcome guests, he quickly unfolded the front bipod, setting the sniper rifle on the roof and uncapping the scope. Derrick scanned the fireboat that was brought in near and clear through the scope, immediately seeing what Harry was looking at below.

"Harry, what're we going to do here?"

What Harry saw on the boat, and Derrick was now focused in on, was a heavily tattooed white male with a shaved head. This individual was standing in the pilot house holding a handgun directly to the head of a man who appeared to be a firefighter standing behind the controls of the boat. There were two other people on their knees in the rear of the boat with their hands on top of their heads.

"Phoenix II, we see that you have company and we certainly do not want to appear rude, but it would be nice to have a little chat," Harry said into the mic without moving the binocs from his eyes. The thug in the pilot house obviously screamed something at the fireman. Harry saw the crewmember lean forward slightly, picking up a radio mic.

Before the firefighter could say anything, the thug grabbed the mic from the firefighter and shouted, "YOU BETTER GET THE FUCK OUTTA HERE BEFORE I START WASTING THESE DUDES! You got no right to be harassing me. I know my rights! I ain't gonna let them things get me! I got to get outta here and this here boat is doing just that! You hear me!" With some alarm Harry saw the thug push the gun into the back of the crewmember's head, emphasizing his point.

Harry took the binocs away from his face enough to rub his eyes. He leaned back in the seat, taking a deep breath and releasing it slowly. "Listen," Harry calmly said into the radio mic after giving the thug a moment to calm down from his rant, "there's enough going on without adding to it, friend. We are all scared but we need to work together to get through this."

That was all Harry was able to say before he heard the sound of a muffled shot. Even through the thick armor of the Bearcat the sound was unmistakable. Quickly raising the binocs to his eyes again, he was in time to see one of the crewmembers slump to the deck at the rear of the boat.

"That nut just shot one of those people!" Derrick said, peering intently through the scope of the sniper rifle, his hands gripped tightly around the stock.

Harry had known anger in his life, especially over the past few weeks, but what he felt at that moment was pure animalistic rage. A rage so powerful that it began in the pit of his stomach and radiated throughout his being. His hands trembled slightly as he held the binocs to his eyes.

"Harry ..." Frank began, but a radio transmission from the fireboat interrupted any further discussion.

"YOU SEE WHAT YOU MADE ME DO! I'm serious SO BACK THE FUCK OUTTA HERE before I waste more of these guys!" It was the thug, and the tone of his voice was nearing the point of being panic-stricken.

Without removing the binocs from his eyes, Harry reached down and picked up the radio mic that had fallen into his lap. Depressing the transmit button he very calmly replied, "Okay, take it easy buddy, we're leaving."

"Frank, back us up. Very slowly," Harry instructed.

Frank started the big truck and put it in reverse, smoothly backing up as instructed. This garnered the attention of several infected again on the outer edge of the group, who immediately turned toward the sound of the heavy engine and started in the men's direction.

25

Continuing to watch the activity on the boat, Harry saw that the thug had moved slightly away from the crewmember he had been holding the pistol on during the radio exchange. Apparently the thug thought he no longer needed a shield.

"Derry, do you have the shot?" Harry asked, knowing that Derrick would still be looking through the scope of the sniper rifle. Training would have taken over and he would be prepared to take out a target of opportunity. In this case, one heavily tattooed white male with a shaved head standing in the pilothouse.

"I have the shot," Derrick intoned coldly.

"You are cleared to take the shot," Harry said in the same deadly calm voice he had used to speak to the thug just moments before. Before he was able to inhale after giving that order, there was a crack from Derrick's rifle. Harry watched through the binocs as the thug's head whipped back and the body slumped to the deck floor.

"Harry, we have company," Frank said nervously as he brought the big truck to a full stop. Lowering the binocs, Harry saw that there were now at least two dozen infected quickly making their way toward the Bearcat, with several others from the horde also turning their attention toward the source of their brethren's interest.

"Derrick, button up. Frank, take us away from the area and hang a left on Broderick. Go up a few blocks and we'll circle around and try to lose these things," Harry said while staring through the windshield, watching the infected advance toward them.

"Got it Harry," Frank replied while putting the truck in gear once again; he started toward Broderick which was just one street down from their current location. He quickly closed the distance and made the left hand turn as Harry had directed, accelerating just as the radio came to life, startling both men sitting in the front seats.

"Fireboat to SFPD, do you copy?" a rather shaky voice said over the radio.

Picking up the mic, Harry said, "Fireboat we copy, this is Harry Lancaster. Are you alright?"

"Yeah, we're good, considering. Never experienced anything like that before though. What a rush! My name is Philip Sanchez. Phil. I'm a paramedic assigned out of Station 2. Wow, I can't believe you took that guy out. He was standing right beside me! Damn, there's blood all over the place! Anyway, a couple of the other guys and I were able to make it to the Phoenix just as one of the crew was taking it out. One of the guys didn't make it though. Too many of those things running around. What's up with all these people? Haven't heard much news because I've been moving around the City. These things are everywhere! Almost didn't make it a few times. Are you leaving? Hey, you really need to help us …"

Frank had been quietly listening to Phil ramble on, but finally glanced to Harry with a puzzled look on his face and asked, "Is that guy alright?"

Harry nodded slightly, acknowledging Frank; he knew Phil's rambling was a direct result of what he had just gone through. On top of what he must have already experienced over the past couple of weeks in the City. Post-traumatic stress. Harry had seen this many times over the years in victims of crime. People are not usually prepared for traumatic events that life can sometimes throw up in the middle of a perfectly good day, let alone the current state of affairs.

"Harry," Derrick began, looking out of the rear door armored windows, "we need to pick up the pace. They're gaining on us."

"Frank, get us moving. Go up to Beach Street and jog around," Harry said.

Frank accelerated down the relatively clear street, only having to swerve around a few vehicles. He reached Beach within a couple of minutes, slowing as he approached to make the left-hand turn. This time he was forced almost to a standstill as he navigated around a MUNI bus that blocked part of the intersection.

"Let's go down two more blocks and start heading back toward the marina," Harry said to Frank as he depressed the mic button to speak. "Phil, I need for you to maintain radio silence for a few minutes while we lose the tail we have attracted, and then I'll let you know what we need to do. Do you copy that, Fireboat?"

"Copy that," Phil said, sounding like he had regained his composure a bit.

Derrick had moved from the back window up to the front passenger compartment while listening to the exchange, and now said, "So what is it exactly we are going to do, Harry?"

"No clue yet," Harry replied, looking intently through the windshield and frantically trying to come up with something. He knew they had to get back to the marina and try to organize those people. He also knew that they could not just keep driving around the City trying to avoid the infected. Their luck would run out eventually. Harry watched as Frank made the left onto Beach and remained quiet until they'd gone several blocks east.

"Stop here, Frank. Turn the engine off and let's sit it out for a few minutes and see what happens," Harry said. He desperately hoped that without the noise from the big engine those things in pursuit would either lose interest or would be unable to find them. At least long enough for him to come up with a plan.

"Gotcha," Frank said as he stopped the truck and then turned the key to kill the engine. The silence was almost deafening, and all three men jumped when Phil's voice came through the radio speaker.

"Sorry to break radio silence here," Phil intoned, "but you guys better come up with something soon. It looks like there are more of those things arriving, and the fog is beginning to roll in through the Gate." Phil was referring to the entrance to the Bay from the Pacific Ocean around the Golden Gate Bridge.

"THAT'S IT!" Harry shouted, startling both Frank and Derrick again.

"WHAT!" Derrick shouted his response as Frank simply stared with his mouth slightly agape.

"I've got an idea," Harry said, then keyed the radio mic. "Okay Phil, we copy. I think I have an idea but you need to get somebody who can operate that boat at the controls."

"No problem. Jimi is one of the boat's crew and as soon as he helps me finish getting Gus patched up I'm pretty sure he can take care of that," Phil said.

"Who the hell is Gus?" Harry quickly asked.

"He's the firefighter who got shot. It was a through and through wound to the upper shoulder. Looks like no major damage but he's going to be hurting for a while, that's for sure. I've got some stuff in the med kit that should take care of that for now, though."

"Yes!" Frank said while doing a fist pump.

Harry's relief was beyond description. He'd been sure the guy had been killed when the thug shot him. Glancing first to Frank and then back to Derrick, both with huge smiles on their faces at the news, Harry replied, "That's fantastic news, Phil! Take care of Gus, then ask Jimi to get ready to move the boat as close to the bayside of the marina entrance as possible. Can you ask him how hard it is to use those two forward monitors?"

"Sure thing, hold on just a sec," Phil replied.

"What are you thinking, Harry?" Derrick asked while waiting for Phil respond.

"I'm thinking we can use the fog and some high pressure water to disperse the crowd from around that main gate a bit," Harry said excitedly. "If the same thing happens that I saw getting to the station, the fog should disorient them, and with the added water from the monitors we should have a nearly straight shot to that gate. We're going to get wet but I think we can make it."

"Harry, I don't know about this plan of yours, buddy," Derrick said a bit apprehensively.

"Hey Harry, Jimi said that both of those forward monitors can be operated very easily. All we have to do is switch on the hull intake pumps and we're good to go. Once he gets the boat into position he and I can operate them well enough," Phil said through the radio, interrupting Derrick. "What do you have in mind?"

"That's great, Phil. I need you to let me know the minute you guys are ready to move. I don't want you to rush attending to Gus, but time is of the essence here so do your best to get it done quickly," Harry replied through the mic.

"We'll be ready in about ten minutes. I'll let you know when we're moving," Phil said.

"10-4," Harry said.

Harry glanced toward Frank. "Head us back toward to the marina. Hopefully the boat crew will be moving by the time we get there."

Without replying, Frank started the truck and made the first left turn he came to. This section of San Francisco, referred to as the Marina District, contained a maze of smaller streets that to those not use to navigating could be very confusing. Short winding streets sometimes abruptly changed names, although appearing to be the same street. Luckily Frank knew the area well and was having no difficulty finding the quickest route. Just as he turned onto Retiro Way, the men in the truck saw a woman and a child run into the street about ten houses up from their location.

Although she could not be heard through the thick metal and bullet resistant glass of the truck, it was obvious she was screaming. Equally obvious was the fact she was not infected. She was pushing a young girl in front of her and was looking over her shoulder. The three men in the truck also saw what she was looking at. Eight or ten of the infected were closing in on her with only about twenty-five yards separating them.

"Oh shit," Frank said, stepping on the brakes of the truck hard enough to throw Harry and Derrick forward, both men grabbing onto anything they could to keep from impacting with the dash.

"They're not going to make it," Derrick said after quickly recovering from the violent forward motion. He stared out of the front windshield in the direction of the running duo.

Harry had recovered only slightly faster than Derrick and, while opening the passenger side door of the truck, he quickly said, "Get the truck rolling and follow me, but nobody else is to get out!" Before Frank or Derrick could protest, Harry grabbed his AR-15, jumped down from the truck, slamming the door shut, and ran to meet the woman.

As he approached her and without breaking stride, Harry shouted, "GET TO THE TRUCK!" With that he ran past her and the kid. The girl, rather. She looked directly at Harry. The terror in her eyes was beyond question, but he did not have time to stop and console. Running further past them a few yards, he saw that six more infected had joined the small horde which was rapidly closing the gap. He could hear the truck behind him but did not look back to see its exact location. Bringing the AR-15 up to his shoulder, he sighted in and began firing.

Harry's complete focus was forward and through the sights of the weapon. Firing short bursts at first one of the infected and then another, he dropped each of his targets. Although he began to realize that the group did not appear to be getting smaller, and they were now only ten feet or so from reaching him! "I am seriously getting too old for this shit," he once again reminded himself when he realized the rifle was empty. Allowing the AR to drop on the sling attached to his tactical vest, he swiftly drew the Glock from its holster and resumed firing. With one shot, a head exploded and the target went down. Shooting again, he hit one of the infected in the shoulder, spinning it around. The group was close now and Harry began to think he was done. "You may finish me," Harry said with determination while hitting another of the things and dropping it in the process, "but I am going to take a couple more of you out before you do!"

At that moment, the air horn from the Bearcat sounded directly behind Harry, startling him enough to nearly cause him to jump squarely into the putrid outstretched arms of the infected rapidly closing in on him. Instead he leaped to the left, feeling the Bearcat pass with what felt like mere inches to spare with a rush of air as it did so. While struggling to regain his feet, he glanced toward the group of infected in time to watch the truck collide directly with the cluster that had not been as quick to move, apparently not caring that the nearly eight-ton vehicle was bearing down on them. Bodies flew in all directions, with one sailing completely over the top of the truck and landing with a solid wet *thwack* on the pavement. The head exploded upon impact, spattering the area around the body with gore.

Harry finally got his feet back under him and rose from his sprawled position. One of the infected lay only a foot or two in front of him. With both legs obviously shattered, it was nonetheless still struggling to crawl. Harry walked up to it and calmly fired a single round from the Glock into its head. That immediately and permanently ended any further movement from the thing.

The truck had backed up from the carnage and Harry watched as both front doors opened and Frank and Derrick jumped out. Frank quickly collected the woman and the kid and ushered them to the rear of the truck. He opened one side of the double doors and helped them both get in. After closing and securing the doors, he ran around the left side and stepped back up and into the driver's side, slamming the door.

Derrick was on the right side of the truck firing single unhurried shots, so Harry assumed anything that had been mobile enough to run or walk was now down. Rounding the front of the truck, Harry's assumptions proved correct. Derrick was standing near the open passenger side door firing at the bodies that were on the ground but still moving.

"That's good, Derry," Harry said. "Let's get out of here." With that, Derrick holstered the handgun he had been using and climbed into the passenger side door with Harry right behind him. Harry waited a moment as Derrick climbed over the center console and into the back of the truck, then sat heavily back into the passenger side seat. Closing his eyes for a moment, he took a deep breath and slowly released it to calm himself. "I am just too fucking old for this shit," he mumbled to himself for what seemed like the hundredth time since the outbreak.

"Are you okay?" Frank asked as he started the truck and began driving.

Glancing toward Frank and then returning his focus to the street ahead, Harry said, "Other than needing to change my underwear I'm good. But damn, I thought you were going to take me out with the truck before those things did."

Frank laughed. "Naw, you had at least good six inches between you and the truck."

Harry chuckled at that and said, "Glad I didn't sneeze is all I'm going to say. That was good driving, kiddo."

"Thanks," Frank replied. "What about the two in the back?"

Harry had momentarily forgotten about the woman and child. Looking over his left shoulder into the rear compartment, Harry saw that Derrick was quietly talking to the two new passengers. Derrick was listening intently to the woman as she spoke, but Harry couldn't make out what was being said. She seemed to be completely composed now, at least in demeanor. She was an attractive woman, appearing to be in her late 40's, and bore a striking resemblance to the girl so it was possible that the child was her daughter. Her short brown hair was disheveled, clothes road-worn, and there was a smudge of dirt on her face. Otherwise she seemed unaffected by the recent events she had just experienced. The child, similarly dressed and looking exhausted, also seemed calmer although she was clinging to the woman's arm. Harry was now able to determine that the girl was much younger than he had initially thought. As Harry was looking back at the trio, the girl glanced up and over toward him. She smiled briefly, then quickly lowered her head.

Harry knew this was going to happen. He had tried to push it out of his mind but he'd known that sooner or later they were going to have direct contact with other survivors in the City. He had been amazed to see so many on the boats at the marina, but rescuing these two brought home the understanding that there were others still alive, and not infected, out there. It was a realization that their task was daunting, to say the least. Harry couldn't fathom how he and his two companions could hope to do more than stand by and watch as people continued to die. Or worse.

26

The woman finished whatever she had been saying to Derrick and leaned back, resting her head on the wall of the truck, and closed her eyes. The girl laid her head in the woman's lap but appeared to stare off without focus. Harry was thinking how exhausted they both must be when Derrick came forward. He sat down in the jump seat just behind the front compartment and leaned forward so he could talk to Harry.

"So what's their story, Derry?" Harry asked, still looking toward the two in the rear.

Derrick rubbed his hand over the short-cut hair on his head a few times, then looked up at Harry. "Man, you're going to be amazed at what those two went through over the last week. I just can't get my head around it."

"What did she have to say?" Harry questioned, but stopped as he glanced up and saw the woman gently lay the now sleeping girl's head on the cushion of the seat she had just moved from. She made her way from the rear compartment of the truck toward the two men.

"I'll tell him, Officer Washington," she said with a warm but tired smile as she patted Derrick's shoulder.

Derrick and Harry returned her smile as Derrick rose from the jump seat to allow the woman to sit down. He moved to the back, taking a seat on the wall bench just across from the sleeping girl.

"A couple more blocks and we'll be at the west entrance to Yacht Road, Harry," Frank stated.

"Okay, that gives us about five minutes to chat here," Harry replied while looking directly at the woman.

"Oh, I shouldn't think it would take longer than that to tell you what has happened, Officer Lancaster," the woman replied.

Realizing that Derrick would have told her both his and Frank's names, her addressing him by name was still a bit surprising. Especially with the familiarity in which she'd used it.

"Please call me Harry, ma'am. I think formalities are a bit overrated in the current situation," Harry responded with a chuckle.

"My name is Wanda, Wanda Pettigrew. That is my granddaughter, Nevaeh. As in heaven spelled backward," Wanda said with a warm smile, extending her hand. Harry shook it briefly, feeling the firm grasp.

"You two must have been through a lot, Wanda. Don't feel as if you need to talk about it right now," Harry said.

The smile slipped from her face as Wanda began speaking without further hesitation; Harry said nothing further, just listened intently.

Wanda and her granddaughter actually lived in New York State, in the capital city of Albany, approximately two-and-a-half hours north of New York City. They had been visiting Northern California to help a close friend with funeral arrangements for her mother who had passed away recently. Wanda had also been assisting in the sad yet necessary steps of going through personal effects and selling the house which her friend had grown up in.

"We were at McKinleyville," Wanda continued. "That's right on the coast and about a hundred miles north of here. I know because Nevaeh and I had never been to San Francisco, so we flew into San Francisco International Airport and stayed in the City for three days before renting a car and driving up to my friend's. We took Highway One almost the entire way and we both had a great time." She paused to gather her thoughts. Harry took that opportunity to glance through the front windshield and saw they had slowed a bit to navigate around several stalled cars in the street. He didn't see any of the infected just yet, but knew the sound of the truck was certain to attract their attention soon enough.

Harry turned back to face Wanda and noticed she was also looking through the windshield. "Where are we going?" she asked.

"To the marina. We have some boats waiting to take us out to one of the islands," he replied. "But please continue."

"Oh, yes, where was I ..." Wanda said, still looking beyond Harry and into the street. Turning her gaze back to Harry, she continued.

"Anyway, longer story short, we arrived in McKinleyville. Hard to see my friend under those circumstances, but we got through the funeral okay. Very simple service. Her mother had been ill for some time, so there was not a great shock at her death but it was still hard.

"There was a mountain of stuff to go through in the house but it was mostly junk. Ended up deciding to call a service to clean it out. I don't think the woman classified as a hoarder but near enough." At that Wanda laughed. "Although my friend grew up in that house, she lives in Oregon now, or did, and she'd decided to sell the property. She already had a few people interested by the time I arrived but still had some open houses she wanted to do.

"She needed to meet with a banker or insurance person, don't remember which now, and she asked me if I would do the last open house scheduled. I said I would, of course, and met with two couples. Both seemed really interested, too." Wanda paused again for a moment, looking down at the floor of the truck. "I was just closing the door to the house after showing it to a nice young couple who had just been married. I was watching them walk to their car when five or six people ran up to them out of nowhere! They started tearing into them like wild animals! I've never seen anything like it except in the movies. For a couple of seconds that's even what I thought was going on! I was on some movie set that had been set up, or this was some sort of prank! I really had no idea what to do. I should have done something but all I ended up doing was locking that door!" Tears threatened to fall from Wanda's eyes but she took a deep breath, wiping at them with her fingertips.

"Believe me, Wanda, there would have been absolutely nothing you could have done," Harry said in an attempt to comfort her a bit. "These things are nearly unstoppable even with guns. Being by yourself and unarmed, there just wasn't anything you could have done."

Wanda looked back up to Harry and said, "I suppose not. What I've seen since has been much worse, but they were looking right at me as I closed that door." She didn't elaborate on what she had seen, but Harry was fairly clear about what it had been like. Harry understood all too well the turmoil she must be experiencing. How many people had he watched die through his apartment window in the early days of the outbreak, never attempting to help a single one of them. He knew intimately what haunted her, but a hundredfold.

"Anyway," Wanda began again, interrupting Harry's thoughts, "I waited until things quieted down outside. I was sure those things had seen me but I guess not. After an hour or so, they seemed to disappear as quickly as they had arrived. The house was completely empty except for a hand stapler. Not sure why there was a stapler but there it was. I didn't think that would have proven to be much of a weapon." She sighed "I was worried sick about Nevaeh and had decided that I was going to get to her one way or the other. That's when I realized those things had finally left.

"I ran out to my car, which was thankfully parked on the side of the house. I didn't have to look at what was around the couple's car out front. I must have dropped my keys at least half a dozen times before I could get the damn door unlocked. Finally did though." Wanda paused to look back at her sleeping granddaughter.

"I must have gone sixty miles an hour down those narrow streets," Wanda began again, looking back up and out of the windshield at the passing scenery. "There was nobody around at all, which was really creepy. It was as if the whole town's population had suddenly disappeared. I didn't think much about it at the time. I could only think about the mile or so back to the hotel where Nevaeh and I were staying.

"It didn't take long to get there, and thankfully those things were nowhere to be seen when I pulled into the parking lot. I grabbed Nevaeh and we got out of there quick. I really didn't have a plan so we just headed out of town. Almost made it, but ran into a pileup of cars a few blocks before an onramp to the highway. Looked like a lot of people were trying to leave town as well, from the size of that mess." Wanda took a deep breath.

"Harry, we're only a block away," Frank interjected.

Harry glanced over to Frank and said, "Copy that Frank. Wanda, maybe you should take a few minutes to rest. We have a lot to do in a very short amount of time." With that, Harry quickly outlined what they had planned.

"That sounds like an interesting idea and I think it will work," Wanda said with a level of conviction that surprised Harry.

Harry snickered. "I would say I appreciate the vote of confidence, but the way you said that seems as if you are more assured than I feel about this right now."

"I am, actually," Wanda replied. "I know those things don't like water."

"How so?" Derrick asked from behind Wanda. He was still sitting on the wall bench with his eyes closed, but obviously had been listening to the conversation.

"I saw the effect it has on them up close and personal," Wanda said, glancing toward Derrick, then back to Harry. "When we stopped at that pileup I saw a sign indicating that there was a small marina not too far from where we were. Not sure why I thought it a good idea, but decided we needed to go there. I guess I figured people had to be somewhere and if they weren't in town that was as a good a place to look as any. Unless anyone left had managed to get out before that wreck at the onramp.

"Nevaeh wasn't thrilled about leaving the car, and neither was I, but we had to get someplace safe. We sat there for a few minutes just to make certain nothing was going to pop up. I rolled down my window a bit to listen. The only thing I heard were birds. Seagulls, I think. I knew we were close to the ocean so figured we only had only a couple of blocks to walk to get to the marina. I remembered that in all the zombie movies I have seen over the years it was a good idea to have some sort of weapon. Not sure what I would actually do with one, but thought it might be a good idea to have something. I popped the trunk on the car and found a tire iron. Figured it was better than nothing.

"We struck out and were okay until we neared the end of the last street where we saw the marina entrance sign. We found where all the people had gone. There was what looked like a large warehouse of some sort at the far end of the marina. The place was surrounded by fifty to sixty of those things! At least that was what it looked like from what I could see. There were no windows in the building, but they were pounding on the walls and doors. It didn't make any sense, but since they weren't looking in our direction we headed for the docks. Thinking back on it, I'm pretty sure there must have been people in that warehouse. People those things were trying to get at." Wanda paused for a moment to shake her head before resuming.

"Made it as far the dock entrance and the ramp where all the boats are pulled up to. Unfortunately there was a fence that surrounded the entrance, and a gate that was locked. With a fairly hefty-looking padlock."

"Excuse me ma'am," Frank interrupted. "Harry, we need a go or no go here. We're ready to cross Bay Street."

Harry quickly glanced through the windshield to see where they were, knowing that once they crossed Bay they would be committed. Frank had gotten them to Baker and Marina Boulevard. Once they crossed Marina they would be on Yacht Road and only minutes to the main gate of the harbor.

"Okay Frank, shut us down right here for a few. I want to hear the rest of Wanda's story, and contact the fireboat to make certain they're ready," Harry directed.

Frank brought the truck to a stop and turned the engine off. Both Harry and Frank scanned the immediate area for any company they might have attracted. It seemed clear of any infected for the time being. But they now also had a very clear view of the dozens that milled around the harbor area right across the street. Marina Boulevard was one of the widest streets in the City, with two lanes running in each traffic flow direction. This allowed for a fairly decent separation between the truck's location and the horde. For the time being, at least.

Looking back to Wanda, Harry said, "Please continue."

"Well, we needed to get through that gate," Wanda began. "Not sure what else to do, I started whacking the hell out of the padlock with the tire iron. Seemed to work in the movies so thought that was the best course to take. Not so much, it turned out. The noise immediately brought us to the attention of some of those Zs. Yeah, good name since these things seem more like zombies than just people with some sort of crazy infection. The noise brought us to the attention of the Zs. Not all of them seemed interested, but enough."

Harry had not really thought about what to call those things other than 'infected' but Wanda was right. They were more like zombies, Zs, than people.

"That was really scary, too, Gran," Nevaeh, now awake, said as she slid from the wall bench to sit at Wanda's feet, wrapping an arm around a leg.

""It sure was, honey," Wanda said quietly to her granddaughter. "But we made it."

"So there I was, banging away on that padlock like I knew what I was doing, with Nevaeh telling me to hurry. I was proud of her though. She really kept her cool," Wanda said while caressing the girl's head. "I knew we either had to get through that gate or we had to run. I gave that padlock one final good blow and it popped open! I stood there for a second or two just staring at it! I think I'd just said something stupid like 'it worked' when Nevaeh reached for the gate and removed the broken padlock. She grabbed my hand and we went through, closing it behind. Several of those things were nearly at the gate by then, so not really thinking I jammed the tire iron between the gate latch and the side post, wedging it closed. I didn't think it would hold for long, but was most sincerely hoping long enough.

"We ran down the dock ramp until we reached the end. I wasn't certain where we were going, just trying to put some distance between us and the increasing group of Zs at the gate. They were really pushing on it by then and I knew we didn't have much time. We reached the end of the ramp and just jumped on this boat that was sitting there. The other boats we'd passed seemed difficult to get on, or they were covered. The boat we found at the end was tied to a pole with a single rope, had what appeared to be a covered area where it could be steered from, and, like I said, it was the last boat. Not much choice left other than swimming at that point.

"I did a quick search of the boat to make sure it didn't have any of those things on it, then jumped back onto the ramp to untie the rope that secured it in place. Just as I got the rope off the post they broke through! I heard what sounded like a loud metal crash and looked toward the gate. They had broken the entire gate down and were pouring through the opening like a swarm of bees! I use that comparison because the sound of so many together was almost like a buzzing." Wanda stopped and took a deep breath, exhaling slowly. "The ramp was fairly narrow and although many of those people, those things, were falling off as they clamored to get at us, enough of them were quickly making their way down the ramp!

"I pushed at the front of the boat to try to get it away from the dock and out into the open water. I've seen that done in movies, too. I really think I've watched way too many of those action movies!" Wanda laughed for a moment, with Derrick and Harry joining in.

"I suppose there won't be many of those movies being made now," Wanda said quickly sobering to that reality. "Anyway, the boat moved a little but not as much as I'd thought it would. I jumped back on the front part of the boat, the deck I guess you call it, and headed up to where the steering wheel was located."

"By the time Gram was back on the boat I'd found the key near the steering wheel," Nevaeh interjected. "I even put it in the slot where it's supposed to go!"

"That's right honey, you sure did," Wanda said, smiling proudly at her granddaughter's quick thinking. "That saved us a bunch of time, too." At the praise from her grandmother, Nevaeh returned a smile with an obvious look of satisfaction on her young face.

"I take it you were able to get the boat started and out of the slip?" Harry asked Wanda.

"Yes we did," Wanda replied with a smile. "Thank God there was a small diagram next to the ignition that showed how to start the boat. Flip a switch, put a lever in neutral, and turn the key. Worked like a charm, too! The engine started right up except we were still facing the ramp.

"At about the time I was wondering how to put the boat in reverse, a couple of those things jumped on the front of it! I had been so focused on getting the boat started I wasn't paying attention. Hadn't realized the front portion of that group had made it to the boat so quickly. We felt the weight of them hit the boat causing it to dip a bit in the front! I figured we were done for. But something happened that I still don't understand. Somehow the few that had managed to get onto the front slipped off and fell into the water! It's kind of hard to describe, but the front of the boat was enclosed. And there was nothing for them to hang onto or get caught up in.

"When they fell off, somehow it actually pushed the boat back enough away from the ramp that I was able to get the boat moving forward. As I said, we were at the end of the ramp with nothing blocking us in and were able to head out toward the opening of the marina. I thought for sure those things would jump in the water after us! A bunch were pushed because of the sheer amount of them crowding the ramp, but the reaction I saw was amazing. They knew we were still there and it was very clear they wanted to come after us. But they only stood on the ramp with their arms outstretched, uttering that god-awful moaning. They did not jump in the water after us! The ones that had fallen in the water were going crazy! Thrashing around like they had fallen into acid, then slowly sinking beneath the surface. That's when I figured out they were afraid of water." Wanda paused with a distant look on her face as she recounted those events.

"I nearly ran us into the rocks that surrounded the boat dock area while I was watching those things, too!" She took up the story again. "But I was able to somehow get us out into the open water and away from that marina. Not really knowing which way to go, I decided to head south, staying along the coast as closely as possible since I really had no idea how to navigate a boat in the ocean. Talk about a white-knuckle ride! I don't know how long we were out there but it was at least a day and a night. There were no gauges of any kind by the steering wheel, so I really had no idea how much gas we had, but I figured we'd just keep going as far as we could.

"I was beginning to panic just a bit when we finally saw the Golden Gate Bridge. Just rounded a point and there it was! I figured we could find help around here so I steered us toward it. Let me tell you, that bridge is something when you're driving over it, but to see it from beneath is incredible!" Wanda looked at Harry with a slight smile. "That thing is huge!"

Harry chuckled and said, "That it is."

"Anyway", Wanda resumed, "once we were past the bridge a good distance I decided it was time we got off that boat and onto dry land again. I saw what looked like a beach area to my right so I headed directly for it. I told Nevaeh to hang on and I let the boat run right up on the sand. We were going fast enough that we hit pretty hard, but at least the boat was stuck in the sand afterward and I didn't have to worry about it slipping back out from under us."

"That must have been the Crissy Field Beach," Frank said absently as he continued to scan the area outside for any threats.

"Oh, I didn't know that," Wanda replied, glancing toward Frank.

"I cracked my head on the side of the boat when we hit the sand, too!" Nevaeh said, looking up toward Harry and rubbing lightly at the spot. "Hurt just a little but I didn't tell Gran."

"You are very brave, Nevaeh," Harry said smiling.

Wanda again stroked the girl's hair and continued with the story. "I knew we had to move right away. I'd left the tire iron back at the boat ramp, so I took a minute to look for something else. Apparently the owners of that boat didn't prep well for these sorts of situations. Couldn't find a thing. Not really certain what I would have done with a weapon, but would have felt a lot better if I'd had something.

"It was beginning to get dark and really cold. Fog was coming in, too, but thought it might be better if we waited on the boat until full dark. I'd found a flashlight, so at least we could see. By the time it had gotten dark there was a heavy fog in the area. It almost felt like it was drizzling rain. We climbed off the boat and headed toward what I thought at the time was the main part of San Francisco. That was some scary shi…" Wanda began but caught herself, glancing to her granddaughter. "That was some scary stuff. We saw a lot of shapes in the fog but it seemed as if they weren't paying much attention to anything. That's because of the fog, isn't it?" she asked, looking to Harry.

Harry nodded. "It appears that the Zs want nothing to do with water on any level. The fog seems to disorient them."

"Good thing for us. I'm not sure what we would have done if those things had decided to come after us!" Wanda replied with a visible shudder. "We got as far as the street where you found us, and were able to get into a house. Found some warmer clothes and something to eat. There was also a battery-powered radio that we listened to. I couldn't believe what was happening! The world seemed to be going mad. Like something straight out of a horror movie.

"We've been there for almost a week. Lots of those zombies, things, infected, whatever you call them roaming around. Saw some pretty bad things happen to some folks, too. But there was nothing I could do to help them." Tears had once again formed in Wanda's eyes. "I just stopped looking out of the windows when I heard the screams. That is, until I heard your truck. When I saw you were the police I figured that if we didn't run out we wouldn't make it much longer. That's our story in a nutshell."

Wanda took a deep breath and leaned back, closing her eyes. Harry could only wonder what she had left out of the story for her granddaughter's sake. Regardless, he knew she was an extremely strong woman who had faced nearly impossible odds, and all for the sake of this child. Harry could understand that bond quite well. Thoughts of his own nephew, Eric, popped into his mind with clarity so strong that tears of his own formed. "No time for this right now," he muttered to himself.

27

"Harry, we need to move soon," Frank said.

"Right," Harry replied, shaking the unbidden emotions off as he reached for the radio mic. "Phil, this is Harry. Do you copy?"

"We're here, Harry, go ahead." Phil's voice came through the speaker almost immediately.

"Are you guys ready to roll?" Harry asked.

"Good to go," Phil replied. "Jimi said it would only take a few minutes to get the boat started and in position. He said the water is deep enough around the docks that he can bring the boat almost to the shoreline if necessary. We are still not real clear on what you have in mind, though."

Harry thought about that for a moment, then said, "Copy, Phil. Ask him to get the boat to the breakwater side nearest the harbor entrance. I need you close enough that when the monitors are turned on the water stream will reach at least twenty-five to thirty feet onto land and maintain a width of about fifty feet. We are going to be coming from the west side of the marina on Yacht Road. As soon as we clear the parking lot we are going to head directly for the gate that leads to the boat slips. I need you to make certain you are flooding the area around that gate. Once we have the truck in position, I need you to maintain a steady flow on and around us. We are going to walk right through the gate. Do you copy all that, Phil? It is extremely important that you do not allow that water stream to stop until I give you the word!"

Harry released the transmit button on the mic and waited for Phil's acknowledgment. Several seconds passed, and Harry began to wonder if something was wrong on the other end.

"We understand, Harry. Jimi just said that would be no problem, but are you sure this is going to work?" Phil finally asked. "I mean, there are dozens of those things around the fence and gate. Jimi said we will be too far away if you are thinking that we can use water pressure to knock them down long enough for you to get through!"

"That's not exactly what I had in mind," Harry said with a slight chuckle. "I think if the fog is heavy enough and we can get enough water flowing in a concentrated area, the Zs are going to part like the Red Sea. They *really* don't like water." With that said, Harry quickly outlined what both he and Wanda had observed. He followed off by telling Phil what he had in mind to get those people on the other boats out of the marina.

Phil responded much more quickly this time once Harry had completed outlining his plan. "That sounds kind of dicey for you guys. Although now that you mention it, I've seen how those things react to water ... but this still seems damn risky."

"We don't have much choice," Harry replied. "We have to do something, not only for those folks on the boats, but ourselves."

"Here's to luck, then," Phil said. "We're maneuvering the boat into position now. Give us the word when you want us to start the waterworks."

Although not in line of sight, Harry heard the big diesel engines of the fireboat start in the distance – a distinct rumbling sound followed by a brief plume of black smoke rising from the exhaust, which was quickly carried away in the brisk wind that had picked up. He then heard the boat's engines as they revved, indicating it was moving.

Harry's anxiety was beginning to mount. He knew they would soon be past the point of no return but he did not, in fact, see any other options. With that thought he took a deep breath and said, "10-4, Phil. The party starts in a few minutes. We are heading toward your location now. Be ready with the monitors."

Harry turned around and faced the occupants in the back of the truck. "Okay folks, you heard the plan. Everyone get ready to move when I give the word. We are going to drive the truck right up to the entrance and into the water being sprayed by the fireboat. It might be hard to see and hear with that much water pouring down on us, but I want you to remain calm.

"Frank, once we're in the water I want you to get this big bastard turned around and backed up to the gate. Leave enough room so the rear doors can swing open.

"Wanda, I want you and your granddaughter to stay near Derrick. Do not move unless he does.

I'm going to get out first and go around to the rear. I don't want anyone to move until I give the word! I would assume that gate is secured somehow, so grab me a pair of bolt cutters, Derry."

Derrick reached over to a wall-mounted cabinet, opened it and removed a short-handled set of bolt cutters. He handed those up to Harry.

"Thanks," Harry said, speaking directly to Derrick as he placed the cutters on the floorboard in front of him. "Hopefully that is all I'll need. Derry, once that gate is opened, get Wanda and her granddaughter to the nearest boat while Frank and I stand guard. We'll move as much of the equipment and supplies out of the truck as possible once the ladies are secure. If things turn ugly, we leave whatever we can't carry. I don't want to lose the supplies, weapons, or ammo, but we won't worry about that. Our lives are more important. When I say leave, we leave. Everyone clear?"

Although there was great concern in Wanda's eyes, she gave Harry a single nod, indicating she'd understood. Neveah was obviously frightened but gave Harry the thumbs up sign.

"We're good to go, Harry," Derrick said while giving both Wanda and Nevaeh a reassuring smile. "These ladies are going to stick to me like glue and everything will be just fine."

Harry hoped Derrick was right.

"Okay, Frank, you heard the man. My rear end is numbing up from all this sitting, so let's go so we can stretch our legs a bit," Harry said while he snapped his AR onto the tactical harness and once again dropped the clip to make certain it was full.

As Frank started the truck, he simply said, "Copy that."

Saying a silent prayer to whoever might be listening, Harry said, "Let's get this done. Phil," he said into the radio mic, "let me know when the boat's in position, and as soon as it is, start pumping water."

"We're almost there now, Harry. Good luck, man!" Phil replied.

Harry glanced toward the west end of the Bay and saw a large fog bank rapidly making its way toward them. He fervently hoped that he was not leading his people to their deaths. "Don't start second-guessing yourself now, Harry ole boy," he murmured to himself while looking at the throng of infected directly across the street.

"Did you say something, Harry?" Frank asked.

"Nothing Frank, just talking to myself," Harry said in a distracted tone, still staring out the windshield.

Derrick, who had squatted down behind the center console between Frank and Harry, said, "Yeah, remember, Rook, the elderly do that sometimes. Let's just hope he isn't talking to his imaginary friend again!" Harry glared at Derrick for a moment before all three men broke into laughter, breaking the tension if only for a moment.

"Some of the best conversations I've had are with myself, you know!" Harry replied after recovering a bit. "You'll understand in a year or two, Derry." With a large grin on his face, Derrick reached forward and patted Harry on the shoulder.

"There's the fireboat," Frank interjected.

Harry looked back out of the windshield in time to see the front end of the Phoenix come into view. It was coasting along slowly. Harry could see about a quarter of the bow beyond where he was certain the gate to the harbor was located. The rest of the boat was covered from view by the San Francisco Yacht Club building.

Moments after the boat came to a stop, Phil's voice came through the radio speaker. "We're in position, Harry. The pumps are ready to switch on and we have two of the heavy monitors pointed toward the gate area. There sure are a lot of those fucks around. I know I've said this several times now, but you guys be careful!"

"Copy that, Phil. We're ready out here and this should be a cake walk," Harry replied in a tone he hoped sounded confident. "No sense in keeping the good folks on those boats waiting any longer. Activate the monitors and let's get this done."

Harry had just replaced the mic on its dash clip when he watched a huge bloom of water suddenly engulf the gate area that led into the harbor proper: a wall of water that blocked out the front portion of the drive, the gate, and the infected.

"Oh my God! That's awesome!" Frank said, staring raptly at the waterworks display a few hundred yards from the truck's position. "Look at the Zs though! They sure don't think much of the show!"

28

Both Harry and Derrick saw very clearly the effect the water was having on the infected. They were scattering in all directions to get away from the flow. It was obvious that those in the rear of the group were not cooperating well with those in the front. Or they didn't comprehend what was happening. Those in the front of the pack were knocking those in the rear over like bowling pins in their haste to create some distance between themselves and the water that was flooding the area.

The leading edge of the fog bank, which had been working its way inland, finally reached the harbor. It was moving fast and quickly covered the area in a blanket of greyish mist. This further added to the chaos within the ranks of the Zs. The infected that had been lining the outer fringes of the harbor near the shoreline started to scatter, arms flailing about as if to ward off the offensive cloud of the fog that was engulfing them. Their reaction to the fog was not as dramatic as it had been to the stream of water being poured onto shore from the fireboat, but the fog was nevertheless effective in getting the Zs' attention.

"Go, Frank!" Harry said urgently.

With that, Frank put the Bearcat into gear, stepped down hard on the accelerator and raced across Marina Boulevard and onto Yacht Road. He could not help running into bodies as they shambled about in their attempt to escape the water and fog, but he kept the momentum of the truck moving forward. The impact of the bodies was hard to ignore but he knew if he slowed, they could be surrounded and bogged down, forcing the truck to a halt.

Harry had seen the reaction of the infected to fog during his foot journey to the police station, but had been too busy at the time to really take in the effect it had on them. He watched in rapt astonishment as the infected walked into obstacles they apparently did not see in their path. This included other Zs, fences, or vehicles. Some actually appeared to be covering their heads while others simply stood, waving their arms about. But something else he observed concerned him a great deal.

"Guys, those things are still running through the stream of water. We need to be very careful when we get out. They might be unable to see *us*, but if they run into one of us we might be in serious trouble," Harry announced.

"I was noticing the same thing," Derrick said with evident concern in his voice.

Frank was still concentrating on driving but added, "Yeah, I agree. It looks like the ones doing that are from the outer edges and don't yet realize what's going on."

Moments after Frank concluded his remark, the truck was in front of the gate. Water cascaded around it as if they had driven under a natural waterfall. Frank maneuvered the truck around so that the rear was facing the gate, then slowly backed up using the side-view mirrors the best he could. Harry was intently watching the monitor on the dash which displayed the rear camera view. He could make out shapes passing behind the truck but could not see the gate yet.

"Derry, how wide are the back doors?" Harry asked without taking his eyes off the monitor. "We need enough clearance between the gate and the truck to open them."

"Three foot six inches each," Frank answered absently.

Derrick was halfway to the doors when he stopped in front of Wanda. Looking at her with a smile, he said, "Now why am I not surprised he would know that." Wanda returned his smile and shrugged her shoulders.

The infected continued to run into the sides of the truck with loud thuds both heard and felt within. This did not serve to ease the mounting tension of the occupants, but everyone remained calm. Even Nevaeh sat quietly albeit with her eyes closed, and clung to Wanda.

Harry finally saw the gate come into focus on the monitor and said, "I see the gate! Slowly now, Frank!"

Frank had not been backing up fast but now he brought the truck to a near crawl.

"Okay, stop here," Harry said calmly. "I need to see how close we are. Get ready to back up a bit more if necessary."

"Copy," Frank replied.

Harry reached down and picked up the bolt cutters that were resting by his feet. He then removed himself from the passenger side seat and quickly made his way to the rear of the truck. He gently placed a reassuring hand on Nevaeh's head as he passed her and Wanda. Harry was rewarded with a smile from the girl.

Derrick unholstered his Glock and quickly checked to make certain he had a full magazine, then positioned himself just behind Harry. Wanda moved toward the front cab of the truck, with Nevaeh in tow, to get out of the men's way.

Harry tucked the short-handled bolt cutters in his duty belt, then repeated Derrick's motion, pulling his handgun and checking the mag. Glancing back to Derrick to ensure he was ready, he reached for the right-hand door of the double set. Slowly pulling the latch handle up to disengage the lock, he pushed the door open and waited a moment to see what would happen. Other than the inundating flow of water, the area seemed clear outside.

He slowly pushed the door open further and stepped down onto the running board of the rear bumper. He was just beginning to step out of the truck when one or more of the infected collided with the open door with such force that Harry was knocked back onto his butt. To his immense relief, whatever had hit the door appeared to continue on, since nothing appeared in the doorway.

"Damn, Harry, be careful!" Derrick said from behind as Harry recovered.

"I think I'm going to need a change of clothes after all this and not just because I'm going to get wet here," Harry replied with a brief chuckle, still aiming his Glock at the gaping opening in front of him. The amount of water being pumped had forced the door back and open. He was half expecting a monstrosity to jump in at him at any moment. "Okay then, let's try that again."

Harry pulled himself up one-handed, still holding the Glock in the other, and carefully peered out of the open door. Not seeing anything in the immediate vicinity, he slowly climbed out of the truck and was instantly drenched with water. It was difficult to see clearly but the outline of the gate was still in front of him. Harry guessed the truck was about five feet from the gate and he wanted to close that distance a bit.

"DERRY! HAVE FRANK BACK UP SLOWLY UNTIL I GIVE THE WORD!" Harry had to shout over the roar of the cascading water. He guessed Derrick had heard him as the truck almost immediately began to reverse toward him.

Just as Harry thought everything was going smoothly, he took a heavy impact, as if he'd been hit by a freight train. It was a Z who had run squarely into him, knocking them both to the asphalt between the moving truck and the gate. Harry was on his back with the large male Z laying on top of him. Harry thought that if the infected were capable of emotion, this one would be expressing complete surprise. The Z was only inches from Harry's face, bearing what might have been a confused look. The thing recovered fairly quickly, however, once it realized what it was looking at.

Harry heard the thing emit a low, guttural groan, then saw its mouth slowly open. The mouth continued to open to an almost impossible width and it began to lower its head. Harry was certain its intention was to chew his face off. Since he was not keen on that action, Harry raised his right hand, still holding the Glock, and shoved the end of the gun into that gaping mouth. Without a moment's hesitation he pulled the trigger, removing the back of the thing's head. Instant panic hit when he realized the full weight of the thing was still on top of him, making it difficult to move.

Derrick had seen a dark shape take Harry down and out of sight below the rear of the truck. "STOP!" Derrick shouted to Frank as he headed toward the door.

Frank brought the truck to an immediate stop and threw the gear selector into park. He then climbed over the center console and into the rear compartment. "Are we ready to go?"

"NO!" Derrick exclaimed. "Something hit Harry. I'm going out." Just at that moment Derrick heard a muffled shot.

Looking out of the rear door, Derrick could see a body lying on top of Harry. He quickly jumped down and pulled the thing off.

"Damn it, Harry, we don't have time to play around here!" Derrick yelled while Harry grasped his outstretched hand to be helped to his feet. "Are you okay?"

Although still a bit shaken, Harry replied with a trace of angst in his voice, "Yeah, I'm good, but I *am* too old for this shit!"

At that moment both Harry and Derrick heard a shot from the rear door of the truck. Both men looked back in time to see another body fall at their feet. Frank was at the open door with gun in hand, looking to the right of the truck.

"One of those things was just about on top of you guys," Frank called out to the startled men.

"Good shot, Rookie!" Derrick said to Frank, giving him a quick thumbs up. Frank retuned the gesture, then resumed careful watch for further threats.

Harry leaned into Derrick so he could be heard over the water and said, "Get back in the truck, Derry. Help Frank keep watch while I get this gate open."

Derrick nodded once, then climbed back up into the rear of the truck. Since Frank was watching the right area, Derrick took the left side.

Harry pulled the bolt cutters from his belt and approached the gate. Realizing he had forgotten which way the gate swung, he silently cursed. He knew that if the big gate swung out they would have to move the truck again. Their luck could not hold out indefinitely and they had to get behind the relative safety of that fence soon.

With the water continuing to inundate the area, nearly blinding him, Harry was able to locate the single padlock that secured the gate. The padlock was fairly hefty but the short-handled, sharp bolt cutters made quick work of cutting through the shaft. Harry removed what was left of the lock, dropping it to the ground, and moved the latch on the gate upward. He was vastly relieved when the gate moved away from him as he pushed it.

Harry heard several shots in rapid succession behind him. Glancing over his shoulder, he was able to make out more figures on the ground between him and the truck. What was more disconcerting were the Zs he could not see but knew were there. The ones that posed the greatest danger. He suddenly realized that trying to move Wanda and her granddaughter from the truck was going to be too risky. Leaving the gate ajar, he quickly made his way back to the truck and climbed up.

"Change of plans," Harry began once he was inside the truck, water dripping from him and creating a large pool at his feet. "Frank, get back up front. We are going to back the truck through the gate entrance. Derry, you and I will get out and stand guard on each side of the entrance as Frank backs it up. Once the truck is through that gate, we close it and Frank will pull the truck right up to it. We will probably have company come through with us, so we clear the area before this truck is opened again. Questions?"

Frank did not hesitate and quickly moved back to the cab and back into the driver's seat while Derrick clipped his AR onto his tactical vest. Harry picked up his own rifle from the wall bench. As both men checked their weapons, Derrick looked at Harry.

"Listen, Harry," Derrick said, "if something goes wrong, I want you to know …"

Harry interrupted him. "Save it, brother. You and I still have a lot to do with miles to go. This shit is deep and I think it's only going to get deeper before it's over. We need to take care of these people and I sure can't do that alone, so keep your head in the game, *Sergeant*," the last said with a mock authority.

"Copy that, LT," Derrick replied with a lopsided grin.

Harry turned his attention to Wanda. "Have you ever fired a weapon, Wanda?"

Wanda looked at him with some surprise and replied, "That's out of left field but yes. A shotgun, but that was years ago."

"I should have thought to ask before now, but I think it might be best if you have a weapon. Do you think you could handle one of those?" Harry asked while pointing to a Mossberg 590 shotgun attached to a wall mount just behind the passenger seat. This particular model Mossberg had an over length of forty-one inches and weighed only about eight pounds, so he thought that Wanda might be able to carry and fire it easily enough. With a slight grin Harry briefly wondered if that particular weapon happened to be the same shotgun Frank had been carrying when they'd first met in the police station.

Wanda looked at the weapon a bit dubiously and said, "Yeah, I think I can handle it. I used to go skeet shooting and duck hunting with my grandfather. The shotgun I used then was a lot longer than this one."

Harry nodded, then said, "Derry, please show the good lady the finer points of the Mossberg operation, if you would."

"My pleasure," Derrick said as he moved forward and removed the shotgun from its mount while Harry kept watch from the open rear doors of the truck. Derrick quickly unloaded the 12-gauge double-aught shells from the weapon and gave Wanda a very quick overview of the operation.

Wanda listened carefully, asking only a few questions, then took the weapon from Derrick. She exclaimed at how lightweight it was compared to what she had shot in the past.

Derrick showed her how to load the weapon using one shell. Wanda then took the remaining five shells and with what appeared to be practiced ease finished loading the shotgun. She racked the first round into the chamber, as Derrick had shown her, checking to make certain the safety was engaged.

"You handle that like a pro, Wanda. Just remember it has a kick, so be prepared if you have to fire," Derrick said approvingly.

"Thanks, Sergeant, but I do have one question here; which end do I point at the target again?" Wanda asked. She then burst out laughing at the expression on Derrick's face. "Only kidding!"

"Wanda, you had me going there for a second," Derrick replied with a laugh. "You do fit into this little group quite well!"

Harry had been listening to the exchange between the two and smiled while keeping his attention focused on the activity outside. He was continuously amazed at the ability of this group to remain calm and maintain their sense of humor in the face of such dangers. He knew all too well this could have gone in a completely different direction.

Derrick moved back to stand by Harry at the doors. "She is one tough person, Harry. I think she'll be okay with the Moss," he said.

"Yeah, I think so, too," Harry said, then suddenly fired his AR into a face that had appeared at the open doors.

"Damn, I am seriously getting tired of those things," Derrick said with a disgusted expression after he watched Harry's round remove most of the upper portion of the thing's head.

"Miles to go, buddy, miles to go," Harry responded.

With Derrick now at the rear doors, Harry moved back to Wanda and Nevaeh. "Okay, Derrick and I are going out and shutting the doors. You two do not open them until you hear me pound on them twice. There may be some shooting outside while we get things in order, but I need you to understand that those doors are not to open until you hear the signal. If things don't go well, Frank is going to head out of here and find you ladies a safe location." After which he glanced up to Frank, who was looking back over his shoulder toward Harry. Speaking directly to Frank, Harry then said, "You do not leave the cab until the truck is on the other side of that fence back up against the gate. If we can't secure the area I want you to drive this thing through the gate and out of the area. Is that clear?"

Frank continued to look into Harry's eyes for a moment. It was clear that the guilt and grief he felt over losing his training officer still laid heavily on his soul; Harry could see that Frank did not want to even think about losing two more people he had come to know not only as fellow officers but friends. However, Frank took a deep breath, then said to Harry, "I understand, Harry. I'll get them somewhere safe."

Harry smiled at Frank and nodded. He knew that Frank would do the best he could to keep Wanda and her granddaughter safe, but also knew that alone his chances would be slim. Harry had no doubt that their survival depended on them all staying together. This infused new determination into his resolve. Once again he was reminded that their options were few.

"We understand, Harry," Wanda said in a reassuring manner, forcing Harry's attention back to the moment. "We'll be ready when you and Derrick get things in order out there. You two just be careful."

"We will," Harry replied, giving Wanda a reassuring nod.

Moving toward the open rear doors again, Harry said over his shoulder, "Okay Frank, fire this beast up and let's go to work. Give it a slow five count then start backing up!" With that he placed a hand on Derrick's shoulder momentarily, signaling they were to exit the truck.

29

As the two men jumped down and closed the rear doors, Harry heard the Bearcat come to life again as Frank started and put it into reverse. The brake lights came on along with the backup lights which helped illuminate the area. Harry saw several bodies of the infected, all dead, lying between the truck and the gate. He hoped that they would not impede the truck but he knew they did not have time to clear them. The sound of the truck engine would become a beacon, and the Zs were sure to hone in on it so they needed to move fast.

Harry and Derrick immediately rushed toward the gate, with Derrick taking a defensive position at Harry's back. Harry pushed the gate open enough to allow the slowly moving truck to clear the gate. Harry remained on the right side of the truck with the gate, and Derrick took up a new position to the left. Derrick began firing his AR almost immediately. Some of the infected were finding their way through the open gate.

Frank continued to maneuver the truck in reverse until he could see Harry by the gate. The water flow on this side of the fence was not as intense, so both men could see each other fairly clearly. Attempting to keep an eye out for unwelcome guests, Harry directed Frank back until the front end of the truck cleared the gate enough to allow it to be closed. Using one hand, he pulled the gate back to the fence line, then motioned for Frank to pull forward again. Once the front bumper was against the gate, Harry waved the fingers of his hand under his chin, indicating to Frank to stop and shut down. Harry then walked over to the truck and stepped up on the side running board of the driver's side, and Frank opened the door enough so Harry could talk to him.

"Radio the Phoenix and have them kill the waterworks," Harry instructed Frank. "Derrick and I will check the area inside the fence once we can see what we have to deal with."

Frank gave Harry a nod and closed the door. Within a few moments a single short blast from the fireboat's air horn was heard, then the water flow ceased. The silence was almost deafening. Harry realized that the fog had completely covered the marina now and was fairly thick, but he could still see about twenty feet in all directions. Much better than it had been just a moment ago with all the water flooding the area.

Once the water from the fireboat had stopped, the infected surrounded the fence line in front of the gate. Their moaning was almost as loud as the roar of the water had been. Most, if not all, still showed signs of being disoriented by the fog, but Harry could tell they were still aware enough to know that something – or *someone* – was in the area. Harry wondered for the thousandth time since this all began what drove the infected. What made them pursue those not infected? Was it to feed, or were they simply driven to spread the infection that consumed their own bodies? How were they able to so easily hone in on those not infected, even while being apparently blinded by fog? These questions and so many more haunted Harry, although he realized the answers might never be known. If this was in fact happening around the globe, humanity was in serious trouble.

Harry had removed his radio after they'd picked up Wanda and her granddaughter, as it had been cutting into his side. He didn't remember seeing one on Derrick recently either. He walked back to the driver's side door, motioning for Frank to open it again.

"Can we talk to the fireboat on our hand units?" Harry asked, indicating the portable radios they had brought from the police station.

"Sure, no problem. Give me a second and I'll hand you one out," Frank replied, closing the door once again.

Several seconds later, Frank cracked the door and handed Harry a hand radio. "You're good to go. I programmed our handhelds with the fireboat frequency on Channel 3."

"Thanks, kid," Harry said as he accepted the hand-held radio, snapping it into place on the clip of his tactical belt. "Make sure you have one of these and hand me another for Derrick."

Frank tapped his shoulder, indicting the mic attached to the shoulder epaulette of his jumpsuit. He then handed Harry another radio and closed the door. Harry walked over to Derrick to give him the unit, then continued to the opposite side of the truck closest to the water line.

Depressing the transmit button on his own shoulder mic attached to the radio, Harry said, "Phil, this is Harry, do you copy?"

"We're here, Harry. Frank told me you were alright. We couldn't see a thing through the water we were laying on you! Glad that's over."

"Yeah, it was intense," Harry replied. "But we're all good. Can you please have Jimi maneuver the fireboat to the other end of the harbor? I have no idea what we are going to find down there, but we should be ready for anything. And Phil, I really want to thank you guys for helping us!"

"No problem on both, Harry. We look forward to meeting you guys in person! We'll get going now and see you on the other end."

"Copy that, Phil. See you soon," Harry said, and with that clipped the mic onto the tab of his jumpsuit.

"We have company, Harry," Derrick said, gaining Harry's immediate attention.

Harry glanced over to Derrick, then turned his gaze past him. There were a small group of forms emerging from the fog in front of the two men.

"POLICE, IDENTIFY YOURSELVES!" Harry shouted while bringing his rife into firing position. He could make out at least six people approaching. Or what he hoped were 'people'.

There was no response from the group which was now only about twenty feet in front of him. Harry shouted again, "IF YOU DO NOT STOP AND IDENTIFY YOURSELVES WE WILL FIRE UPON YOU!"

Harry finally received a response to his demand. That all too familiar moaning. Except this time Harry was shocked to see two of the forms break into a run, arms outstretched and seemingly headed directly toward him. Harry fired his weapon into first one then the other runner, taking them down instantly. Derrick followed seconds later, firing into what remained of the group. Harry adjusted his position and added to Derrick's fire and between the two of them the group was taken out within seconds.

"Well that was interesting. That's the first time I've seen those things actually run. That explains why those folks on the boats didn't try to come ashore. With the gate closed and locked, this would have made a fairly decent area to regroup. But with those things running around I get it now," Derrick said from his position to the left of Harry while pointing to the bodies lying on the ground.

"I wondered the same thing when we first saw them. But if they don't have weapons I can understand why they didn't want to risk going hand-to-hand with those things. I've seen the infected move fairly quickly but not in a full-out run. That's not good at all! Let's do a sweep, get Frank and the ladies and get down to the boats," Harry concluded, turning his attention to the fringes of the fog for further threats.

Harry and Derrick spent the next ten minutes or so checking for any infected that might have been in the area before or after they'd opened the gate. They did not feel it necessary to enter the few buildings that were on their side of the fence, the large structure housing the San Francisco Yacht Club being one of those. The men hoped that if there were any of the infected inside those few buildings, they did not have the ability to open doors, although they kept a wary eye out just in case.

Satisfied that the immediate area was secure, Harry and Derrick returned to the truck. Harry grew more concerned as he saw the number of infected that were gathering on the other side of the gate in front of the truck. He knew that sooner or later the sheer weight of all the bodies pressing against the fence would bring it down. He did not want to be there when that happened.

Harry pounded twice on the rear doors of the Bearcat and they almost immediately opened. Harry found himself looking straight into the business end of a shotgun, with Wanda on the other end.

She immediately raised the weapon and said, "Oh my God, Harry! I'm so sorry! I just wanted to make certain one of those things wasn't ready to jump in!"

"Damn, I wish people would stop pointing guns at me!" Harry said, but took the bite out of the remark with a halfhearted smile.

"What do you mean by that?" Wanda asked, a bit confused.

"I'll tell you later, Wanda," Frank said with a laugh from where he was standing behind her. It didn't go unnoticed by Harry that Frank also had his Glock in hand. "Harry seems to attract a lot of suspicion lately."

"Yeah, whatever, kid. You're lucky there are ladies present!" Harry replied.

Harry jumped up into the truck and helped Frank gather up some supplies into two tactical bags that were empty, concentrating on ammunition, emergency ration energy bars, and a few bottles of water. He noticed a few wrappers from energy bars laying on the bench where Wanda and Nevaeh had been sitting, along with two empty bottles of water. Harry realized that he had eaten very little since leaving the apartment building. He actually could not remember the last time he'd eaten, and he was hungry.

"Frank, please toss me a couple of those energy bars and waters," Harry asked.

Frank passed Harry the bars and water. Harry thanked him, then stepped back out of the truck and walked over to Derrick.

"You hungry?" Harry asked, handing him one of the brick-like bars that passed for emergency rations, along with a bottle of water.

"Now that you mention it, I could eat," Derrick said as he readily accepted the food and water. "I think I can even eat this crap!"

Harry and Derrick ate in silence while continuing to scan the area for any unwelcome surprises. After consuming his bar in a couple of bites, Derrick commented, "That was extreme back there. You know we have all been damn lucky so far, right?"

Harry knew that Derrick was not just referring to their recent adventure, but to all of their experiences from the beginning of the insanity up to this point: each person starting out on their own, facing and overcoming their individual challenges, all of which had brought them together to this point in time – behind a flimsy wire-link fence that threatened to collapse at any moment.

"You're right, my friend," Harry replied, staring at the seemingly-pulsating mass of bodies that were packed around the fence and gate. "It seems as if we have definitely had luck on our side. It also feels as if I have been in the middle of this mess for months instead of just a couple of weeks." Harry paused and looked at Derrick. "I'll tell you something else that has been gnawing in the pit of my stomach. I think if we don't get into open water soon that luck is going to give out."

"I've had the same feeling for a few days myself, bro. But we're almost there now," Derrick replied as he tossed his wrapper and empty water bottle at a nearby trash can. He missed the wide opening on top of the can by at least a foot.

"I'm glad you shoot better than you play basketball!" Harry said with a laugh.

Derrick's response was a single finger salute as he bent to pick up the trash, successfully getting it into the can on the second attempt. Harry followed suit with his empty wrapper and bottle. Old habits were hard to break, even in the middle of an apocalypse.

"Okay. Let's get everybody gathered and head out. I hope that fence holds long enough for us to get the girls to safety, then come back for the rest of the supplies," Harry said anxiously while adjusting the equipment he had strapped or clipped to his body.

"Let's do it," Derrick replied.

Walking the short distance back to the open rear doors of the truck, Harry got everyone's attention, then motioned them out. "Let's take a little stroll down the marina here and see when the next tour boat departs, shall we?" He smiled, attempting to ease the concern that was evident on Wanda and Nevaeh's faces. Not to mention the apprehension that had taken firm hold of his own emotions.

"We're ready, Harry," Wanda said, returning his smile and cradling the Mossberg across her arm like a professional hunter. Harry knew she was trying to convey confidence to Nevaeh but it also helped him a great deal as well.

Harry looked at each person for a moment. "We're going to proceed to the end of the dock and try to make contact with those folks on the boats," he finally said. "Frank, you and I will lead. Wanda, you and Nevaeh will follow us, and Derrick will take up the rear. Nevaeh, if anything happens I want you to crouch down right away, okay? Out of the line of fire."

"I will," Nevaeh replied softly, flashing a quick thumbs up. Harry winked at her, then turned his focus back to Wanda.

"You stay in the middle and try not to shoot me in the butt," Harry said to Wanda with a lopsided grin. Although he hoped she knew he was quite serious in that request.

"I'll do my best, but no promises," Wanda replied, shaking her head and emitting a short laugh.

Harry then directed his attention to Frank and Derrick. "Speaking of butts, you guys watch your own. We don't have a clue what we're going to find up there. Procedures are out the window from this point on. We are not going to take any more risks than we have to. If something even looks like a threat we take it out. Understood gentlemen?"

"You know rank suits you quite well. You should have done this a long time ago!" Derrick replied in a comical manner, giving Harry a very sloppy salute.

Frank was attempting to stifle an outburst of laughter and waved a hand to indicate he had understood.

Harry glared at Derrick for a moment, then said, "Okay boys and girls, let's go."

With that the five headed east, walking slowly toward the end of the harbor and toward the access to the moored boats, Harry and Frank in the lead, the girls in the middle and Derrick bringing up the rear. Each of the adults kept their heads on a swivel watching for any threats, each thinking that a mass of infected was sure to burst from behind a door to engulf them. But nothing set upon them as they closed the last hundred yards toward the small, gated entrance that would take them into the dock proper where the boats were berthed.

They had only taken a few more steps when suddenly more forms emerged from the edge of the heavy fog. Frank and Harry immediately stopped and brought their ARs to shoulder. Derrick had also seen the shapes coming toward them and moved up to join Frank and Harry. Wanda maintained her position but turned to keep watch for anything that might appear from the rear.

30

Although Harry had said they were not going to take chances going forward, his conscience would not allow him to simply open fire. "POLICE, STOP!" he shouted.

The forms were a bit more distinct now as they got closer; at Harry's words they immediately froze in their tracks. All three men breathed a sigh of relief but kept their fingers on triggers.

"DON'T SHOOT! WE'RE NOT ONE OF THOSE THINGS!" This came from a male voice in the group.

"I NEED YOU TO SLOWLY APPROACH WITH YOUR HANDS AWAY FROM YOUR BODY!" Harry shouted his command, then lowering his voice said to Frank and Derrick, "Watch them closely. They've been given their only chance here."

Harry watched as four men approached, their features becoming clearer as they neared. He saw three younger men and one older. All four of the men had their hands up as they closed the distance.

"That's far enough, gentlemen," Harry ordered when the men were about ten feet in front of him.

The older man, a black male in his mid-to-late 60's with thinning gray hair and neatly trimmed moustache, took in Harry, Derrick, and Frank. Almost as if he were inspecting them. Then addressing Derrick directly, he said, "I am glad to see you and your men, Sergeant."

The man's voice was not unfriendly but wasn't overly hospitable, either. "I assume by the gunfire we heard that you removed that group of zombies, or whatever they are, that has been keeping us off the harbor. Those damn things are relentless. They hadn't moved from the gangway entrance until they heard the brouhaha you and that fireboat created. No matter, damn glad to see you! My name is Cecil Fremont, Colonel U.S. Army retired." Cecil had lowered his arms as soon as he began to speak, and stepped forward with his right hand extended to Derrick.

Frank and Harry had put their rifles at a low ready position as the colonel addressed them. Although appearing nonaggressive, the men could quickly bring the weapons back into firing position if things did not go well. The colonel gave them a glance, and Harry was certain that the message had been delivered quite clearly.

Derrick reluctantly shook Cecil's offered hand as he glanced at Harry a bit sheepishly and said, "My name is Derrick Washington, sir, but I'm not in charge here. This is Lieutenant Harold Lancaster and Officer Frank Lewis." Derrick nodded to the two men to his left. "Lieutenant Lancaster is the officer in charge."

"I see," Cecil said while looking directly into Harry's eyes, then glancing at his collar. "My apologies, Lieutenant. I saw Officer Washington's sergeant chevrons and assumed he was in command since I did not see rank on your uniform."

Harry chuckled, thinking back to the conversation he'd with Derrick at the station while insisting he pin the chevrons on his collar.

"No apologies necessary, Colonel Fremont," Harry said while extending his hand. "We've dropped the formalities given the recent turn of events. Please, call me Harry."

Cecil shook Harry's hand as he said, "I can appreciate that, Harry, and I'm Cecil. Who are these lovely ladies?"

Harry introduced Wanda and Nevaeh, then Frank. Cecil shook each person's hand in turn and offered a few words of small talk. He was a very engaging person with an easy smile. Harry could see the tension visibly leave Cecil's body as he briefly chatted with everyone.

"This is Walter, Bill, and David," Cecil said as he introduced each man from his group. All were very tired-looking, visibly jittery, but friendly enough. It did not go unnoticed by Harry that each man, including Cecil, bore a weapon of some type tucked in their belts: a large hammer, a wrench, and two crow bars. "Walter and David actually worked at the San Francisco Yacht Club. Bill was on vacation in San Francisco, as I was. Since all of us are ex-military, we fairly quickly became a team of sorts. Not much we could do with these weapons but they offered some sense of security among the other folks over there," Cecil gestured toward the boats.

"How many people are with you?" Harry asked.

Cecil took a breath, releasing it while contemplating his reply. "There are one hundred twelve men and women along with eleven kids. There were others, but we had an outbreak and had to deal with them. Unpleasant business that, but we had no choice. We had no idea initially what was going on and didn't pay much attention to those coming in. Not that we know much more now, but we learned quickly that people can turn after being in close contact with those things out there. Some of the movies we have all seen are good guides, I suppose. If one of those things bites or scratches you, breaks the skin, you do become infected. I've watched it happen."

Cecil stopped talking, gazing off into space and obviously remembering the events he was describing. Harry did not interrupt Cecil's wool gathering as he had experienced those periods himself over the course of the past couple of weeks.

"So, Lieutenant Lancaster – Harry – what do you suggest here? Frankly, I am at loss," Cecil asked, resuming the calm demeanor he had exhibited earlier.

Harry glanced toward his left and watched as the fireboat maneuvered to the entrance of the harbor, about three hundred yards out, then came to a stop by reversing its engines. He was trying to get his head around what Cecil had just told him. One hundred and twenty-three survivors were more than he had expected, having only seen a few dozen on the boat decks when they'd first arrived. He should have known that others would have been hiding inside the boats.

Harry looked back to Cecil, who was patiently waiting for him to respond. Harry could see what he thought was a glimmer of hope in this man's eyes, which did not help Harry's comfort level at all. They had gotten this far, however, so he was determined to see this through to whatever end awaited.

"I saw an interview a few days after all this started about a group in Southern California and what they were doing. A guy by the name of Scott Allen outlined some very interesting information about the infected." Harry spent the next several minutes or so explaining his plans. He also told Cecil what had happened on the fireboat in detail, and who was currently manning the boat. This included why Harry had felt it necessary to kill first, ask questions later.

"Initially we had no idea that we would find anyone on these boats when we arrived," Harry resumed after letting what he had just told Cecil sink in a bit. "Although I wasn't expecting so many, I don't think this changes anything. There are obviously enough boats to get us out to open water and onto one of the islands. I think Alcatraz would be the logical choice right now, but I am open to any suggestions. We have weapons, ammunition, and other supplies on the truck that we should get as soon as possible. I'm concerned that fence is not going to hold much longer. If those things get through, we will have no choice but to abandon that stuff and I'd really prefer we didn't."

Cecil nodded his head in understanding. He looked back to the three men who had accompanied him and said, "Bill, you and I will take the ladies down to my boat. Walter and Dave, please get two of those maintenance vehicles you told me about so we can assist the officers with the supplies. I think that will make the transfer much easier and hopefully get everything in one trip."

Walter and David sprang into action without comment. Cecil noticed the slightly perplexed expression on Harry's face. "We have had some time to discuss our own plans, Harry. There are really good people here willing to do whatever it takes to survive this mess. Including listening to an old Army guy well past his prime who has become as much a reluctant leader as I believe you have."

"No truer words, sir, no truer words," Harry replied just as two small vehicles rounded the corner of a nondescript shed not too far from where the group stood. Walter was behind the wheel of one, and David the other. The vehicles were painted a dark green and looked very much like golf carts with extended flat beds attached. They must have been battery powered, as Harry could only detect a faint whirring sound as they approached.

Walter and David stopped the maintenance vehicles by the group. "Looks like these things have about a half charge each," David said. "I think there's enough juice left to get this done. With the weight of the stuff we need to pick up, whoever goes with us will have to walk back though."

"This is great!" Derrick said with obvious relief. "It would have taken us some time to move all that equipment by hand."

"Agreed," Harry replied. "Cecil, are there folks in your group that can actually pilot those boats? The Bay can be treacherous, and we don't need any additional distractions right now with rescues if someone gets into trouble out there."

"Yes, I agree completely," Cecil said. "Most of the folks here actually own the boats they are on. We placed anyone not familiar with boating with those that are. We've actually been ready to move for a few days, but were uncertain where to go."

Harry nodded and thought for a moment before replying. "What I'd like to suggest is that we get the manned boats out of the harbor and into the Bay right now. Have them head toward Alcatraz. They should wait for us to clear the island, but they will at least be in position to start coming in. The dock on the island is small, so we will have to figure out the best way to have folks get off the boats." Harry paused a moment, frowning. "Then there is the matter of what to do with all the empty boats. There is no way they could be left tied to the island's dock, and I don't think it's a good idea to set them adrift. Guess we'll figure something out when the time comes."

"What do you think about having the fireboat ferry people out to the island?" Cecil asked.

Harry glanced toward the Phoenix that was now quietly sitting to the north of the harbor. He thought about Cecil's suggestion, then said, "That would work, but I'm concerned with the time it would take. When those things break through the fence, and I'm convinced that will happen soon, that small gated area leading to the dock slips will not hold them back long." Harry was referring to the small gate Cecil had pointed out earlier. He felt certain the infected would have no trouble breaching that, quickly allowing them to flood the area around the boats.

"I think we should have the boats get into the Bay. We'll need a smaller vessel to load everything from here, then we can transfer the equipment onto the fireboat from that. Once we have the supplies secured we'll head to Alcatraz."

Without hesitation, Cecil said, "Sounds like a plan, Harry. I'll go with the ladies and get everyone moving on the dock. There's an old Swift Boat anchored to the side of the slips that I think would be ideal to haul the equipment." Cecil was referring to a Patrol Craft Fast PCF vessel, better known as Swift Boats. The boats were all-aluminum, fifty-foot-long shallow-draft vessels operated by the U.S. Navy initially to patrol the coastal areas and to prohibit Vietcong movement of arms and munitions during the Vietnam War. "It should be able to get very close to the boat launch area at the end of the marina. She's old, so I think they must have used her for Bay tours."

"I can pilot it," Bill said. "I've had a little experience with those boats."

Harry glanced over to Bill and nodded in thanks.

"Time is of the essence, so I suggest we all get about what we need to do," Cecil said as he turned to head back to the docks.

"Just a moment, Cecil," Harry said, stopping the older man. He removed the Glock from its holster on his tactical belt, reversing the weapon with the grip facing Cecil. "You might want to hang onto this for now."

Cecil accepted the weapon and looked it over a moment. "Glock 21," he said while expertly releasing the mag, thumbing the top of the large .45 caliber rounds, then replacing it into the heel of the grip. He pulled the slide back just enough to ensure a round was chambered. "Nice weapon and excellent stopping power. I'm a P226 9mm man myself, but this will do in a pinch." Cecil was referring to a Sig Sauer model P226 9mm.

He laughed at the glower on Harry's face and said, "Don't get me wrong. A friend once said that a Glock ain't pretty but it'll get the job done. Maybe I should also take a couple of those extra mags there."

"Oh hell," Derrick said, attempting to stifle his own laughter.

"Great, I'm surrounded by comedians," Harry said as he removed two of the extra mags from their belt case and handed them to Cecil. "You do know that weapon doesn't have a safety, right?"

"I am well aware of that, young man," Cecil replied with humor dancing in his eyes. "I will admit I'm somewhat of a horror genre enthusiast and read a great deal. I've always been amused with sequences in books where a character describes switching a Glock off 'safe'. Too bad some writers don't invest more time doing research." Cecil tucked the weapon into the pocket of the coat he was wearing and placed the two extra mags in the opposite pocket. He lost all humor as he said, "I wonder if there will ever be new books written after all this."

Harry could offer little solace to the older man. "I don't honestly know, Cecil. But I do know we are going to do everything we can in the here and now. The future will just have to take care of itself for the time being."

As an afterthought, Harry asked Derrick to give Cecil his radio and suggested that Cecil stay in close contact. Cecil took the hand-held radio and, after a brief explanation of its operation, gave the unit to Bill, who tucked it into a back pocket of his jeans.

Cecil glanced up to Harry. "I'll also radio the Phoenix and make the proper introductions. Okay ladies," he then said to Wanda and Nevaeh, "shall we?"

"Bill, I think you should take this," Wanda said while handing him the shotgun and the extra shells. "I think you can probably use that damn thing better than I can."

Bill took the weapon, giving it a quick onceover, then thanked Wanda. Looking toward Harry he said, "I'll go with Cecil and get the PCF up to the boat launch."

"If you have any issues let us know," Harry replied. Bill nodded and joined Cecil.

Looking to Harry, Derrick, and Frank, Wanda said, "You all be careful." She turned to catch up with Cecil, who had taken Nevaeh's hand and was chatting quietly with her as they walked. Wanda had only gone a few steps when she suddenly turned and ran back to Harry. Throwing her arms around his neck, she said, "Thank you for everything, Harry. Thank you for our lives!"

Harry was touched by her gesture. Holding his rifle in one hand, he used the other arm to return the hug and said, "See you on the other side." Wanda disengaged herself from the hug and jogged to catch up with the others.

31

Harry watched the four disappearing into the heavy fog, then turned to the other men. "Frank, please accompany David and Walter to the truck and get started unloading. Derrick and I will be right behind you."

"On it," Frank said as he jumped into the modified golf cart Walter was driving. The two vehicles then headed toward the Bearcat with a quiet whir of their electric motors and quickly disappeared from view in the heavy fog.

Derrick stood by Harry, still scanning the area around them. Harry removed the radio mic from the tab on his jumpsuit and radioed the fireboat. "Phil, do you copy?"

"Right here Harry," Phil responded immediately.

"There's going to be several boats coming out of the dock shortly. Cecil Fremont will be in touch with you directly on the radio. He's a retired Army officer who has organized these folks and he seems to know what he's doing." Harry paused a moment as he thought he caught movement in his peripheral vision, causing the hairs on the back of his neck to stand up. He quickly brought his rifle up in the direction of the movement, allowing the radio mic to drop on its cord.

"See something?" Derrick asked, also bringing his weapon to a firing position in the same direction.

"Not sure. Thought I saw ... something," Harry replied as he continued to scan the area. Nothing moved and everything remained quiet. After several seconds he lowered his rifle and brought the mic back up.

"Harry? Are you there?" Harry heard Phil's voice coming through the mic speaker.

"Sorry Phil," Harry replied into the mic, still looking intently at the area now in front of him. "We're going to unload some equipment from the truck. I want to load it on the Phoenix, then head out to Alcatraz."

"Not sure how close to land we can get, but do you want us to move into the harbor?" Phil asked.

"Negative," Harry replied. "There's a boat over here that we think will work for the transfer. If not, we'll figure something out, but for the time being remain where you are."

"Copy that, Harry. We'll stand by here," Phil said.

"10-4. Look forward to meeting you in person, Phil. Talk to you shortly." Harry replaced the radio mic on his jumpsuit tab as he turned to Derrick. "You ready?"

"Let's go. I've never been big on boat rides, but I have to tell ya I am looking forward to this one," Derrick said, nervously scanning the area.

Harry gave him a pat on the shoulder and both men started walking toward the Bearcat.

They made quick time getting back to the truck. The outline of the Bearcat and faint images of Frank and the other two men moving around the rear began to appear through the thick fog. Harry was just about to radio Frank of their approach when he heard something behind him. He turned his head toward the sound as a figure came running at him.

Harry had no time to bring the rifle up as the infected man closed the distance between them. He allowed the thing to get within arm's length, then side-stepped, extending his left leg and tripping the moaning creature. The thing went face down onto the pavement. Harry brought the rifle up and delivered a blow to the back of the infected man's head. There was a sickening pop and the thing fell limp.

Derrick's attention had been drawn to the struggle but he could not get a clear shot. As Harry delivered the blow to the infected man's head, more figures emerged from the fog line.

"DOWN, HARRY!" Derrick shouted.

Harry dropped to the pavement without hesitation and rolled to his right, quickly seeing the approaching threat. There were ten to fifteen figures, all emitting that now all-too-familiar moaning which had become the trademark of the infected. Derrick had already begun firing as Harry rolled. He brought his rifle up, adding to the crescendo of gunfire.

Frank was just exiting the truck with a box of food rations when he heard Derrick's shout, then the shooting began. He dropped the box he was carrying, pulled his handgun, and ran toward the sound. As he closed the distance he could see Derrick firing away and two figures lying on the ground about five feet in front of him. Frank had no idea what was going on but quickly added his share of lead being flung into the group of people closing in on their position.

The battle was over in minutes, with only two of the infected getting close. The amount of firepower the three men had expended quickly decimated the horde, leaving them in a bloody heap. Harry slowly rose from the ground, absently rubbing his elbow which he had banged on the hard pavement.

"Where the hell did they come from?" Derrick asked, breathing heavily as adrenalin still flooded his system. "They didn't make a sound until that guy came at you!" He motioned briefly to the figure closest to Harry.

Harry was also confused at this new behavior. "I don't know, Derry," he said while still scanning the fog line, waiting for something else to pop out at them. "I thought I'd seen something back there but nothing came at us. What also concerns me is the speed of that thing as it came at me," Harry motioned to the figure on the ground.

"This thing must have been around when we were with Cecil. Why didn't they hit us then? Were they stalking us?" Frank asked, still holding his Glock in a standard Weaver shooting position, the gun in his outstretched hands moving where he looked while scanning the fog line.

At that moment, the realization that something had changed in the behavior of the infected hit Harry hard. Had these things somehow gained the ability to coordinate their attacks, or was this just a coincidence? What alarmed him the most was the speed of the runner they had just encountered.

"I don't know, Frank," Harry said. "Something is different about this one but we don't have time right now to piece it together. Let's get that truck emptied and get off this jetty."

"Harry, this is Cecil, do you copy?" Cecil's voice came through the small mic speaker.

Without removing the mic from the tab on his jumpsuit, Harry reached up and pressed the transmit button. "Go ahead, Cecil."

"Bill has the Swift Boat at the launch. You guys will be able to unload the equipment right into it. Also, I have everyone ready on this end and we're heading out in just a couple minutes. I heard the gunfire. Everyone alright?"

"Copy that, Cecil," Harry replied. "We ran into a bit of unexpected company here but everyone is fine. Please tell Bill we are headed to him right now. Get everyone moving and we'll see you all shortly."

"Moving out now, Harry. Talk soon," Cecil said.

Harry and the other men heard the sound of boat engines starting in the distance. The infected obviously heard the sound as well and redoubled their efforts at the fence.

The size of the horde had increased tenfold since the men in the Bearcat had come through. The ones closest to the fence were being pressed against it with such force that flesh and fluids from exposed parts of their bodies were oozing through the links. The fence itself began to produce a metal groaning sound as it bent forward under a weight it was never designed to handle.

Harry glanced into the rear of the truck and saw a few cases of water and food rations still sitting on the floor. Making a quick decision, he said to the other men, "Leave what's left and let's move, guys. That fence is coming down any second."

David and Walter moved to their carts and instantly took off. Frank gave Harry a thumbs up as he jumped onto the back of the cart driven by David. Harry watched the two small vehicles as they disappeared into the heavy fog, then quickly turned toward the fence as he heard the distinctive sound of popping metal. A section of the chain link fence was now bowed inward at the top where several of the wires holding it onto a cross bar had broken.

"Harry …" Derrick began.

"We need to go NOW!" Harry said, interrupting his friend.

Both men took off at a run toward the boat launch area at the end of the San Francisco Harbor Mole. They held their rifles across their chests, ready to engage anything that got in their way. Although both men fully expected the infected to rush them at any moment, they made it to the boat launch unmolested.

David, Walter, Frank, and Bill were hurriedly loading the Swift Boat with the equipment and supplies when Derrick and Harry arrived. Derrick was breathing heavily but otherwise didn't appear to be fazed much by the mad dash he had just made. Harry, on the other hand, thought he was going to have a heart attack. Although in fairly decent shape for a fifty-year-old man who worked out regularly, he had never been an endurance runner. While Derrick stood beside him watching the area from whence they'd just come, Harry bent over, placing his hands on his knees, and took deep gasping breaths.

"You okay, buddy?" Derrick asked, smiling, knowing Harry would not see the gesture. "I guess you should have ridden on one of the carts and left us younger guys to jog."

Harry did not look up as he was still trying to catch his breath while wondering when someone was going to pull the knife out of his side. He was able to say through deep breaths, "I … am … too old for … this shit!"

Derrick patted him on the back in reply and chuckled. Harry was just beginning to get his breath under control and was finally able to straighten up. He was going to say a few more choice words to Derrick when there was an explosion of sound coming from the direction of the truck. It was quite apparent that the fence had finally broken and the infected were coming. Seemingly hundreds of them would reach the boat launch within minutes.

Harry glanced back to the three men unloading and realized there were still several cases of supplies on one of the maintenance carts. "That's it!" Harry said with urgency. "Those things are on the way. We need to leave right now! Get on the boat and let's go!"

32

The leading edge of the infected broke the outermost fringes of the fog and became visible. Derrick opened fire with his AR, dropping bodies with each burst he sent into the crowd. Harry brought his own weapon to shoulder, adding to the carnage as the horde continued to advance. Harry was relieved that so far no runners had appeared out of the mass yet. Unfortunately that relief was short-lived, as six of the fast-moving infected suddenly broke through the ranks of their slower brethren.

"Runners!" Harry exclaimed, instantly taking two of the things down with the AR-15.

Derrick took another one down with his next volley. Frank, who appeared to Harry' right, shot two more of them as Harry finished the last. All six had fallen heavily and skidded a bit when they hit the pavement.

The bodies the men had already shot lay as a small barrier in front of the advancing horde. This served to slow it a bit as others behind this barrier began to trip and fall, causing a slight domino effect. But further to the rear the infected began to simply walk up and over the bodies in front of them.

The small diesel engine of the Swift Boat came to life with a rumble as Bill started it.

"In the boat, now!" Harry exclaimed, the three continuing to fire into the horde as they slowly stepped backward. "It looks like they're tripping up but others are coming over the top!"

The three men continued backing up as they fired. Their shots were true, bringing more of the things down. But with the number of infected surging toward them their efforts did very little to stem the tide. As they finally reached the bow of the Swift Boat, the horde was within fifty feet of their position.

"You guys get on the boat. I'll cover you," Harry said to Derrick and Frank in a tone that held little room for argument. The two men broke off their fire and climbed on board. Just as Harry was about to join them, at least a dozen runners suddenly appeared at the top of the pile of bodies. They leaped over those bodies, quickly closing the short distance between them and the men at the boat.

"HARRY, COME ON!" Derrick shouted, beginning to get out of the boat to join his friend.

"STAY IN THE DAMN BOAT AND GET OUT OF HERE!" Harry returned the shout as he continued to fire at the runners that were now only twenty feet in front of him and closing that gap rapidly. "NOW!"

Harry was once again brought to the realization that his time was up. That calm which had taken hold of him the last time he'd thought he was going to die as they were rescuing Wanda and her granddaughter. He slowed his breathing and took better aim, determined to take out as many of the infected as he could before they got to him. But he had lost count of the rounds he had been firing and the next pull of the trigger did not bring about the desired result of a round leaving the barrel.

"Well, that's not good," Harry said to himself as he quickly reversed the rifle, grasping the extremely hot end of the barrel in a two-handed grip. He was still wearing tactical gloves which helped somewhat, but he could still feel the heat creep through toward the palms of his hands. He did not have time to concern himself with that little discomfort however. Unable to insert a fresh mag into the rifle, and without his Glock, he prepared to bludgeon the first infected to reach his position. "COME ON YOU SONS OF BITCHES!"

The runners were now ten feet from Harry, and as he brought the rifle up into what resembled a baseball player's stance preparing to hit a home run, he heard the earsplitting blast from an air horn to his right. Seconds later he was knocked off his feet and onto the ground by a tremendous surge of water. His head impacted with the pavement hard enough to cause him to momentarily lose consciousness.

* * *

The thick fog limited Phil's view of the strip of land that made up the mole of the harbor. But he had been keeping a watchful eye on the area after he had spoken to Harry on the radio. Without the engine of the Phoenix running it was fairly quiet, the only sound the lapping of the Bay waters as it hit the breakwater of the mole and the sides of the fireboat. Phil had heard the racket of the fence being taken down, and even without binoculars he was able to see the infected clearly enough once they emerged from the fog line. As soon as he saw the mass of infected surge forward he had immediately told Jimi to get the Phoenix as close to shore as possible.

It took Jimi only a few moments to start the powerful engine and engage the propeller of the Phoenix. Phil was nearly thrown from his feet as Jimi sharply turned the boat toward the breakwater of the harbor at full throttle. As the fireboat got closer to the mole, Phil watched as the three men began firing into the leading edge of the horde bearing down on them, although with little effect. He watched as two of the men broke off firing and jumped into the smaller boat at the edge of the boat launch. The third man continued using his rifle in a vain attempt to hold back the advancing mass but it was obvious his efforts were not slowing the onslaught.

As the fireboat closed to fifty yards from the entrance to the docks, Phil saw a large pack of the infected suddenly break from the horde and begin running toward the men's location. Although there was a pile of bodies that had accumulated from the men taking the things out, the runners seemed to have little difficulty in getting over it. Phil watched in horror as the man suddenly grasped the end of his rifle, placing the stock on his shoulder as if he were preparing to swing for the fences. The runners were now very close, and if Phil didn't do something soon that man was going to die.

"JIMI, GET THE PUMPS GOING RIGHT NOW!" Phil shouted as he grasped the forward water cannon he now stood behind, aiming the nozzle toward the space between the infected and the man. Within seconds, Jimi yelled back that the pumps were on and the cannon was ready. Jimi let lose a blast of the Phoenix's air horn to let the men ashore know that the fireboat crew was trying to help. Phil activated the water cannon, sending a heavy concentrated jet of water between the man and the runners. He could not see what was happening through the water, but he hoped it was enough to at least distract the infected long enough for the man to get onto the boat behind him.

* * *

Derrick and Frank also heard the air horn, followed by the heavy flow of water coming from the fireboat. Harry disappeared under the onslaught. Derrick did not hesitate as he leaped from the boat and ran to Harry's last position, with Frank right behind.

Harry came to his senses as he felt himself being dragged to his feet. Thinking the worst, he swung his arms wildly to fend off the infected he was certain surrounded him. The response shocked him, however.

"Damn it Harry that hurt! I'm trying to help you here!" Derrick said, although his voice was somewhat muffled by the roar of the water. "You need to get your ass moving, old man!"

Harry finally shook off what remained of the fuzziness in his head and realized what was going on. It was obvious that somehow the fireboat had rendered assistance, and at fairly close range given the force of water being pumped. Derrick was now half-dragging and half-supporting Harry, leading him to the Swift Boat and helping him aboard. Frank was right behind, keeping a close watch with his rifle at the ready and pointing toward the direction of the horde. Bill helped get Frank back in the boat, then raced to the pilot house.

Starting the Swift Boat, Bill reversed it away from the launch, then out into the open Bay at full throttle.

Harry laid on his back, trying to catch his breath as the Swift Boat sped out of the harbor. "What the hell happened?" he asked Derrick

"We had our butts saved is what happened," Derrick replied. He looked toward the Phoenix as the Swift Boat passed. He could clearly see a man standing behind the water cannon at the bow of the boat and someone in the pilot house. As the Swift Boat passed, Derrick raised his arm and waved. The Phoenix gave two short blasts from its air horn and the water cannon shut down. Derrick glanced back toward the launch area. What he saw made his blood run cold. Hundreds of bodies crowded the edge of the launch, arms outstretched toward the Bay and the escaping men on the boat.

"Help me up, Derry," Harry said, extending his hand. Derrick grasped the outstretched hand and helped him to his feet.

Harry was still a bit unsteady. "Wow, head rush," he said as he gingerly touched the knot on the side of his head.

"That looks a bit painful," Derrick said, indicating the goose egg.

"Yeah, but luckily my head is harder than that pavement," Harry replied while reaching to where the radio mic should have been on his jump suit. Not finding it, he looked down toward the radio on his tactical belt. He saw what was left of the mic cord simply dangling from the obviously damaged radio. "That's unfortunate," Harry muttered.

"What?" Derrick asked.

"I must have landed hard on the radio back there. Ripped the mic from the cord. Smashed the hell out of the top, too," Harry said as he removed the radio from its belt case and examined it.

"Here ya go, Harry," Frank said as he made his way to the two men still standing at the bow of the boat and handed Harry his radio.

"Thanks, kid," Harry said as he tossed the useless radio into a box at his feet while taking the operating radio being offered.

"Phil, this is Harry," he said into the radio. "Man, we really owe you guys!"

"Glad to be of service. You know the San Francisco Fire Department has one of the quickest on-time responses in the Bay Area," Phil replied with a laugh.

"You have sure proven that point clearly today, my friend. Seriously, thank you," Harry said with deep sincerity.

"No problem, Harry. What's our next move?" Phil asked.

"We head to Alcatraz. Break, Cecil, are you monitoring?" Harry said.

"Right here, Harry," Cecil's voice replaced Phil's on the radio. "We're already at the dock on the east side of the island and we have a problem here."

Harry glanced to Derrick and Frank who were now both standing in front of him and said into the radio. "What do you mean, we have a problem?"

"There appears to already be some unwelcome inhabitants here. Please head over and we'll decide what to do," Cecil replied, frustration obvious in his voice.

Shaking his head, Harry could only imagine one thing that could create that tone in Cecil's voice. "Copy that, Cecil. We're on the way. Break. Phil, follow us over and be prepared to go to work again," Harry said.

"10-4, Harry. Right behind you," Phil responded

Harry looked back toward Bill at the controls and pointed toward Alcatraz. Then, using a chopping motion with his hand, he indicated that Bill should head toward the island. Bill nodded in acknowledgment. The diesel engine of the Phoenix come to life then, and the fireboat quickly caught up to the Swift Boat. All eyes were now on the island made famous in history as a prison and in numerous movies.

It took twenty minutes for the two boats to reach the eastern side of Alcatraz and the only dock to get onto the island. Harry saw the various boats from the marina bobbing in the wake of the Bay waters several hundred yards from the island. One boat was only about fifty yards from the dock, and he assumed that was Cecil's.

"Phil, cut your engine and maintain a position here while we meet Cecil," Harry said through the radio. The fireboat stopped and maintained a position just to the south of the dock and approximately a hundred yards out.

"Okay, Harry. We'll stand by here," Phil responded.

"Harry, this is Cecil. We're the small speed boat up here. Pull up alongside us but don't approach the dock. You'll understand why as soon as you get closer," Cecil's voice came though the radio speaker.

33

Harry was now standing next to Bill as he began to maneuver the Swift Boat next to Cecil's smaller boat. Harry had already seen activity around the dock and the shapes he had been watching became clearer as they neared the island. To his dismay, he watched as dozens of infected milled around the dock and upper landing.

Derrick turned toward Harry with a questioning look. Harry simply shrugged his shoulders. He had no idea what they were going to do now.

Bill quickly brought the Swift Boat alongside Cecil's. They were close but still could not talk directly, so they continued to use the radios.

"This is not good. We counted about fifty of those things up there," Cecil said calmly through the radio Harry held. "Even with the weapons we have, I think we would have a difficult time clearing them out enough to land."

Harry had not taken his eyes off the small horde that now nearly covered the small dock. The activity from the Swift Boat had garnered their full attention. He could not hear them from this distance, but he was certain the moaning they emitted must be attracting other infected from the area.

Harry's thoughts were a jumble. He had not thought past this point in his plan. Alcatraz had seemed to be the most logical location to find safety. It was apparent that others had thought the same. Maybe these were people who had made it to the island seeking a safe haven. They could have run into a group of infected when they arrived, and as in Cecil's group on the marina, the infection spread before it could be contained.

Derrick and Frank were now standing next to Harry staring at the dock. Frank was looking through binoculars, scanning the area.

"They're definitely infected," he said "I also see several in the windows of the building directly above the dock."

"I don't think we can handle this, Harry. There are just too damn many of the things," Derrick said.

"I agree." Harry took the binocs from Frank and brought the dock and surrounding area to closer view. "They seem to be coming out of the woodwork."

Harry handed the binocs back to Frank and turned to look toward Cecil to find out what he suggested. But like an elephant in the room not previously noticed, something caught his eye – a large land mass to the north of their location. Another island he knew well, but for whatever reason had not considered. A large island which, like Alcatraz, sat in the Bay, isolated and only accessible by boat. Angel Island.

Harry had been to the island many times over the years. He enjoyed the feeling of wilderness so close to the city. AI was a tourist destination as well, but he could still find solitude on the many trails that spanned the large land mass. With sadness once again surrounding him like the fog they now sat in, he remembered the many times he had taken his nephew to the island to spend a day exploring. He'd delighted in his young nephew's reaction to the history of the island. Harry once again felt the urgency to get these people somewhere safe so that he could go find his own family.

Shaking himself out of the funk he was swimming in, he radioed Cecil. "I think we need to bypass Alcatraz. We don't need to risk the lives of these people trying to clear the island. We might be able to do it, but at a cost I am not willing to gamble."

Cecil replied immediately and said, "I agree completely, Harry. But we can't just float around the Bay."

"Agreed. But I think we may have another option. Look to the north at that large land mass. That's actually an island,

Angel Island, and frankly I think it would offer a better location for us than Alcatraz. There is only one way that I know of to get onto the island and that is Ayala Cove. It has several boat docks we can tie up to, and offers a much larger area should we run into the infected. Along with many buildings that could be used for housing, there's also a Coast Guard Station on the point to your right. Point Bunt. Not sure if anyone is still manning it, but there might be additional supplies that could be secured."

Harry saw Cecil turn and look, then heard his voice reply through the radio. "I think we have no other option right now. Speaking of the Coast Guard, have you heard anything from them or if they are still in the area?"

"No idea. I made contact with the chief of police before we headed to the marina. He said the Coast Guard was still here but we don't have the radio equipment to make contact." Harry glanced to Frank who was shaking his head, confirming what he had just said, and then continued relaying the information to Cecil. "The chief said they were trying to secure the Oakland Port the last time they had been in contact. I got the impression that they were not to be messed with."

"We haven't seen anything of them as well," Cecil replied after a few moments. "Not even helicopters. I wish there was a way to contact them. They have to be able to provide help in some manner."

"Here again, I don't know, Cecil," Harry said. "Maybe we can find radio equipment at that Coast Guard station once we get these people on the island."

The moment Harry released the transmit button, a female voice came over the small radio speaker he held in his hand. "Mr. Lancaster, this is the Coast Guard Cutter Tern. Please stand by one for the Captain."

Harry could not believe it. He looked to Derrick and Frank who both stood with mouths open, looking first at him, then at the radio in his hand.

"Mr. Lancaster, this is William Overton. I'm the captain of the Tern and in overall operational command of the military assets in the area. That is, what is left of the military assets here, which is not much." Overton sounded tired, his voice tinny through the small radio speaker.

"Captain Overton, I can't tell you how happy we are to make contact!" Harry said with relief. Here was someone to take the responsibility of people's lives off his own shoulders. He quickly reported what had happened up to that point, including what they had seen in San Francisco and the infected they had found on Alcatraz. "If you could give us instructions as to where you would like us to go, we can get started right away," Harry concluded.

"I understand your situation, Mr. Lancaster. We've been monitoring your radio communication since you left your station," Captain Overton began. "To answer your last statement first, we are not going to meet. At least not at the moment. You should continue with whatever plans you have, and I would agree that Angel Island is a good place to secure if you can. We are well aware that Alcatraz is overrun. We did a few flybys of the island at the onset of this mess and were able to determine that fact. I don't have the time to explain everything to you in detail, so I need you to listen very carefully.

"I have been ordered to secure the Port of Oakland by the military command in Southern California. They think the Port contains supplies that will be vital in the weeks to come. Personally I think it's a clusterfuck, but I am not in a position to question orders at this time. What I do know is that I have lost nearly half of my crew since the shit hit the fan and can barely hold what we have here, let alone help others. I realize that sounds harsh. This goes completely against everything I believe as an officer and a human being, but I have little choice at the moment. I refuse to lose any more of my people engaging in fruitless actions and putting those I have left at further risk."

Overton went silent for a moment, although Harry could tell the transmission button was still open on the captain's side, not allowing him to ask the questions that were quickly forming. Harry was reeling from what had been said thus far, but could only wait for Overton to continue.

"Treasure Island is also completely overrun," Overton finally said. "I had ordered the entrances off the Bay Bridge blown once it was determined we could not screen the people coming in. But it was too late by then. Too many of the infected had gotten into the refugee camp that had been established, and it fell to them quickly. We think there may be a small group of National Guard that have survived. We lost contact with them, so cannot confirm their status at the moment. The last communication we received said they were barricaded in an apartment building on the west edge of the island. That was two days ago and we have heard nothing since.

"I have confirmation of one other fact that I regret to pass along. Chief Ekers and those with him are presumed dead, and the Hall of Justice is teeming with the infected. There was a short radio transmission from his group reporting a breach, and we were unable to make contact afterward. We still maintain very limited satellite imagery access and have been monitoring San Francisco along with the surrounding areas. I was given a set of photos not an hour ago from the last flyover of San Francisco by the satellite. Those photos clearly show the infected in and around the Hall. You may find some consolation in the fact the streets surrounding the building are littered with bodies. Chief Ekers and his men had obviously taken out hundreds of those things. My sincere condolences, Mr. Lancaster." Overton paused once again, leaving the mic open.

Harry could not get his head around the news he'd been given. He had just spoken with the chief a few hours ago, and now his friend was gone, along with many others Harry had known. The coldness of these facts chilled him more than the damp fog that surrounded him.

"I want to make one other thing perfectly clear, Mr. Lancaster, and you should pass it along to those with you," Overton said in a commanding manner. "Do not attempt to sail past the Bay Bridge nor approach my ship. You and those with you are to remain on the west side of the Bridge. We do not have the time nor the resources to screen for the infection, and as I said earlier I am not going to put my people at further risk. If anyone attempts to approach this ship I will blow them out of the water.

"History will judge my actions accordingly but right now I intend to make certain my people survive this mess to the best of my ability and experience. There will come a time, God willing and hopefully in the near future, that we can all reclaim our humanity. But for the time being we have been thrown back into the dark ages, replete with the ugliness that I have come to realize was necessary during that period. I consider myself a fair and good man, sir, proudly serving this country for the better part of thirty years. I do not take lightly the decisions I have made nor the orders I have issued, but my resolve is absolute.

"I realize you must have many questions but frankly I have very little in the way of answers for you at the moment. I can confirm some pertinent information that may prove useful however. This infection was the creation of a terrorist group and was released worldwide in a coordinated attack, and yes, from all indications every part of this globe has now been affected. It was some sort of mutated viral rabies strain. The name of that group and their reasons for the attack is really a moot point now.

"There were many people who were immune to the virus when initially delivered, but apparently it has mutated again. Those initially immune can now contract the infection. Scratches and bites from those already infected are the methods of transmission. I believe that is what happened on Treasure Island.

"As for the United States, it is in total anarchy and it has been confirmed that the infected are in every part of the country. Large cities like San Francisco are teeming with the things, but smaller towns have not fared any better. The military and local law enforcement agencies are splintered at best, or simply nonexistent at worst. There has been little to no contact with Washington D.C. and I am not certain if there is a structured government remaining. The military command element in Southern California seems to be the only governmental authority right now. At least on the West Coast."

Overton broke off, the sounds of small weapons and machinegun fire in the background. With the radio still open on Overton's side, Harry could hear this very clearly along with the captain giving orders.

"Concentrate fire to the west of that dock!" Overton said. "Don't let those damn things get any closer!"

The heavy gunfire continued for almost a full minute. It sounded as if dozens of weapons were being fired at once. Finally Harry heard someone shouting, "CEASE FIRE! CEASE FIRE!" Then silence.

Harry was looking at the deck of the Swift Boat while listening to the radio, a deep frown creasing his face. He could not transmit to the Tern, so all he could do was continue to listen and wait.

"Sorry for the interruption, Mr. Lancaster," Overton finally said. "We had a breach in one of the barriers we constructed and those things were pouring through. I need to attend to that momentarily.

"I apologize for this one-sided conversation but frankly I do not have the time to get into a drawn-out discussion right now. But I thought you deserved to get what little information I have. Find somewhere to secure and keep your heads down. Don't allow people you do not know to join your group." Overton could be heard taking a deep breath and slowly releasing it. "You should understand that you are on your own for now. There isn't anyone coming to help you. Do what you have to do to stay alive, Mr. Lancaster! That's all any of us can hope to accomplish for now. Survive and hope that humanity will rise from the ashes. God speed and good luck to you, sir. Luck to us all."

With that, the radio transmission with the Tern went silent. "Captain Overton?" Harry said into the radio. "Overton, do you copy?" The radio remained quiet.

34

"What the hell is this, Harry?" Derrick said angrily. "They can't just leave us out here! What the hell are we supposed to do now?"

Harry's own frustration had grown with each passing moment as Overton had spoken. How indeed could anyone comprehend being left to defend against the chaos that had befallen humanity? Harry turned to face Derrick, Frank, and Bill. They were looking to him as if he had the answers.

"Harry, we heard what Overton had to say," Cecil's voice came through the radio. "I do not agree with the captain completely, but I understand his position. Would probably do the same thing if I were forced to do so. Be that as it may, we have people here we need to help. I'm an old man well past my prime, but give the word and I'll do my best to heed at least part of what Overton said. Stay alive and help as many folks as possible to do the same thing. You up for that, Lieutenant?"

Harry felt the burden of responsibility weigh heavily once again. He slowly looked at the various boats that were sitting in the Bay waters filled with the survivors who had already faced horrors beyond imagining. They had no idea yet what he had been told, that they would have to continue to face this dreadfulness as a group, unable to rely on anyone other than the person standing next to them. His anxiety was building by the moment, eager to get started toward his family in Indiana. But how could he turn his back on all these people who had families as well. He sat down heavily on one of the benches built into the Swift Boat, with elbows on his knees and arms extended in front of him.

"We've come this far, Harry," Frank finally spoke up for the first time. "I say we stay focused and do what we can."

Harry looked up to Frank for a moment, then to Derrick.

"I agree," Derrick said with a grin while laying a hand on Frank's shoulder. "I think the rookie here wants to take a tour of Angel Island. Who am I to deny the kid?" Then dropping all pretense of humor, he said, "You know we stand together no matter what you decide, Harry, but we need to do what we can for these folks." He gestured toward the waiting boats.

"I'm getting too old for this shit," Harry said while getting to his feet.

Looking toward Frank, Derrick said, "I knew he was going to say that!" then laughed. Frank smiled at Harry, who was once again in awe of his friend's ability to lighten the mood of just about any situation.

"Right," Harry began. "So we do what we can and get these people on dry land. But you both need to know that I'm not staying for long. Not certain how just yet, but I'm heading inland. My family is alive, at least they were a week or so ago, and I have to get to them."

"That's what you guys were talking about awhile back?" Frank asked, remembering the cryptic exchange between Derrick and Harry at the truck before they'd started out for the marina.

"Yes, Frank, it was," Harry answered. "I received an email from my nephew right before I headed to the station. He said they were okay at the time but I have this gnawing feeling that I need to get to them as soon as possible. Once these people set up on the island, I'm leaving."

"*We* will be leaving!" Derrick said, crossing his massive arms on his chest and staring Harry down as if that gesture concluded further debate on the subject.

Frank glanced quickly to Derrick, then back to Harry and said, "Yep, we're all leaving." With that he also crossed his arms, attempting to emulate Derrick but not quite having the same affect.

"Look guys, I appreciate ..." Harry began.

"I believe the discussion is decided, Lieutenant," Derrick interrupted.

"I could order you to remain, Sergeant!" Harry replied, attempting his best authoritative voice.

"You could do that, but then I would have to disobey that order. You'd have to take my rank for insubordination and I'd still go with you. We would both win!" Derrick replied with a huge smile on his face.

Harry knew that Derrick wanted nothing to do with rank, although the chevrons on his collar meant little now.

"Besides," Frank interjected, "You keep saying you're too old for this shit so you'll probably need our help at some point anyway, right?"

"Oh I like the way this rookie is proceeding through his training, don't you, Lieutenant?"

Derrick quipped.

Harry knew this was going to be a losing battle for now. Shaking his head he said, "One thing at a time then. First let's see what's on Angel Island."

Harry radioed Cecil and then made certain Phil was listening in. He suggested that they get underway, then head around the island and into Ayala Cove on the north side. Cecil suggested that he proceed ahead of the flotilla of boats and scout the area. Harry and Phil agreed, but insisted that Cecil not go ashore until more firepower could be made available.

As if on cue, the fog bank which had engulfed the survivors since before they'd left the marina began to roll back, exposing Angel Island.

Once the general plan was set in place, Cecil sped off in the Bayliner as the Phoenix brought her engine up to running speed and began to push forward through the Bay waters. Those at the controls of the other boats figured out what was going on and started following. A few at first, but soon the rest of the small flotilla fell in behind the large red fireboat.

"Let's see if we can catch up with Cecil, shall we?" Harry said to Bill after he made his way back to the pilot house.

The Swift Boat came to life and headed toward Angel Island at full throttle, passing the boats who were maintaining their positions to the rear of the Phoenix. The Swift Boat rounded the island on the west side, giving Harry a fairly clear view of the shoreline. With the fog line receding, he could see several buildings dotting the landscape closest to shore but nothing more. If the island contained the infected, they were not making themselves known. That concerned Harry a great deal; he thought back to the infected on the marina and how they'd appeared to be actually stalking their victims. But there was no more time for contemplation; they had arrived. They rounded the final point on the north side of the island and entered Ayala Cove.

The next twenty-four hours was a blur of activity. The survivors landed after Harry, Derrick, and a few others proficient with weapons made a sweep of the island. They ran across several of the infected but dispatched them quickly and without incident. Harry speculated that they might have been part of a tour group that had been on the island at the time of the initial attack. There were a few wearing National Park Ranger uniforms who must have been assigned to the island. Harry was surprised that there were not more of the infected, and no survivors, but he was quite happy the island was clear.

They checked the buildings next to the docks, including the large visitor's center. These too were found to be free of any unwelcome inhabitants, although a family of raccoons were found in the basement of the visitor's center. Momma Raccoon was not happy with their eviction and made her protests known as Derrick herded them out of the building. Harry and the others took great pleasure in watching the antics of the large man trying to wrangle six small animals while he cussed and threatened to shoot them if they didn't 'move your little furry asses.'

Once the other survivors landed, weapons that had brought from the police station were dispersed among those who could handle them, but only after passing a review by Derrick and Frank. The firearms that remained, along with extra ammunition, were secured in a locked room in the visitor's center.

Harry had the opportunity to finally meet Phil Sanchez, Jimi Johnson, and Gus Franks face-to-face. Ayala Cove was deep enough to allow the Phoenix to pull up to the refueling dock, so once the all clear was given Jimi maneuvered the big boat in and shut her down. Derrick, Frank, and Cecil were part of the welcoming committee that awaited the San Francisco paramedic and firemen. Hugs and expressions of gratitude were shared between all the men, each knowing that without the other none of them would have gotten as far as they had.

Gus was still in a great deal of pain from the bullet wound he had received, but was able to walk the short distance to the visitor's center where his care would continue. Jimi was fortunate enough to run into a friend who had been among the survivors at the marina. Both he and his friend were assigned to the security detail that Cecil put together. They would also tend to the generator and other maintenance issues on the island. Jimi's friend was a building engineer who'd worked at the Transamerica building for many years.

Cecil organized people into several groups, each responsible for completing a particular task: searching the buildings for usable supplies; inventorying the supplies and weapons on hand; collecting firewood to provide heat and cooking. Others kept the children occupied, with Wanda in charge of that activity. Everyone pitched in and there was very little complaining, although everyone remained on edge. One or two out of each group was now armed and their primary responsibly was to keep watch for any surprises. Especially with those who were tasked with entering buildings. Harry had them mark each building as they cleared it, but everyone still remained on high alert.

They located a large generator which they were able to use to provide electricity for the visitor's center and a few other buildings. Harry and Cecil, along with a couple of others, had spent the better part of an hour trying to get it started without much success. That was until Frank happened to be passing the shed where the generator was housed. He watched the men at work for a few minutes, then walked over to the tank that held the fuel supply for the large unit. He glanced around the tank until he found the supply line which fed the fuel to the generator. Reaching down, he located a small red valve labeled 'ON' and 'OFF'. Frank turned the valve to the ON position and said, "That should do it." He then calmly walked out of the shed to resume what he'd been doing. Harry and Cecil looked at each other and busted out laughing at their oversight. The generator started with the first try, producing very welcome electricity to power lights and some of the other basic essentials like refrigeration and heating. Everyone worked throughout the night, and by morning the island resembled a small community.

Cecil decided to call an impromptu meeting of all the survivors after he and Harry had discussed the need to set up a structured leadership. Too many questions had begun to arise from others in the group as to who should be asked what in regard to assignments and other matters. Harry found himself answering far too many of those questions, and he wanted no part of the decision-making. Cecil had argued that Harry had little choice in the matter, as the other survivors looked to him as the primary reason they had made it to the island in the first place.

Word went out about the meeting and spread quickly. After the survivors had a chance to clean up and eat, they started trickling in to the visitor's center. Everyone was expected to be in attendance, with the exception of Derrick and four others who would remain on roving patrol outside.

Inside the visitor's center the main room had enough chairs brought in for everyone to be able to sit; the room was buzzing with conversation as people filed in. Phil, Frank, Wanda, and Jimi were sitting toward the back of the packed room. Gus was sitting in a wheelchair near the front, chatting with a nurse practitioner who had been among the survivors. She had helped set up a small clinic in one of the buildings.

Harry and Cecil were the last to enter the room, and when they did everyone rose to their feet in thunderous applause. Both men were taken aback by the outpouring. It took several minutes for them to reach the front of the room, as they were stopped to shake hands and receive accolades from those present. Many of the survivors were too emotionally overcome with gratitude to do more than shake hands and offer a simple thank you. Once the men were able to stand before the group the applause was renewed.

Harry had insisted that Cecil oversee the meeting, and he was finally able to bring the room under control. "Thank you all. Please be seated."

After the room quieted and everyone found a seat, Cecil continued, "I believe I speak for everyone in this room when I say the last week or so has been, to say the least, the hardest which we've ever had to endure. Our nation, the world, has been brought to its knees. I spent many years in the military and I thought I had seen the worst that humanity could inflict upon itself. I was sorely mistaken." Cecil spent a few minutes relaying what Captain Overton had told them. Harry and Cecil had decided to keep nothing from the group. Most of those present sat in stunned silence at the news. Others quietly wept.

"Regardless, we in this room and the few outside have made it this far and survived," Cecil said, looking around the room. "We are part of a group that luck, the universe, or God has decided should continue on. To remain the survivors of the dead and set up this safe haven. Not sure what is to come, but I do know that we will face it together – and together we will do our best to rise from the ashes! I remember something that Winston Churchill once said that I think is appropriate. *'We shall draw from the heart of suffering itself the means of inspiration and survival.'* The room once again erupted in applause, and this time Cecil was unable to bring them back under control.

After several minutes, everyone finally settled back into their seats and Cecil was able to continue. "I want to introduce you now to the person who was able to reach us at the marina and who, along with his team, literally saved our lives. Many of you have already met him, but for those of you who have not, this is Lieutenant Harold Lancaster from the San Francisco Police Department. I asked Harry to relay to you what he has heard and learned."

Harry had not been paying close attention to what was being said, as he'd had something weighing on his mind since they'd arrived on the island. Sitting on the edge of a table in front of the room, he was a bit startled when he heard his name and once again watched everyone rise from their seats, applauding.

"I'm seriously too old for this shit," he said under his breath as he got to his feet and joined Cecil.

35

Harry felt more uncomfortable than ever. Raising his arms and motioning everyone to sit did little to curb the group's enthusiasm. As he waited for it to play out, he glanced at Cecil who could only grin and shrug his shoulders as if to say 'it's not me'.

The applause finally faded and the room became quiet, allowing Harry to speak. "Thanks folks. I know you all have been through a great deal, and what Cecil has just told you does not make this any easier. But you all have to keep in mind that we are not alone in this. There are others that have survived this. They are still fighting and even making gains." Harry spent several minutes telling the group about the GNN interview he had seen and what Chief Ekers had told him. A few of the other survivors had seen the same interview.

"You all need to understand clearly that there is no help coming. At least not in the foreseeable future. The continued survival of this group depends solely on each of you working together. You are relatively safe for now, but you need to remain vigilant as you continue to get the island fully operational and secure. To that end, Cecil and I wanted to put a few ideas in front of the group."

For the next two hours, the survivors discussed everything from medical supplies to food. How they could get the word out that Angel Island was a safe haven, and what procedures to be put into place for acceptance of any new arrivals. This created the most debate, as some felt anyone arriving had the right to be part of the community. That was laid to rest when it was pointed out how quickly Treasure Island had succumbed to the infected. The nurse practitioner said that she could develop a very simple blood screen for the infection once she had the proper equipment. Until that could be accomplished, it was decided to set up a closely guarded quarantine location for all new arrivals. There were several buildings on the island well-suited for that purpose, although not in the best of conditions. As harsh as it seemed to some in the group, it was decided that new arrivals could decide whether they wished to go through quarantine or not be allowed to land on the island.

The discussion finally turned to the establishment of a governing body for the island. It was decided to establish a five-person counsel with one of the five being a chairperson. That person would make the final decision should the counsel be unable to reach a consensus on a particular matter.

Cecil and Harry sat quietly during this discussion and allowed the survivors to decide how to set this up. To both men's surprise, the group not only settled on a five-person committee to act as this new governing body, but they made their choices as to who would serve on that committee with very little disagreement. Cecil was unanimously chosen to be on this committee, and was elected its chairperson. These people had put their lives in his hands at the marina and they trusted him. That, along with his extensive military experience and even temperament, made him ideal to head the committee. With a great deal of humility, Cecil accepted the responsibility and gave his assurances he would act in the best interest of the island and its inhabitants. The five-person committee stood before the group of survivors who once again stood and gave them a round of applause.

Harry had asked Cecil, Derrick, and Frank to meet him at the boat dock right after the meeting. He'd been thinking about what Overton had said, that the National Guard might still be on Treasure Island. It had been several days since the last contact had been made with them, according to the captain, but Harry felt an obligation to find out whether or not they were still alive. The others readily agreed, and a plan was quickly developed. This plan would include Jimi and Phil, as Harry was going to take the SFFD Fireboat Phoenix on this mission.

It only took an hour or so to get everything set and in motion. Phil and Jimi did not hesitate in their support. Jimi had the diesel topped off and the fireboat ready within fifteen minutes. Harry and Frank brought a few basic supplies on board, along with spare ammunition, and Derrick found two additional people willing to go. One was an Alaska state trooper who had been on vacation in San Francisco, and the other the nurse practitioner who had proven her proficiency with firearms. She, along with Phil, should be able to handle any medical issues if necessary.

There were several others who readily volunteered, including Cecil, but he had been dissuaded by Harry who pointed out they needed to limit the number of those on this expedition. If something should go wrong, the loss of a few would not impact those left on the island. Although Cecil could not argue with that logic, he was still not happy being left behind.

"You are going to be much more valuable to this group by remaining and continuing to get things set up, Cecil," Harry said. "You know as well as I that these people need to have someone they can look to. We also both know that fear of the unknown can be one of the biggest threats to the success of what we've begun here. These folks are a great group of people, but they still need to have the voice of reason near them for now. You, my friend, are that voice, and you have become the most vital asset this group has at the moment."

Cecil had been looking at the Bay as Harry spoke, clearly lost in thought. "Alright, Harry," he'd said after taking a few moments to let Harry's words sink in. "I understand your point. Just get there and get back and don't take any unnecessary risks." After shaking Harry's hand, Cecil walked toward a group of survivors who were sorting through supplies they'd found in one of the buildings.

Harry joined the six other people now waiting on the Phoenix. Jimi maneuvered the fireboat out of the cove with expert ease, and headed toward Treasure Island at full throttle. It was a clear and sunny afternoon, and if not for current events, this would have been a beautiful day to take a Bay cruise. Everyone on the fireboat knew the bright sunny day masked the horrors that were still present.

Treasure Island sat approximately a half mile southeast of Angel Island. Since the small flotilla of survivors had arrived on the island along the western side, Harry directed Jimi to go east of Angel Island this time so they could take a look at that side. Jimi slowed just a bit while Harry and Derrick scanned the island with binoculars. Both men saw a building as they rounded the northern point, passing China Cove and Immigration Station. They continued to scan the shoreline for anything of possible value or the infected. Frank kept careful notes as Harry and Derrick called out locations for Cecil to investigate.

As they neared the end of the island and Point Blunt came into view, Harry was shocked to see something on the sandy beach. Sitting, eerily abandoned, was a helicopter painted a bright yellow with the words San Francisco Bay Tours printed on the tail boom. The nose was facing the Bay waters, and there was barely enough room on the small beach for it to have landed.

"What's up with that?" Derrick asked, seeing the helicopter at the same time as Harry.

Harry continued to scan the area as he replied, "I have no idea. It's obviously a tour copter but I don't see any signs of a struggle. It looks like someone just landed the thing and left."

"Can I look, please?" Frank asked. He had been squinting at the bird with a hand over his eyes to shield them from the bright sun. Taking the binocs, Derrick handed him, Frank gazed at the helicopter for a few moments.

"That's a Bell 412 and looks to be only a few years old. Very nice bird," Frank said.

Derrick glanced to Harry, then said, "Should I ask how you know that, Rook, or do I already know the answer?"

Still looking at the helicopter, Frank replied, "My dad had one. I earned a private pilot's license when I was seventeen and was working toward the add-on for rotorcraft right before I moved out here to attend the academy. I had enough hours at the stick to take the test but never got around to it."

Harry looked at Frank with some surprise and said, "You're telling us you can actually fly that thing?"

Removing the binocs from his eyes, Frank turned to Harry and replied, "Yes, I sure can. As long as it's airworthy and, of course, has fuel. Whoever flew that Bell may have had to set down over there because they ran out. I can't be certain from this distance, but the bird looks like it's in good condition."

"If that thing runs, do you think there is enough room to land it near Ayala Cove?" Harry asked.

Frank thought for a moment then said, "The rotor blade on a 412 is forty-six feet in diameter and the fuselage is just under forty-three feet long. Yeah, I think the beach area to the right of the docks could handle it."

Harry looked toward the distant east, thinking of his family in Indiana again. Frank and Derrick had already made it clear that once Harry decided to head inland, and that time was rapidly approaching, they were going with. The men had no ties to the West Coast and the bond the three had developed ensured that there would be no separating them at this point. Harry had tried to argue that they would be better off remaining, even stating he could travel faster alone, but that strategy had failed. Derrick had made it clear that they left together or he would simply follow Harry. Frank had readily agreed with Derrick.

Without answering Frank's direct question, Harry asked one instead. "Assuming it's in good operating order and has fuel, or we can get fuel, how far will it fly on a full tank of gas?"

Frank did not hesitate in answering. "Approximately four hundred forty miles with favorable weather conditions. That's the rated flight distance at least."

Harry nodded, then said, "I think we may have found a way to close some distance between here and where I need to go. If everything works to our favor, that helicopter could at the very least get us over the mountains and halfway through Nevada. Maybe further if we're able to locate a fuel source. But let's keep our heads on what we're doing right now. We'll work this out once we get back."

"I'll check it out then, Harry," Frank replied with obvious excitement.

"You sure you know how to fly that thing?" Derrick asked with a trace of anxiety in his voice. He watched as the bright yellow Bell 412 grew smaller as the fireboat picked up speed, again heading toward Treasure Island. "I mean, are those things really safe?"

"Damn, Derry, I forgot you had a fear of flying!" Harry quipped as he winked at Frank.

"I don't have a fear of flying! I just never understood how a helicopter stays in the air!" Derrick retorted.

With a slight smile on his face, Frank said, "Don't worry Derrick. I've got enough hours logged to handle that bird. Not to mention it almost flies itself. Oh, there was this one time though that ..."

"Okay, I don't want to hear about that!" Derrick interrupted. "Can you fly the damn thing or not!"

Frank raised his hands in a surrendering gesture and said, "Just kidding! Seriously, I am comfortable in that helicopter or I wouldn't try to fly it. We'll be fine. For the most part." He could not resist one final jab.

Derrick just stared at Frank as Harry attempted to keep from laughing. "You're real funny there Rookie. All those points I said you got recently? You just lost them all!"

Harry couldn't contain himself any longer. His laughter was contagious and Frank was soon bent at the waist, laughing hysterically.

"Oh, you guys are just a riot," Derrick said in disgust as he turned and headed toward the pilot house to join Jimi. "Have a good laugh, but you just remember that I voiced my concerns when we crash our asses into the side of the damn Sierra Nevadas because you know that's where it'll happen!" That just made Harry and Frank laugh harder.

36

It took twenty minutes to reach the western tip of Treasure Island. During that time Harry wondered how they'd know which building the Guardsman were in – and hoped they were still alive. He wracked his brain for facts about the island. He'd read somewhere that it was over five hundred acres in size and man-made, first constructed for the 1939 World's Fair Golden Gate Exposition and then taken over by the U.S. Navy in 1942.

As they neared the island, they saw its breakwater and a two-lane road which separated the Bay waters from the apartment buildings, now clearly in view. What was also clearly in view were dozens of the infected surrounding one particular apartment building. There would only be one reason to draw their attention like that.

"Frank, do you think we can use our radio to contact anyone on a military frequency?" Harry asked.

"No, unfortunately our equipment is not compatible unless they happen to be listening." Frank was taking in the scene before them through binocs. "We could try to send out a general broadcast. Maybe someone might be monitoring on the other end, or the Tern will be listening again and relay."

"I'm not putting much hope on that right now," Harry commented more to himself than to Frank. After a moment's consideration, Harry said, "I think we need to get their attention first." Making his way quickly into the pilot house, Harry instructed Jimi to sound three sets of three long blasts from the Phoenix's air horn at his signal. Derrick, who had been watching the activity on shore from his position alongside Jimi, was preparing his sniper rifle. Harry then had

Phil man one of the forward water cannon and stand ready to flood the area.

"If we could get whoever is in that building through a back window, I can easily cover them with the cannon at this distance," Phil said as he made ready to open the heavy stream of water. The fireboat was now only about ten yards from the rocky breakwater.

Harry made his way back to Frank and told him to be ready to start broadcasting the fireboat's position and that they were here to render help. "You know what to tell them once the water starts and what to expect." Frank nodded his understanding and went into the pilot house to use the fireboat's more powerful radio.

The last instructions Harry gave were to the state trooper and the nurse; he had them position themselves at the bow of the boat with their rifles. He reminded them that visibility was going to be extremely limited due to the water, and told them not to fire at anything unless they absolutely were certain of the target. Both indicated they understood and got into position.

Making eye contact with everyone, Harry finally gave Jimi the go for the air horn. The blast was nearly deafening, but it immediately got the attention of a large number of the infected around the building. The second series of blasts got them moving away from the building and toward the sound. The last series just seemed to agitate them. Harry made the decision to try to clear some of the things, so he joined the other two at the bow, reminding them not to burn through their mags and to make each round count. All three began to fire, with Derrick adding to the efforts with the sniper rifle. Each round sent into the horde brought a body down. But for every one downed, at least two fought to occupy the space that had been vacated.

Harry looked back toward where Frank was standing in the pilot house. It was obvious he was frantically relaying a message through the mic, then pausing to listen for a reply. Frank saw Harry looking in his direction and shook his head, indicating that he had not received a reply from anyone on shore.

Harry motioned for everyone to cease firing. There was no reason to waste more ammunition than was necessary. He was just turning to make his way back to join Frank when he heard a shot ring out from the direction of the apartment building. He let his rifle drop on the tactical sling and quickly brought the binoculars to his eyes just as he heard another shot. This time he saw one of the infected toward the back of the horde fall. It took him a couple of moments to pinpoint the location of the gunfire but finally looked to the roof.

There were five soldiers waving frantically and a sixth using a pair of binocs looking straight at Harry. This soldier waved and Harry returned the gesture. Harry watched as the soldier then said something to the others on the roof. They stopped waving and just stood looking toward the fireboat.

"We found them!" Harry said excitedly. Everyone except for Jimi, who was maintaining the Phoenix's position, rushed to the bow.

"Now what?" Derrick asked, watching the mass of infected that now crowded the road, half focusing on the fireboat sitting out of reach and the other half still clawing at the apartment building.

Harry was watching the Guardsmen on the roof. The soldier with the binocs shrugged his shoulders in an exaggerated manner, as if to ask the same question that Derrick had just posed. "Phil, do you think you can create a wide enough gap with one cannon for those people to get through the infected?" Harry asked.

"It would be better if we used two," Phil replied, indicating the second water cannon on deck. "One would work but two would allow us to cut a wider path through those things."

"I'll get on the other one," William, the state trooper offered. "I worked a fireboat out of Anchorage and these water cannon are similar." Phil quickly outlined the pattern he had found worked best at the marina and made certain William knew how to operate the water cannon.

Harry had been formulating a plan as he continued to scan the horde, the apartment building, and the people on the roof. The soldier was looking fixedly through his binocs toward the fireboat. Harry finally came up with what he thought might work.

"Phil," Harry began, still looking through the binocs in his hands, "I want you to put some water into that crowd for a couple of minutes, then shut 'er down."

Without further comment, and while Harry continued to look at the other soldier, Phil activated the powerful cannon, sending a heavy high-pressure stream into the horde of infected. Dozens were knocked off their feet, while those to the right and left of the heavy flow of water scrambled to back away from it. Harry was relieved to see that the jet of water nearly reached the apartment building before Phil shut it down.

The soldier on the roof immediately gave a thumbs up, indicating that he understood what was going to be tried. After which he extended his hand showing all five digits, closing it once, then repeating. Harry assumed the soldier meant they would be ready in ten minutes.

Harry told everyone what he had seen and they all got into position: William and Phil on the water cannons, with Harry, Derrick, Frank, and the nurse shoulder-to-shoulder at the Phoenix's bow to add whatever support they could, although they would be unable to fire directly into the horde. The soldiers would be on their own getting to the Bay. As an afterthought, Harry had Jimi maneuver the fireboat as close to the breakwater wall as possible, since the Guardsmen would have to jump into the water once they reached the breakwater. There was no way Harry could land onshore with that many infected milling about, and he was concerned if the fireboat got too close some of the things might jump aboard.

Once the fireboat and everyone on board was in position, all they could do was wait. Harry had the binocs fixed to his eyes waiting for a signal from the survivors on shore while the ten minutes seemed to pass very slowly. When that signal came, and Harry had no doubt it was the signal, it took him by surprise. Gunfire erupted from the lower floor of the apartment building, increased to a crescendo, and was then followed by three very loud explosions that rocked the horde closest to the structure.

"That sounded like flash bangs!" Derrick said from Harry's left side.

"NOW!" Harry shouted to Phil and William.

Within seconds, thousands of gallons of high-pressured water poured into the horde. Phil and William gradually widened the gap down the middle of the infected like the parting of the Red Sea. Almost immediately after the water began flowing, Harry watched as six figures emerged from a large window in the building about ten feet above the ground. The six soldiers dropped down, formed a line and began to run the gauntlet between the two walls of infected flesh created by the water streaming from the fireboat.

The precision with which the soldiers executed their escape impressed Harry. He could clearly see three with weapons pointed to the right and three pointing to the left, all six firing into the horde as they ran. Each soldier carried a large pack, but two of them had what appeared to be equipment strapped to their backs.

Harry heard the report of Derrick's weapon from his left and saw a runner brought down to the rear of the fleeing soldiers. There were three more shots from the sniper rifle before the soldiers made it to the breakwater wall and jumped into the cold Bay waters. Everyone on the fireboat held their breath as each of the heavily-laden soldiers popped to the surface and began their swim toward the Phoenix.

The soldiers made it to the fireboat and were helped on board, each dropping their packs and stripping out of their fatigues after being handed survival blankets to wrap up in. Harry could but marvel as he realized how young these five men and one woman were. They were in their early to mid-twenties at best. Once he could be of no further assistance, Harry made his way to the pilot house to have Jimi start the Phoenix back to Angel Island at full throttle. He also radioed Cecil to update him on the rescue.

37

Derrick made the introductions between everyone. Out of uniform and shivering under the silver-colored blankets, he thought they looked more like high school teenagers than the professionally-trained military personnel they were. Derrick felt a great sadness overtake him while chatting with these young people. He wondered what the future held for them and the generations to come. Glancing up toward Harry, Derrick felt a renewed commitment to the man and a deeper understanding of why he was continuing to fight instead of finding a hole and covering it up after crawling in.

Shaking off his melancholy mood, Derrick finished the intros by saying, "The guy by the wheel is Jimi, and that old dude on the radio is Harold Lancaster."

The soldiers exchanged what Derrick thought were confused looks. "I know my humor is sometimes misconstrued, but please understand that I have a great deal of respect for Lieutenant Lancaster," Derrick quickly said, feeling as though he needed to explain his remark about Harry.

"We understand that completely, Officer Washington," Corporal James Woloshin said. He had the dubious honor of being the highest ranking National Guardsman that had survived on Treasure Island. At twenty-five years old and with the rank of corporal, he had found himself in the middle of hell after the outbreak that swept the refugee camp. Within three days everyone was either dead or had joined the ranks of the infected. Everyone except the five others who had placed their lives in his hands.

"Let me explain, sir," James continued, then spent the next five minutes relaying information that, although remarkable, brought a huge smile to Derrick's face, shortly followed by emotions that nearly brought him to tears. Derrick asked a few questions, and the answers he received confirmed beyond a doubt what he had just been told.

After a few minutes of consideration, and looking each of the soldiers in the eyes, Derrick said, "Not one word to anyone! We'll all sit down and talk after we get you settled. Do you understand me, Corporal? That goes for the rest of you as well!"

"Yes, sir, we understand. This is pretty amazing, and the odds of all this coming to together are astronomical," James replied with no small amount of awe in his voice.

"We've experienced some pretty amazing things up to this point, young man. I'd have to classify this under miraculous!" Derrick said with the smile returning to his face.

After Harry completed his update to Cecil, he joined the group at the back of the boat. Derrick introduced each of the soldiers, and as Harry shook hands he picked up an odd sense from them. Nothing negative, and if he had to put a label on the feeling the word would have to be a muted excitement. He quickly shook those thoughts off as he continued to chat with each of them in turn.

The Phoenix pulled into Ayala Cove within twenty minutes after the rescue. Every person on Angel Island who was not involved in a critical assignment was at the docks as the fireboat came to a stop at the refueling dock and shut down. As the cold and half-clothed Guardsmen got off the boat, the applause and cheers from the other survivors was louder than those Harry and Cecil had experienced. Each soldier was welcomed and taken off to find dry clothes and a place to store their gear.

Frank had quickly bonded with the only female soldier in the group. Allison Hernandez reminded Harry of the actor Michelle Rodriguez: beautiful, athletic, and quite capable of taking care of herself. Frank was like a teenager telling his best friends about Allison as he described her to Harry and Derrick later that evening. Allison, twenty-four years old and with an I.Q. that matched Frank's, had spent time in the regular Army where she trained as a Cobra Attack Helicopter pilot. After being wounded in Afghanistan, she'd decided to leave the Army and pursue a career as a commercial airline pilot.

"Okay, so that means she has a real license to fly helicopters, right? Maybe you could get lessons from her then, Rookie!" Derrick ribbed Frank after listening to him go on about how 'cool' she was. Frank just looked at Derrick like he had grown an ear on his forehead. That just made Derrick laugh harder.

At 7:00 p.m. Cecil called a stop to all work for the night. Everyone was running on fumes as they continued to set up the island and he knew they needed to decompress. The people who had taken over as cooks created a fantastic meal out of some very basic supplies they had gathered, and the survivors enjoyed an evening of relaxation. Genuine laughter was heard as they all pushed the horrors they had experienced out of their minds. If only for the night.

Harry watched the soldiers and Derrick talking among themselves as he ate with Cecil and the other council members. He'd caught them glancing in his direction several times. Curiosity was getting the best of him as he wondered what the hell they were talking about.

Excusing himself, he wandered over to the group and said, "So what's up, folks?"

Derrick looked at James for a moment, then nodded toward the visitor's center. "Harry, we need to talk. Let's go inside the center."

Harry was perplexed as he, Derrick, and James entered the quiet building. Frank came in a moment later to join the small group.

"Okay, what's this all about?" Harry asked

"James has some news he received. News that affects you directly, Harry. I want you to know that I believe what he is about to tell you," Derrick said as he leaned forward in his chair.

Harry looked from Derrick to James. "Okay, son, what do you have?"

"I am not sure how best to begin so I will just say it, sir. I have been in contact with your nephew in Indiana," James said, and suddenly became very uncomfortable at the expression he saw come over Harry's face.

Harry immediately jumped to his feet, his head spinning. "What the hell do you mean you've been in contact with my nephew? Eric? How the hell have you been in contact with him?" Harry grabbed James by the collar with both hands, dragging him to his feet. "What kind of fucking sick joke is this? You had better explain yourself very quickly!"

Derrick was on his feet almost as quickly as Harry had been. Placing a hand on his friend's shoulder, he said, "Harry, you need to hear him out."

Harry's eyes clouded with tears and emotion blocked his ability to speak. He released James as he sat heavily back down. In an almost whisper he managed, "What do you mean you've been in contact with Eric?"

James smoothed the front of his shirt but remained standing as he spoke. "We spoke twice. The first time was several days ago, six days to be precise, and via satellite phone. The last time was two days ago. Apparently your nephew found a sat phone in an abandoned Guard vehicle." Seeing the sheer terror that now creased Harry's face, James quickly added, "But he's okay, sir. At least he was when I spoke to him last."

Harry began to stand again as he said, "Get him on the damn thing! Right now, Corporal!"

Derrick gently kept Harry from gaining his feet and said, "Let him finish, Harry."

James did not wait and continued. "I would have done that the moment we found out who you were, sir. But the battery in your nephew's sat phone died. I could tell it was happening so I got as much information as possible before it did.

"Apparently the group of people he was with came under attack by a large group of infected while they were in transit to a safe zone. The infected were put down without anyone being injured, but the vehicle your nephew, your sister and brother-in-law were in ran off the road during the initial attack and flipped. Everyone on board was fine other than a few bruises, but the vehicle could not be salvaged.

"As they were transferring the people and supplies from that vehicle the convoy was hit by another group of infected. Derrick told us you call them runners. Your nephew and a few of his friends had been helping carry supplies when the infected hit. Apparently they came out of the woods that surrounded them.

"Your sister, brother-in-law and most of the others made it onto a bus that had been brought in, but your nephew and his friends were cut off. They were able to hide until the infected moved on. He did not go into much detail about what happened during the attack, but I got the impression it was bad." James finally sat down and stared at the floor.

Harry sat in stunned shock as tears coursed their way down his cheeks. "What else?" That was all that he could manage for the moment.

James looked up to Harry, and after taking a deep breath he continued. "Your nephew is with his friend Tyler and a few others. This all took place just outside of Carmel. The military had set up a staging area at a place called the Monon Community Center where they had the area residents assembled for evacuation. They were being relocated north of Kokomo to a safe zone that had been established. I don't have all the details, though.

"Once the infected left the area after the second attack, your nephew organized the other teens. They collected the weapons and supplies that had been abandoned when the other survivors fled. That's how they found the sat phone. Here again, I can't give you many details, but the kids made their way to Carmel High School and were able to secure the building.

"Your nephew set up a rotation of the kids to send out brief calls on the sat phone and that is how we picked up the first one. Apparently they started to dial random numbers, trying to reach someone, and our equipment picked up the transmission from the phone, since it is military. After the second call, as I told you, the battery in their phone finally went dead. I was able to pass along some suggestions and answer a few questions about the weapons they had collected.

"I understand your nephew is only fifteen, sir, but with all due respect, he really has his shit together! He asked pertinent questions and seemed satisfied with my answers. I'm not certain how I would have handled all this at his age, but I am sure that he was solely responsible for saving the other kids with him and has kept them alive since!

"You should also know that just before the sat phone went dead your nephew gave me a message for you. Although at the time I had no idea I would ever have the opportunity to deliver it. He said to tell you that he's all right and that he remembered everything you two had talked about. That he would do what he could to keep the others safe." James cleared his throat in an obvious attempt at removing the lump that was quickly forming. "He said to tell you that he loved and respected you more than you could ever know. There was more that he started to say but static garbled it and then the phone went dead."

38

Harry had finally gotten his emotions under control, and was now trying to put what he had heard in some order of understanding. His sister was apparently safe, as was Eric; for now at least. Tyler was Eric's best friend and together they made a good team. Both boys had matured well beyond their ages. They played sports together and many of the other things teens enjoyed, but were both leaders in their group. Eric more so with his good looks, intelligence, and quick wit. He was a natural leader that people were drawn to. Both he and Tyler were over six feet tall, athletic, and easily able to handle themselves. But neither of the boys had ever used their size to intimidate, both being the first to stand against bullying. They were well-liked and respected by their peers and teachers.

They had supplies and were in a safe location. Harry was not going to ponder how long either would last. Carmel High School was a very large campus. Eric's graduating class alone had been nearly thirteen hundred students. Harry had no idea where Eric and the others would have secured themselves in the school, but he knew Eric would find the safest and most logical location.

Derrick interrupted Harry's thoughts. "Harry?"

Harry looked around the room and found all eyes on him. "I'm good, Derry," he replied.

Turning his attention to James, Harry then said, "James, I apologize for my reaction. This is a bit of a shock to say the least. I just can't get my head around the odds! But I want you to know how much I appreciate this information, and thank you for helping Eric with the information you were able to offer. He is a very smart and capable kid and I know you increased their odds greatly."

Harry then turned his focus on Derrick and Frank. "I'm leaving in the morning. I know you guys have said you would go but I'm not holding you to that. This island is safe and I think given time it will become a beacon of hope. Between Cecil and the others, you two could at least find some peace until this all gets sorted out. God knows you've done enough."

Derrick could no longer remain silent, and with very rare tears forming in the large man's eyes, he said, "Harry, you and I have been through some shit not only recently but over the years. Not to mention all the good times we've had. You invited me into your family and they accepted me the moment we met. You are the closest thing to a brother I have, and if you think for one moment I'm going to let you traipse off alone you're just sorely mistaken! We started this together and we are going to see it to the end together!" Crossing massive arms across his chest, he looked to the floor as a single tear found its way down his cheek.

"I told you before, Harry," Frank began, using Harry's first name, "I was going to stick with you guys. Besides, you might need someone a little smarter than two old beat cops!" Frank's ability to break the tension worked once again. Harry and Derrick both looked at him at the same time and smiled.

"Well, he's right ya know," Derrick said to Harry. "You're already too old for this shit and I'm right at your rear bumper on that!"

"I would like to go as well," James said to Harry's surprise. "I'm from Ohio and have no family out here. Maybe once we get your family situated I might head on and see if any of mine are still alive."

Before Harry could answer, another voice joined the conversation from the door of the visitor's center. "You can count me in as well," Phil said as he walked up to join the group. "I didn't mean to eavesdrop, but Cecil wanted to find out if you guys were going to be in here all night." Turning to

Harry, he then said, "I can handle myself, Harry, and I want to help. There's not much holding me here any longer. I grew up in San Francisco and am pretty sure all my family is dead. At least I haven't been able to get in contact with anyone since this all started." Phil went quiet after saying that.

Harry looked at each man in the room. Each of them willing to put their lives on the line for someone else without hesitation. This was no real surprise though. Each man there was a true professional and had always done what needed to be done. A couple of cops, a firefighter, and a National Guardsman. Harry felt a bit of shame for not taking into consideration that each of these men, as well as the other survivors, had lost family and friends over the past couple of weeks.

"I would be honored to stand with each of you, gentleman," Harry said, pushing past the lump that had formed in his throat. "Frank, at first light I want that copter we saw inspected and, if it's operational, brought here. Derrick, Phil, and James, please gather what supplies, weapons and ammunition the island can spare. We need to pack light to be able to move easily." Taking a breath he then said, "We need to get some rest so let's get this done quickly. Tomorrow is going to come sooner than we like."

Each man acknowledged Harry's instructions and went about what they needed to do. Harry met with Cecil and told him what James had to say, and what the men had planned. Cecil shared Harry's wonderment that James had not only been in touch with Harry's nephew but that he was actually among the survivors on Treasure Island, allowing him to give Harry this information.

"I'm not a particularly religious man, but this sure makes you wonder," Cecil said after listening to Harry's story. Harry could only nod his agreement.

At first light, Frank, along with Allison Hernandez and three others, made the hike to the helicopter on the other side of the island. They found it to be in perfect working order with nearly full tanks of fuel. There was no sign of the pilot, a mystery that they contemplated as they flew the bird back to Ayala Cove. While they were on that side of the island, they'd also checked out the Coast Guard Station located on Point Blunt. It was abandoned, but the team was able to make entry into the main building. They did not find much, but were able to collect a few basic medical supplies and found several doors securely locked. Frank passed that information along to Cecil.

It was 10:34 a.m. when Harry, Derrick, Phil, and James walked down to the beach where the bright yellow helicopter sat. Frank and Allison were doing another preflight check as the other men approached. Earlier in the morning, Allison had informed Harry that she would like to go along, offering that she could not only handle weapons but was a much more qualified pilot than Frank. Derrick jumped at the opportunity to kid Frank a bit and said he would be the first one to vote her in. After a bit of argument between Allison and Harry, an argument Harry knew he could not win, she hastily gathered some clothes and supplies and stowed it on the helicopter.

While Frank and Allison went off to inspect the helicopter, Cecil and Harry pored over maps of the U.S. Harry knew they would have to keep away from large cities, so he came up with what he thought to be the best route to cross the nation. There were far too many variables they were certain to encounter, but he felt that the route he decided upon was the most logical. It was twenty-three hundred miles from the San Francisco Bay Area to Carmel, Indiana through a country now devastated and filled with horrors that Harry could not begin to comprehend. He had no idea what lay ahead, but his focus was clear. Nothing would stand in his way.

Cecil had brought up a very good point about the island while they talked about what was happening inland. "How do we let others know we are secure and a safe haven?" he'd asked.

That was a very good point. Both Harry and Cecil knew there had to be other survivors in the area. They weren't equipped to undertake rescue operations, but they could let people know that Angel Island stood ready to offer safety if the survivors could reach it. Cecil had set up two teams that would patrol the coastline by boat from the Bay Bridge to the Golden Gate – teams that would be capable of picking up survivors from predetermined locations – but they needed a way for anyone inland to know where to go.

The equipment that Harry had seen the Guardsmen carrying when they picked them up from Treasure Island turned out to be military grade radio gear. Connected to the island's generator, that equipment was able to transmit at least one hundred miles outside the immediate area but it also had the ability to join with satellite communications. As long as there were still operating satellites. They had already picked up spotty radio traffic from the Bay Area. Some of it desperate calls for help, while others were calmly broadcasting descriptions of what they were seeing. Reports of marauders in Marin County begin to come in as well. That area was just north of San Francisco on the other side of the Golden Gate Bridge.

"I think we should broadcast a message," Harry offered. "Maybe every hour. Let people know Angel Island is here and able to offer help if, and only if, survivors can reach you. We have enough boats to pick up folks from the shorelines, but we need to establish a way to do that. Giving people very clear instructions."

"Any suggestions on what we might say?" Cecil asked after agreeing with Harry's idea.

"Maybe." Harry sat down and hastily wrote several paragraphs on a sheet of paper. Once he was done, he handed it to Cecil who quickly read it.

"I think this is a good start. We'll modify it as things change here, and once we figure out the best locations for pickups, but at least we can use this to get the word out right now," Cecil said. "I'll get this over to the radio room right now."

After delivering the script to the radio operator, the first broadcast from Angel Island was made. This message would be repeated every hour until the island was at capacity or until people stopped answering.

"This is Angel Island San Francisco Bay, located at 37.86N 122.43W. We are a group of civilians that have secured the island and are accepting survivors. For those on land in this area, your best hope is to secure some type of boat and get onto the Bay; we have learned the infected fear water. We are sending out daily patrols as far ranging as possible so we will find you. Ships entering the Bay from the Golden Gate entrance are required to drop anchor, contact us on this frequency, and wait for instructions before proceeding. There are safe docks and anchorages in the Bay, and you will be escorted to one of those locations for intake.

What remains of the Coast Guard and other military assets are spread thin, and so is their patience. If you encounter them, use caution when making initial contact. Yield to their directions precisely. However, do not expect direct assistance of any kind for the time being. You must help yourselves!

Do not, we repeat, DO NOT approach any mainland docks. This includes the San Francisco Marina, Embarcadero Piers, Sausalito, and Tiburon. These areas have not been secured and are infested with the infected. Wait for our patrols to escort you to secure areas.

Survivors are reporting marauders on the Marin County side of the Bay. Additional caution is strongly advised if you are traveling overland in that area. We have not heard anything from the South Bay approach. You should assume all land routes are unsecure. Do not enter San Francisco for any reason. It is completely overrun.

Avoid all contact with the infected by any means possible. Once they have seen you, they will pursue relentlessly. We are all fighters, but for now we must survive.

This is Angel Island. You are not alone."

39

In the end, it took another day to get everything prepared for their departure, but the time had finally arrived. Most of the survivors on Angel Island came to the beach to see Harry and his team off. It took another forty-five minutes to get through the throng of well-wishers. Cecil knew that Harry was very anxious to get started, so he interceded and got everyone back to work.

Wanda had stood with Nevaeh out of sight from those on the beach. She'd already said her goodbyes to the group. She had the very distinct feeling she would never see Harry, Derrick, Frank, or the others again. This saddened her greatly and she offered a silent prayer for them. She then turned and headed back to the clinic where she had been assigned, thankful that she and her granddaughter, along with so many others, had been given a chance to live by those men.

Cecil walked the short distance to the waiting helicopter with Harry, chatting as they went. "You be careful, Harry. I know that sounds silly and I should be giving you a more rousing speech, but that's really all I can come up with at the moment. Other than to thank you for helping give us a chance here." Cecil hesitated for a moment. "You come back here if things don't work out, okay?"

Harry considered what Cecil said for a moment. "I don't know why I feel this way, but I don't think I will be returning, my friend. I am at peace with that, funny as that may sound. I had a dream last night and I can't tell you the last time I had one of those," he said chuckling. "I dreamt that I found my family but then, like an out-of-body experience, I saw them all in great sorrow as they looked at a closed casket." Kicking at a rock he saw on the sandy beach, he then said as he looked into Cecil's eyes, "I wasn't with them as they mourned. At least not standing with them. Anyway, I really have no idea what that means, but when I woke I had the feeling this would be the last time I would see this area."

Cecil had nothing to offer the man in the way of comforting words. He extended his hand and, as Harry grasped it, Cecil pulled him into a hug. "You watch your six. We'll keep you all in our thoughts and prayers. People will never forget now, or in the future, what you and the others have done here, Harry. That I can promise you!"

Harry disengaged himself from Cecil's hug and put a hand on the older man's shoulder, squeezing it slightly. There was just nothing left to say.

Cecil turned on his heel and walked a short distance away from the copter. Harry watched as Derrick and James climbed on board the bird and began to strap themselves in. Derrick looked extremely nervous about being in the helicopter, but was maintaining a brave front. Harry and Frank had been kidding him all morning about the pitfalls of flying in a copter.

Just as Harry was climbing in, he heard something in the distance. A sound he had not heard since the attack, causing him to immediately take several steps back away from the helicopter and look skyward. Harry heard the sound of a small airplane approaching!

Frank and Derrick joined Harry and, as they shielded their eyes against the bright sun which warmed the island, they watched as a small single-engine plane made a low pass over them and banked around to circle the island. Harry had never seen a plane like this one. It was white with a small cockpit that looked only big enough to seat a couple of people. The engine and propeller was attached to the rear tail section above the plane and to the rear of the wings.

"That's a Seawind," Frank said admiringly as the small plane passed overhead. "That thing is a beauty!" He went on to explain what he knew about the plane, but all Harry could understand was that it landed on water and had a fairly long-distance flying capability; and that Frank held the opinion that it was 'sweet'.

"Who the hell is that?" Derrick asked, not expecting an answer.

"No idea," Harry replied.

It sounded as if the plane was returning, and as Harry was attempting to figure out how they could contact the pilot, the Guardsman who was remaining on the island and maintaining the radio equipment came running onto the beach.

"We just made contact with that plane, sir," the young soldier said excitedly as he caught his breath. "That's Scott Allen and he claims to be part of a flotilla of survivors in Southern California. He is requesting permission to land and come ashore."

Cecil had rejoined Harry just as the plane passed overhead. This time Harry was able to see that two people were in the cockpit, albeit not clearly. "Cecil, if this is who he claims to be, your day just became a lot more interesting," Harry remarked as he watched the plane bank around the island once again. "Scott Allen is the guy who gave that interview on GNN. I would suggest that you at least make contact with him. I have no idea why he would be up here, but you should probably find out. I can't delay any longer and need to take off."

"We'll take care of it, Harry," Cecil replied.

Turning to the Guardsman, Harry said, "Please pass on my regards to Mr. Allen. Explain the circumstances and that I can't wait for him. Tell him what he had to say in that interview he did with GNN is why, in part, this island is secure, and that there are survivors here. Hell, just tell him I said thank you!"

The Guardsman immediately took off at a run toward the building which now housed the radio equipment. Derrick and Frank climbed back into the helicopter as Harry said a final goodbye to Cecil. Harry heard the small plane approaching again but this time it was much lower. As it approached Harry's position he watched the wings begin to wag back and forth.

"Guess he got my message," Harry said as he raised an arm and returned the wave as the plane flew overhead. "Good luck, Mr. Allen," Harry said to himself. "Good luck to us all."

Harry got on board and sat across from James and Phil. Derrick was in the seat beside him, and Frank was acting as co-pilot with Allison flying the bird. After the helicopter warmed up for a few minutes, Allison lifted them off the ground. The rotor wash created a small sand storm on the beach as she increased power to the engines. They gained altitude quickly, then turned east, gaining speed as they flew.

"So what now, sir?" James asked

"We continue to survive, Corporal," Harry said through the boom mic attached to the headphones which each man wore. "We continue to fight and do what we can. We rise from the ashes. There are no other options."

Harry looked out the side window at the San Francisco skyline. There was smoke rising slowly from several locations, but the city he had served for so many years was gone. He knew that he would never see it again but was, as he had told Cecil, at peace with that. He had longed for his roots in Indiana and now he was finally on his way. His thoughts turned to Eric and the other kids. "Stay strong, kiddo, we're on the way."

"Did you say something, Harry?" Derrick asked through the headset.

Harry simply nodded his head in response. He refocused on the overwhelming task that lay before this small team. They had miles to travel and he knew untold horrors awaited them. Harold Lancaster had no idea what they would face, but he did know that he would do everything in his power to keep these people among the survivors of the dead.

EPILOGUE

Indiana

"What do you mean you got through, Eric?" Tyler asked as he stared at his best friend in complete surprise while the other kids crowded around.

"I talked to some guy who claimed to be in the National Guard!" Eric replied excitedly. "He said they were on Treasure Island."

"Isn't that the place you told me about that used to be some sort of military base?" Tyler asked.

"Yeah, it is," Eric replied. "I've been there a few times with my uncle, but the military has been gone for a long time." Eric remembered fondly the trips he and his Uncle Harry had made to the island.

"Then how can you be talking to some military dude?" Tyler retorted, somewhat confused.

Eric could only look at his longtime friend and shake his head a bit. Tyler was a very smart fifteen-year-old, but sometimes he needed to be refocused a bit. Especially when he was under stress. "I said I talked to some guy that was *in* the National Guard, Tyler. Forget the island, okay."

"Okay," Tyler replied, looking a bit embarrassed. "Anyway, can he get a message out to your uncle?"

"I've no idea. I explained what happened here and where we were. I told him who Uncle Harry is and he said he'd try to relay a message, but that seems like a stretch to me. I got the feeling he was in trouble there. The guy didn't say anything but I could hear those things in the background pretty clearly. I did get a lot of information about the equipment and guns we collected." Eric sighed as he looked

243

at each of the other kids. "The battery in the phone died before I got much more, though."

"What do we do now?" Tyler asked, looking around the room and seeing the same utter fear on each of the other kids' faces.

"The same thing we have been doing." Eric said, standing up from behind the desk that had been set up as a makeshift command center. "Look guys, we've made it this far. We're safe, we have supplies, and now that we can figure out how to use those guns we can at least take those things out if we have to." Eric let that sink in, knowing the group had been on the verge of panic for the past few days. Panic that could get them all killed. Many of the kids had been talking about leaving the school to search for their parents. He had even considered it a few times himself. But he knew if someone opened the doors the school would be flooded with those zombie things outside.

Tyler had stood with Eric since they'd become separated from their parents and the other adults after the attack at the Monon Center. Stood with him as he always had. Eric had been able to get them this far, and now everyone looked to him for answers. Looked to him as the leader of this band of eleven teenagers.

"We can't stay here forever, Eric. Nobody knows where we are and sooner or later the food and water we have is going to run out," Tyler said with a slight whine in his voice.

"I know, I know," Eric replied as he began to pace, trying to figure out what he could offer the group. He was trying to formulate into words a way to ease the tensions that were building. He was only fifteen, and would gladly run into the arms of his mom and dad, his Uncle Harry. But that was not an option for now.

After a few moments of consideration, he stopped pacing and said, "Right now we are okay. We have more information than we had a few days ago, and at least we know what we're facing." Eric considered his next words carefully. "If we stick together we have a chance. Those things out there can't get in, so we have time to get things together more and plan out what we do next."

"Hey Eric," Joey Benson, the computer whiz in the group, called out from another desk that had been set up. It was piled high with all manner of computer parts he had collected. "I think I can modify this satellite phone and connect it directly to a computer. We would just need to get an antenna on the roof."

Eric and the other kids rushed over to Joey. Looking at the mess atop the desk, Eric said, "Are you sure, Joey? Can you bypass the battery?"

"I sure can." Joey replied, looking pleased with himself. "There's enough juice left in some of these other batteries that if I connect them together we should be good!" He was referring to the stacks of loose batteries that had been collected in a cardboard box next to the desk. "We may only get a few uses out of the phone but it should work!"

"That's great, Joey." Eric said, then turned to the others. "This changes everything, guys! If we can get that thing working again we can send out messages! Somebody will hear those and help will come!" Although he was smiling broadly, he knew having the sat phone working really meant nothing. It took days to reach the Guardsman on the West Coast, but he had to offer his friends something to pull them out of their morose mood.

This small glimmer of hope worked almost immediately. "This is great!" Tyler said. "Okay, Eric, what should we do now?"

Eric, Tyler, and the other kids spent the next few hours continuing to fortify their stronghold in the gym at Carmel High School. Eric relayed what he had been told by the Guardsman about the weapons, and they soon were able to at least load the magazines into wells and dry fire the M16s. The next step would be live round practice, but they had no idea where to do that just yet.

The kids were exhausted, both mentally and physically, after surviving another day. They all ate together in relative silence that evening before bedding down for the night. Muffled crying was heard after some of the battery-powered lights were turned out, but nobody said anything about that. Eric was still wide awake as he made the rounds, checking the doors of the gym they had secured. He had already done that at least four other times earlier that evening, but he was going to make certain everyone was as safe as possible.

He quietly made his way up one set of open bleachers to reach the windows. The kids had covered them with black plastic sheeting they'd found in a storage room. Pulling back a section he had cut when the plastic was first put up, he gazed out into the parking lot that teemed with the infected. They were just milling around and Eric was thankful they were no longer attempting to get through the school's heavy steel doors. Looking out at the mass, he suddenly felt overwhelming hopelessness.

"Hey man, you okay?" Tyler asked as he suddenly appeared next to Eric, startling him.

"Damn, you scared the crap out of me!" Eric said as he glanced at Tyler for a moment before returning his gaze through the window.

"Sorry. I saw you come up here. You looked kind of bummed and I just wanted to make sure you're okay," Tyler said while looking out at the horde as well. "Doesn't look like there are as many of them now." Turning from the window, he sat down heavily on the bleacher with his back resting against the wall. "This all seems so hopeless. What are we really going to do?"

"It's not hopeless, Tyler," Eric replied as he glanced down at his best friend. A calmness had suddenly replaced the despair that threatened to overcome him just moments ago. "What we are going to do is survive! I don't know how I know this but my uncle is on the way. I can feel it. So until he gets here, we are going to keep those guys down there safe, and we are going to make it." Eric reached his hand toward his friend as he had many times. "You and I are going to stay strong for them and wait."

Tyler looked up to Eric, considering his words, then grasped the outstretched hand and allowed himself to be helped up. Once on his feet he simply nodded once in agreement. Eric returned his attention to the window which faced west, looking past the horror that surrounded the school.

"We're going to survive and we're going to wait," Eric repeated more to himself than to Tyler. "We're here, Uncle Harry. Please hurry."

#

Thank you for reading Book One of the series, *SURVIVORS OF THE DEAD*. I hope you enjoyed reading it as much as I enjoyed writing it. The saga continues in Book Two, *THE ROAD UNKNOWN*, following Harry and his team as they cross a devastated country while Eric and his friends struggle to survive against nearly impossible odds! Coming to Amazon Kindle and in paperback in 2014.

ABOUT THE AUTHOR

Originally from Indiana, Tony Baker moved to San Francisco in the early 1980's, where he spent the next thirty years garnering a great deal of insight into human nature – experience which created a perfect understanding of the possibilities that await should an apocalyptic event befall society. Being an avid reader of the horror genre for years, Tony developed a deep-seated desire to write, often jokingly saying, "I think I could write as well as the worst I have read." After years of contemplating that desire, he took the first step on that journey in September of 2012 and began writing *From the Ashes*, the first book in his *Survivors of the Dead* series.

Printed in Great Britain
by Amazon

85185348R00148